Home at Last
Book 3: Abbott Island Series

Penny Frost McGinnis

www.MtZionRidgePress.com

Mt Zion Ridge Press LLC
295 Gum Springs Rd, NW
Georgetown, TN 37366

https://www.mtzionridgepress.com

ISBN 13: 978-1-962862-32-5
Published in the United States of America
Publication Date: August 1, 2024
Copyright: © 2024 Penny Frost McGinnis

Editor-In-Chief: Michelle Levigne
Executive Editor: Tamera Lynn Kraft

Cover art design by Tamera Lynn Kraft
Cover Art Copyright by Mt Zion Ridge Press LLC © 2024

All rights reserved. No portion of this book may be reproduced or transmitted in any form or by any electronic or mechanical means, including photocopying, recording or by any information retrieval and storage system without permission of the publisher.

Ebooks, audiobooks, and print books are *not* transferrable, either in whole or in part. As the purchaser or otherwise *lawful* recipient of this book, you have the right to enjoy the novel on your own computer or other device. Further distribution, copying, sharing, gifting or uploading is illegal and violates United States Copyright laws.
Pirating of books is illegal. Criminal Copyright Infringement, *including* infringement without monetary gain, may be investigated by the Federal Bureau of Investigation and is punishable by up to five years in federal prison and a fine of up to $250,000.

Names, characters and incidents depicted in this book are products of the author's imagination, or are used in a fictitious situation. Any resemblances to actual events, locations, organizations, incidents or persons - living or dead - are coincidental and beyond the intent of the author.

Unless stated otherwise, all scriptures come from The Holy Bible, New International Version®, NIV® Copyright©1973, 1978, 1984, 2011 by Biblica, Inc.® Used by permission. All rights reserved worldwide.

Holy Bible, New International Version®, NIV® Copyright ©1973, 1978, 1984, 2011 by Biblica, Inc.® Used by permission. All rights reserved worldwide.

Dedication

For our grandchildren — true treasures of the heart.

Acknowledgements:

Writing the third novel in the Abbott Island series has been a bit of a struggle, but with the people in my life who encourage me and God's loving kindness, I made it.

First and foremost, I thank God for His mercy and grace. He's the reason I write. He asked me to, so I humble myself in obedience to Him to tell the stories He places on my heart.

My husband, Tim has loved, sacrificed, encouraged, brainstormed, and listened. Most of all, he has believed in me. I'm so grateful to take this daily journey with him.

Thank you to my wonderful children who encircle me with love and support, along with their spouses and my grandchildren. I so appreciate your encouragement.

Thank you, Hannah for brainstorming with me to figure out what Lucy wanted in her future, Stephen for some practical advice on construction, and Michael for directing me to a good resource for treasure hunting.

A huge thank you goes to my publisher, Mt. Zion Ridge Press. Thank you, Tamera Kraft, for giving me the opportunity to publish with you and Michelle and for creating a beautiful cover. Thank you, Michelle Levigne, for your expert editing and making my story better. I appreciate the work you do to publish stories for God's kingdom. I'm privileged to work with these ladies who are not only my publishers, but my friends.

Special thanks to my critique partners, Kathleen Friesen and Kim Garee. Your editing and encouragement mean the world to me. Thank you to my beta reader and dear friend, Bev Cinnamon, for taking the time to read through *Home At Last* and giving me honest feedback.

A huge thank you to my readers. Without you, I wouldn't keep writing. I've met some wonderful folks along the way, and I so appreciate your encouragement and support. Readers are the heart of writing.

I believe God places people in my path to encourage and push me forward. I appreciate each and every one and hope my stories encourage you.

I'd love for you to sign up for my newsletter and keep up on writing news at *www.PennyFrostMcGinnis.com.*

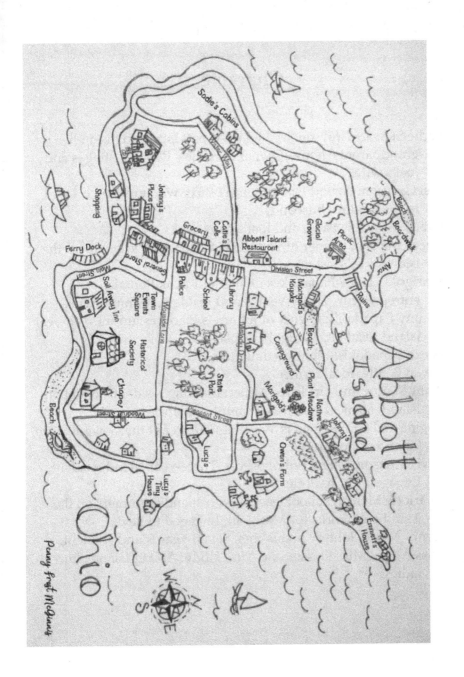

Characters:

Sadie Stewart Grayson: Moved to Abbott Island to live in her grandparents' home. Owner of Sadie's Rental Cottages and Joel's wife.

Joel Grayson: Abbott Island police officer who grew up on the island. Sadie's husband.

Gracie Grayson: Sadie and Joel's baby.

Lucy Grayson: Owner of The General Store and grew up on the island. Joel's sister.

Marigold Hayes-Papadakis: Owner of Kayak Rentals, entrepreneur. Thirty-year island resident. Johnny's wife.

Johnny Papadakis: Owner of Johnny's Place restaurant. Ten-year island resident. Marigold's husband.

Alexa Papadakis: Johnny's daughter.

Owen Bently: local farmer.

Aunt Marley and Uncle Jed Miller: life-long residents to Abbott Island, farmers and Owen's aunt and uncle.

Regina and Gio: Regina is assistant manager at the General Store, Gio is her husband.

Levi Swenson: Island police officer. Three-year island resident. Engaged to Charlotte.

Charlotte Mercer: School teacher who spends summers on the island and works for Marigold. Engaged to Levi.

Henry Marin: Johnny's sous chef. Seven-year island resident.

Miss Aggie, Miss Flossie, and Miss Hildy: Abbott Island church ladies.

My goal is that they may be encouraged in heart and united in love, so that they may have the full riches of complete understanding, in order that they may know the mystery of God, namely, Christ, in whom are hidden all the treasures of wisdom and knowledge.
Colossians 2:2-3

CHAPTER ONE

Waves kissed the sand on the small beach outside Lucy Grayson's new tiny home. The sunrise drew her outside before her morning coffee. On the porch, before she witnessed the sun lift in the sky, she closed her eyes and listened to the calm song of the water. Blessed with the gift of land from her parents, Lucy appreciated the builders who had created a small haven for her and her betta fish, Finnegan. She reveled in making the small space hers and considered investing in a second tiny home to rent to tourists who swarmed Abbott Island in the summer.

Nearby, a motor rumbled and disturbed Lucy's peace.

Owen Bently, a local farmer on the island, parked his truck along the road, stepped out, and unloaded tools from the bed of the orange Chevy S10. Hired to landscape the barren yard, he carried a shovel and rake to the house.

Lucy stepped off the porch to meet him. Late April's wind whipped her long blond hair across her face and blocked her vision. Her foot slipped into a hole she'd not seen in the yard before, then twisted. She collapsed to the ground, her bottom met the dirt, and dust billowed from the earth around her.

"Agh." Inside her boot, her ankle throbbed.

"Lucy? Are you okay?" Owen hovered over her.

With a grunt, she scooted from the hole on her bottom and dragged her foot with her. "No." An earthy odor from the dirt irritated her nose.

The farmer knelt beside her and reached for her leg. "Let me see." The compassion in Owen's kind eyes calmed her, even though she hesitated to accept help. "I'm familiar with ankle injuries from my time in baseball. I can get you into the house and examine it. If you need me to, I'll call the EMTs."

Never one to hide her emotions, Lucy assumed her face showed Owen her stubborn pride, even though she needed his help.

A mumble tumbled from her lips. "Okay."

He knelt and wrapped an arm around her and, with a gentle tug, pulled her to a standing position. "Can you put weight on it?"

Lucy pressed the injured foot to the ground. "Ouch. No, it hurts." She shut her eyes and winced, then opened them and glared at him.

He nodded to the porch. "Is your door unlocked?"

"Yes." She dragged in a breath, then swept her gaze over the yard. A shovel and hole digger leaned against Owen's truck. She twisted to view her helper. "What have you done to my yard?"

His brows raised into an upside-down vee. "I was going to ask you what happened. I brought my tools and the trees you wanted me to plant, but I haven't dug holes yet."

The two of them stared at the yard pocked full of divots and holes. Lucy's voice quivered. "Then what happened?"

He scrunched his forehead. "I don't know. You saw me park and unload the shovels, but someone was on a digging spree."

Her hand on Owen's arm, Lucy hopped on one foot and faced the water. Between her and the lake, at least ten holes marred her yard. Sure, without grass, the place appeared barren, but she and Owen had worked out a landscape plan he drew to put in place. "Could moles do this?"

Owen snaked his arm around Lucy's waist, to keep her from falling. "No. The holes are too big for moles, and they're all the same size. It's like someone searched for something. When you had your tiny house delivered, did any of the builders act overly curious about this area?"

Four contractors had worked on her property. One installed electric, one plumbing, and two had finished the house and completed the project.

"There was one guy who asked a bunch of questions, and another one used a metal detector, but I assumed he was searching for nails and screws. I didn't think anything about it, but maybe they came back for something." She pressed her injured foot to the ground. "Ugh. I need to go inside and look at my ankle."

With one swift movement, Owen pressed his arm under her legs and tightened his grip on her waist and lifted her from the ground.

"What are you doing?" Without thinking, she wrapped an arm around his neck, bringing her close enough to fill her nose with his woodsy scent.

His strong muscles brought her comfort and a desire to be rescued.

No. Lucy Grayson did not need rescuing. She took care of herself. Except, if she tried to move on her own, she'd fall on her tush again.

He jostled her a bit. "I'm carrying you into your house because you can't walk." With his foot, he pushed the door open and deposited her onto her couch. "There you go. Let's get your boot off." He unzipped the ankle boot and slipped it off. He examined her ankle with his fingers. A zing from the gentle pressure traveled up her leg to her belly. The physical reaction startled her. She hadn't experienced an attraction similar to this since high school when she dated Jamison North, which fizzled out when he told her she'd make pretty babies. Other than conversations about vegetables and landscaping at her General Store, she and Owen hadn't spent time together. Sure, she found his blond hair, brown eyes, and trim physique attractive, but she didn't have time to ponder a relationship.

2

Home At Last

Running the General Store and setting up her new home had grabbed all of her time.

Before her mind went into overdrive about Owen and his handsome face and kind soul, she bit her lip to stop the electrical jolt and watched him press on her leg.

He lowered her foot to the couch. "You may have sprained it, but it doesn't appear to be broken. You do have some swelling. I'd ice, elevate, and rest it today and evaluate it tomorrow. If it's not better, you'll need someone more qualified than me to examine it."

She mustered restraint against gazing into his eyes and focused on his chin. "Were you an athletic trainer or something?"

He repositioned his baseball cap. "What?"

She scooted herself to find a comfortable position on the couch. "You mentioned you knew about injuries because of baseball."

He shook his head. "No, I wasn't a trainer. I played some." Before she responded, he stepped to the kitchen. "Where do you keep plastic bags?"

"Bottom left cabinet in the rack on the door."

The sound of ice clinking echoed through the house.

In a few minutes, Owen had rigged an ice pack with a bag, ice, and a dish cloth. "I hope it's okay to use your butterfly towel. It was on the sink." He tucked two pillows under her foot and rested the ice pack on top. "Have you had breakfast?"

Lucy squinted at him. She had hung her favorite new towel yesterday when she finished unpacking, but who cared? Her stomach rumbled, and her system needed a jolt of caffeine. "I made coffee, but I haven't added cream to my cup or eaten. There are granola bars in the upper right cabinet and creamer in the fridge. Help yourself if you want something."

He carried a coffee cup and breakfast bar to her and sat in a nearby rocker. "I don't need anything, thanks. Aunt Marley fed me breakfast this morning, pancakes and ham." He rubbed his stomach.

Lucy swallowed a piece of the granola and berries bar. "How are your aunt and uncle? I haven't seen them in a while." The hearty fragrance of the coffee calmed her nerves.

"They're good. We've stayed busy preparing the farm for spring." He lifted his tall frame from the chair and stood. "So, you need anything else? I'll get the trees planted, and I can fill in the holes, or should we call Joel?"

She raised her hand to say stop. "I'm calling Joel. Something is wrong. Can you hold off on the trees until he takes a look? I need to call the store and tell them I won't be in today. Fortunately, it's mostly locals on the island right now. Regina can handle the customers without me today. My phone should be on the counter in the kitchen."

Owen retrieved the cell phone and handed it to Lucy. "If you're okay, I'm going to go. Call me when you're ready for the trees. Take care." He tipped his hat the way his uncle always did and left.

The essence of spring hung in the air. Fragrance from the spruce trees Owen planted a few years ago, with the hope of developing a small section of the farm into Christmas tree sales, filled the truck's cab. The S10 rumbled along the lane to his aunt and uncle's home and his own small house he'd built last year. Nothing fancy like Lucy's, but at least he had his own space.

He raised a quick prayer for Lucy and her aching ankle. When he'd lifted her from the ground, her body hugged to him, akin to pieces of a puzzle snugged together. Sure, Lucy's Scandinavian beauty made men give her a second glance, but he didn't have time or the desire to get tangled in another relationship. The last one had left him more broken than he had realized until his aunt pointed out how mopey he'd been.

God blessed him with Aunt Marley and Uncle Jed. After his parents and sister moved to Guatemala to help run a school, he had no ties, except Abbott Island. Uncle Jed had invited him to live with them and recover from his injuries and broken heart, then offered him the farm as long as they could live out their days there. Working the land brought him great satisfaction and kept his mind busy and off his disappointments. Adding a landscaping aspect gave him a chance to use his college degree in landscape architecture. The degree he had achieved while playing baseball.

At the farmhouse, he parked the truck, then ambled into his aunt's kitchen. While her back was to him, he sneaked over to her, placed a hand on each shoulder, and kissed her cheek.

"That best be you, Owen." At eighty-four years old, she twisted around faster than a twenty-eight-year-old. "Didn't you have work to do this morning, helping the pretty Grayson girl?" She lowered her chin and raised her eyebrows, then stepped to the table. "Let's sit."

Owen eased into an oak chair and propped his leg across his knee. "I did, but it's delayed. When I got to Lucy's, she had fallen. She twisted her ankle in a hole. The yard is filled with them. We counted at least ten, a lot for a small area. She called Joel to look into what might be going on."

His aunt's frown lines creased her forehead. "Hmm..."

He lowered his leg and leaned toward his aunt. "What are you thinking about?" He scooted his chair closer to her.

Aunt Marley rose from her chair. "Let me get your uncle. There's a story I want him to tell you, and he tells it better than I can. He's outside. Be right back."

In a chair on her tiny porch, Lucy held her niece, three-month-old Gracie, while her brother, Joel, investigated the holey yard. A great blue

Home At Last

heron soared overhead and the waves washed the sand. "What do you think, brother?"

Dressed in jeans and a t-shirt, Joel trudged across the yard, stepped on the porch, and plunked into the other Adirondack chair. "I called Levi, and he's coming over to take photos and measurements. Since I'm off duty today, he said he'd check it out." He smiled at his baby girl. "I can hang with you for a while. Sadie is cleaning the rental cabins, getting them ready for spring tourists. She has a handful of renters before the full season takes off in May. I'm sure you don't mind holding your niece."

Lucy lifted the baby in front of her and pecked a kiss on her cheek, then settled her against her chest. "I don't mind one bit."

"Levi said he'd be here in about a half an hour. Someone on the other side of the island reported evidence of a theft." He rested his hands behind his head. "Miss Flossie's cat disappeared again, and she thinks someone stole him."

A giggle escaped Lucy. "You've got to love her. When she gets together with Miss Aggie and Miss Hildy, they're a hoot."

He lowered his arms and rested them on the chair. "Watch out for them. You know they're on the hunt for more matchmaking fun."

"I'll stay under the radar with those three." She patted the baby's back. If they caught a whiff of Owen helping her, they'd grab it like a cat with a fresh mouse.

Lucy winced when she moved her ankle, then settled it on a small stool. "While you're here, I want to talk to you about something. I'd appreciate it if you'd keep it to yourself." She hesitated about how much to share.

He leaned in and locked eyes with his sister. "Sure. What's up?"

CHAPTER TWO

Baby Gracie gurgled, then smacked her lips. Lucy and Joel waited on the porch for Levi, with the little one wrapped in her hand-crocheted blanket from Marigold.

"I think Gracie is hungry." Lucy eyed her brother, then shook her head. "I'm still amazed you're a dad, and I'm an aunt."

"Me, too." He rustled through the diaper bag situated at his feet. "Let me get a bottle. Sadie pumped this morning and filled this one, and it doesn't need to be heated." He snapped the cover off and passed the bottle to Lucy.

Gracie's eyes opened, and she took the bottle's nipple into her mouth and sucked.

"She's hungry all right." Lucy didn't spend time dreaming of having her own children. She figured she'd help Sadie and Joel with their family but being tied to a store left her with little time for anything extra. When she had purchased the General Store, she believed her dream had come true. Now she wished she had more time to rest and help her family. Plus, weariness dogged her most days. At thirty, she assumed she'd have more energy, but the mental and physical work at the store drained her.

"What's on your mind, Sis?" He tugged a burp cloth from the bag and handed it to her.

She lifted the babe to her shoulder and patted her back from the bottom to the top. Gracie's burp rivaled the ones Joel used to make on purpose when they were kids. "Takes after Dad."

"Yeah, yeah. I know. What did you want to talk about?"

"A couple things." She breathed in, then let out a slow breath. "I think I'm going to sell the store." She studied his face to measure his expression.

His brows lifted and his mouth hung open. "I wasn't expecting those words. Why do you want to sell your money maker? The store is doing okay, isn't it?"

"Yes. The income is good, but I wake up exhausted every day, and I don't have time for anything except work. In the winter, I'm cleaning, ordering, doing inventory, checking out new products. It never ends. I had hoped hiring a part-time assistant would help, but it hasn't lessened my work. Regina is great, but I still struggle to stay ahead." She fed Gracie the rest of the bottle. "I can make enough profit from selling the store to live for a while without work, plus I invested part of the money Nana left me,

Penny Frost McGinnis, Abbott Island Book 3

and it's doing well enough. I can get another job when I'm ready. Travel is on my list of things to do. You know, I haven't had a vacation in years, unless you count spending the weekend at our parents' on the mainland." A dream she'd never shared flitted through her mind, but she brushed it away.

Joel leaned forward and clasped his hands together. "You've worked there since you were fifteen and bought it when you turned twenty-four, which is an accomplishment. Have you asked God for guidance?"

"I'm trying to. I fumble through the words, but I'm asking." Her foot throbbed. "Can you hold Gracie? I need to readjust my foot because my ankle is aching."

He lifted the baby from her, and she adjusted her foot on the stool and applied the ice. Then she gestured to the yard. "This makes me mad. I should be able to step into my yard without falling in a hole."

Before brother and sister continued their conversation, gravel crunched under the police cruiser as Levi pulled into Lucy's driveway.

His lanky frame exited the car. He perused the pocked soil. "That's a lot of holes. Did you hear noises outside last night, Lucy?"

She pushed her arms against the chair to stand, then dropped herself into the seat. Frustration flooded her. "No." She barked out the word. "I'm sorry. I didn't mean to yell, but no. I didn't hear a thing. I'm a pretty sound sleeper and with the lake lapping the beach, I don't hear anything else." Extra security might help. "Joel, can you add a floodlight to the porch? Something like you put on your house when Sadie had trouble?"

"Of course." He cuddled baby Gracie. "Whatever you need. You're more exposed on this property than we were at Mom and Dad's house."

A shiver ran up her spine. "I hadn't thought about the easy access to the property from the road. I mean, it's good for the rental, if I add one." Who would want to dig a bunch of holes and leave them? What were they searching for?

Levi grabbed his camera from the cruiser and snapped several photos of the property. "I found a couple footprints, probably boots, but otherwise there's not much evidence." He continued to the beach area. "No holes on the beach."

Joel passed Lucy the baby and joined Levi. "I've never seen anything like this since I've been an officer. Could be kids playing a prank or someone believed a crazy treasure story, and they're trying to find it. People tend to believe islands have buried treasures. You know, all those pirates on Lake Erie back in the day." Joel laughed.

Lucy raised her voice for Joel to hear her from the porch. "There was a kid I didn't hire for the summer because I have a full slate this year. Lots of my employees are returning. I doubt he would do this."

Levi and Joel finished their work and stepped onto the porch.

8

Home At Last

Her brother squeezed her shoulder. "You don't know what a person might be capable of or why they'd do something like this."

He lifted Gracie out of Lucy's arms and handed her to Levi. "You need practice for the near future. After you and Charlotte tie the knot."

"I hope not too soon." The younger officer held Gracie with an awkward cuddle.

"I need to get that little one to her Momma. Let's get you inside, Sis." Joel lifted Lucy from the chair and helped her balance. Levi followed him inside.

Joel made Lucy cozy on the couch with a blanket and a new bag of ice. "Sadie wants to bring dinner later."

"Thanks. I appreciate it. Did you bring the crutches you had?"

He ran his hand through his short, blond hair. "Yes. Let me grab them. Be right back."

Levi bounced Gracie in his arms and looked around the tiny house, every room within sight except the bathroom. "You sure like pink."

A smile split Lucy's face. "I love pink. It's such a happy color, and I wanted the kitchen to sparkle." For a moment, she focused on her pink kitchen opposite the living space. A sense of peace passed over her, then flew away.

Crutches in hand, Joel stepped inside. "Here you go."

"Thanks, brother."

Joel reached for Gracie and swaddled her tight, then kissed Lucy on the cheek. "Try not to hurt yourself any more than you already have, and we'll finish our conversation about selling the store later."

She poked out her bottom lip. "I hope you figure out what's going on." Why on earth would anyone target her?

~~~~~

Seagulls sailed overhead on the mainland, carried by the breeze, and a few tourists wandered the grounds. A man stretched his arm across a bench under the watchful eye of Marblehead Lighthouse. He punched numbers into his cell phone, then lifted it to his ear.

"Did you find anything?" He played with the leather strap on the watch he carried but never wore.

"Nope. Nothing. Didn't want to poke around and dig too much last night. The blond lady moved into the little house. I was afraid we'd wake her. Didn't get to fill the holes in."

"What do you mean you didn't fill them in?" He growled through the phone.

"No time. The sun came up, and I'm not risking going to jail."

The man squeezed the leather. "I'm not asking you to go to jail. I'm asking you to do what I'm paying you to do."

"Maybe if you had a better map, instead of letters with clues, we

Penny Frost McGinnis, Abbott Island Book 3

could find it."

"I don't need to listen to you. Don't do another thing until I tell you to." He clicked off and jammed his phone into his pocket.

~~~~

Aunt Marley's kitchen transported Owen back in time. The fake brick linoleum, avocado green refrigerator and stove, and the high-back chairs around the scarred wooden table carried him to a time when he clomped around the table dragging his wiffle bat, at five years old. Aunt Marley had prepared hundreds of meals in this kitchen and fed as many people. The grief he had suffered over his failed baseball career found balm within these walls.

The screen door rattled and Uncle Jed and Aunt Marley swept into the kitchen. "Do you have to walk so fast?" Uncle Jed muttered under his breath.

Aunt Marley huffed. "If I wanted you to get in here, I did." At the refrigerator, she lifted out a pitcher of lemonade, set it on the table along with three glasses from the cupboard and poured them each a glass.

Uncle Jed plopped in a chair and dragged his hat off his head. He fingered the bill, then hung it on the back of the chair. Aunt Marley offered the lemonade to Owen and her husband, then sat beside him. She poked him in the arm.

"You gonna tell him the story?"

"I am." He lifted his glass and took a long, slow drink. "Okay, now I'm ready."

He rubbed a hand over his comb over. "So the tale goes like this."

Owen frowned at his uncle. "Wait a minute. What tale?"

"I reckon she didn't tell you there's a story involved." He scratched his ear. "It's about the holes in Miss Grayson's yard. Or at least it might be."

He leaned away from the table and crossed his leg over his knee. "In 1897, folks took off for the Yukon. A brother and sister from around Sandusky traveled west and made the trek over the Chilkoot Pass. They say the wind cut like a knife and the snow piled so high they had to dig their path as they went. With packs on their backs, they climbed the icy, snowy trail and found their way to a camp. From camp, they trudged along in the knee-high whiteness and met with the folks who searched for gold." He stopped and gulped his lemonade.

Owen leaned in and clasped his hands on the table. "You're telling me people from northwest Ohio traveled to the Yukon to hunt for gold?"

"Yes indeed. A lot of folks headed there in the freezing cold. Even women and children. Whole families made the trip and ladies went without their husbands. According to legend."

"Are you going to finish the story?" Aunt Marley gave Uncle Jed a *let's get on with it* look.

He scratched his head. "Anyway, they got themselves there, and from what I've heard, found a good sock of gold—the name they called their findings. I was told the sister cooked at one of those hotels the ambitious people built for the packs of people who traveled north. I believe it was the Grand Forks Hotel where folks moving through stayed a while before they trekked in or out of the gold fields. The sister made money, bought food, and hiked to her brother's camp. They'd mine for a few days, and she'd do it all over again the next month or so. The last time she made her way to him, the other miners broke the bad news he had died. Not long after, the sister packed and carried the gold home, alone. It's said she brought the gold home in a bentwood box, about the size of a small strongbox, made of cedar decorated with a Tlingit tribe design, with carved animal faces."

Owen leaned away from the table. "What happened to it?"

"Rumor says the box is buried on Abbott Island somewhere. People say the sister came home to Sandusky and her family was afraid to have the gold in their home. They feared somebody might break in and try to steal it. Their relatives had left them a piece of property on the island, so the girl took the box to Abbott Island and buried it with a plan to return and take out a few nuggets at a time as they needed them. Far as I know, the gold's still buried."

"What a crazy story. I've read about the people who pursued the Klondike Gold Rush. They had to be tough with the winter weather and mountains. I can't imagine." Owen carried his glass to the sink and rinsed it out. He turned to his uncle. "Are you sure the gold was never found, if it's even real?"

Jed tapped his fingers on the table. "Not to my knowledge. People have searched the island, but I'm not sure anyone knows where it is."

Aunt Marley covered the lemonade pitcher with clear wrap and stored it in the refrigerator. "Folks are still searching for it. A few years ago, a couple came nosing around here, and I shooed them away. If it's true, the box could be anywhere."

Uncle Jed popped his hat on his head. "I've got work to do." He looked at Owen. "Since you're not planting trees, mind to come help me? I want to prep the garden and plant a few early vegetables. My sweet wife loves fresh peas." He patted Aunt Marley's bottom.

Her cheeks pinked. "You ornery old man, get to work." Her stern expression bowed into a smile.

Owen followed his uncle out the door. Could treasure seekers have torn up Lucy's property? Why choose her place? Had anyone checked the county records to figure out who these people were related to?

"Uncle Jed, what family owned the island property and who were the siblings?

Jed hooked the tiller onto the tractor. "Don't rightly know."

Hidden treasure on Abbott Island seemed far-fetched, but his dad used to say anything was possible.

CHAPTER THREE

The taffy pink in Lucy's kitchen buzzed with energy, while the celeste blue of her loft bedroom calmed her and hugged her with peace. Except today. Instead, camped out on the couch, her ankle awakened her early on Tuesday morning with a dull, achy pain.

The memory of the holes in her yard raised her ire. Before the anger bubbled over, she propped herself on the edge of her temporary bed and examined her foot and lower leg.

"Not too much swelling, Finn."

Finnegan, her betta fish, cruised around the aquarium Lucy had splurged on. The rimless, self-cleaning tank adorned with blue and white stone and fake greenery gave him a warm, clean place to play.

"I see you, buddy."

Finn darted about and paused when he heard Lucy's voice. At least she believed he did. Thank goodness the little guy lived without too much attention to detail. Even though she'd love to have a dog like her sister-in-law's Rosie, her busy schedule left little time for pet care.

Lucy wiggled her foot and touched the puffy area. Good, no sharp pain. She edged off the couch on her crutches and rested her healthy foot on the floor. In slow motion, she touched the other one on the gray vinyl planking. With all her weight on both feet, she balanced and stepped forward. Her slight, painful limp cinched her decision to stay home. Later, she'd call Regina and ask her to open the store from noon to five. With hope to return to work tomorrow, she hobbled to the kitchen and popped a medium roast coffee pod in the Keurig.

After coffee and toast, Lucy dressed, wrapped a lightweight blanket around her shoulders, tucked the crutches under her arms, and limped to the front porch. The holes glared at her. She lowered into the Adirondack chair. Her usual smile turned down and morning cheerfulness refused to make an appearance.

Red clusters of buds hugged branches of the red maple, and bluish-green cedar trees clustered between the beach and the scraggly foliage that separated her property from her neighbor.

"Good morning." Marigold's voice echoed across the yard. She stepped onto the porch. "I heard your foot met a hole yesterday. How are you today?"

No doubt Sadie had filled her dear friend in on her ankle's fate.

"There's less swelling, and I can put a little pressure on it." She patted the arm of the other chair. "Come sit."

Her fifty-something friend settled in the chair beside her. "I brought you a house-warming slash sorry-you-injured-your-foot gift." She lifted a basket from her lap and passed it to Lucy.

"You didn't need to bring me anything." For the first time today, a grin crossed Lucy's face. Inside the basket, she found three mason jars with a candle poured into each one. She lifted the teal-colored one and unscrewed the lid. "A sunny day at the beach in a jar. Lemony and a light sweet fragrance." She lifted a pink one, and a pale green one. "Let me guess. Strawberry and lime?"

"Not quite. The pink is cherry almond, and the green is lime and ginger. I've been experimenting with making homemade candles. Johnny encouraged me to try it. I've wanted to for a long time, and I believe I have these three ready for the public."

Lucy twisted the caps off the other candles. "They smell wonderful. I can't wait to burn them." She replaced the lids and placed the candles on a small table between the chairs, then returned the basket to Marigold. "Thank you so much. I needed something to brighten my day, and you always know how to add cheer to any day."

Marigold rested the basket on the floor. "Sadie told me about the holes." She pointed to the yard. "Any idea why someone would dig in your yard?"

"Nope. None. I'm hoping Levi and Joel can find more clues, but I kind of doubt they will. The culprits didn't leave breadcrumbs." Her eyes surveyed the yard. "A couple of them are in places Owen will plant trees, so that's a plus." She rolled her eyes.

A chuckle rose from Marigold. "Always the optimist."

Lucy gave her a sideways glance and burst into laughter. It lightened her mood, then she quieted.

Thank goodness for her friends, Marigold and Sadie. The two of them had rescued her from herself so many times. God had blessed her with friends and family, yet loneliness sneaked into her days. Just once, she wanted to know what it was like to have a guy she could depend on and go places with, a man besides her brother. She loved hanging with Joel and Sadie, but the third wheel rolled solo. Time to date eluded her. Owen's handsome face popped into her mind, and she shoved the image away. Why would anyone with his calm demeanor want to date her craziness? Besides, the store buried her with work, and the tiny house project and move had added stress. She prayed for wisdom. Did she take the leap and sell now and hope for the best results, or did she hang on longer?

Marigold's voice broke the silence. "Deep in thought?"

Home At Last

"Too deep." Lucy lifted the cherry almond candle, removed the lid, and breathed in the fresh scent. "This one goes in my kitchen. Want to come in? You haven't visited since I put everything away."

Marigold nodded, gathered the candles, and followed Lucy as she navigated into the house on her crutches.

She touched the kitchen counter. "All the pink in here inspired me to create the cherry candle. Where did you buy the refrigerator? I've not seen one so small with a vintage style and color. It's adorable."

Lucy's heart fluttered. Her kitchen brought her joy. "Mom found it for me. She discovered a company that makes appliances with a vintage appearance, the perfect size for a tiny home. It's a great fit in the small space beside the stove. The inside has the perfect amount of room for one person to store their cold food. There's a small freezer at the bottom. I bought the pink stove from them, too. It's too much for most people, but I love the color."

"Me, too." Marigold adjusted the hand-crocheted shawl she wore. "Is there anything I can do for you before I go? I've got more crafts to finish for a show in a couple of weeks."

"Would you set the other candles in the living room? I can't carry them with the crutches."

"Do you think you'll need the crutches long?" Marigold tagged behind her.

"I hope not. I'm using them as a precaution today." Lucy stood and balanced herself.

Marigold deposited the jars on the end table, then they stepped outside. "Take care and if you need me, call me, please."

"I will." Lucy watched her friend walk away, before her attention moved to the beach where the water lapped the shore. The cloudy sky reflected on the water's surface with a bluish cast. She longed to walk to the water's edge, but feared the holes might trip her again. Instead, she watched the seagulls putter along the sand. Rest today, then go to work tomorrow. She'd will her ankle to heal by tomorrow morning.

~~~~~

A crutch under each arm, Lucy worked her way from her Jeep into the General Store on Wednesday morning. A few business owners unlocked their doors or waved hello. The sound of the boat's horn announced tourists who arrived by ferry. Willpower propelled Lucy up the steps and onto the porch of her store. From there she spied the lake and found the water smooth and the day calm. With a click, she unlocked and opened the door. Inside, she flipped on the lights, then hobbled to her office. Regina had left her a note about yesterday's business and a neat desktop. So grateful for her new employee and friend, she made a memo to thank her with chocolate for taking the reins for a few days.

15

Penny Frost McGinnis, Abbott Island Book 3

After she maneuvered from her office to the front counter, Lucy plunked into a folding chair and sorted boxes of souvenirs Regina had left for her behind the counter. Tourists bought key chains, magnets, and stickers more than other items. This year, she added an ornament with a kayaking Santa to her inventory, inspired by Marigold's kayak business. She held one of them in front of her and giggled. She needed one for her tree, but where would she put a Christmas tree in her tiny house? In front of the window or beside the couch? She flicked her wrist in an *I don't care* movement. *I'll think about a tree in November.*

After a few hours, Lucy leaned under the counter and the bell over the door jingled. She lifted her head to see who had arrived. With a clunk, she bumped the back of her skull. "Ouch!" Her eyes closed, and she pressed her hand on a small knot.

A deep voice said, "Are you okay?"

She pressed her lips together and stood, and dizziness swirled through her brain. Her hands grasped the counter, and she righted herself.

"I'm fine." *I have to be.*

"You look pale."

The stranger's Hollywood, bad boy handsomeness accentuated by a dark beard and green eyes gave her pause.

She shook off her dumbfounded expression and forced a neutral veneer. "How would you know I'm pale, since I've never met you before?" No wonder she never had a date. Her snarky responses would put off potential suitors. "I'm sorry. I've had a tough morning, but it's not your fault. How can I help you?"

He shoved the brown waves of his hair away from his face. "I'm Andrew. Nice to meet you." He stuck out his hand, and she shook it. "I'm hoping to talk to the owner of the store. Can you tell me when he'll be here?"

Lucy raised her chin and stood taller. "I'm the owner." Good looking? Yes. Winning points with her? No. "What do you want to know?"

"I didn't expect a person so young to own the store."

"Or a woman?" Lucy cringed.

He rested both hands on the counter. "You got me. I was expecting an older gentleman. Sorry, I didn't do my homework."

Her ankle ached. She stepped back and sat in her chair. "No you didn't. I've owned the store for more than five years and worked here since I was fifteen. Want to sit down?" She moved a box from the seat next to her and patted it.

"If you aren't too busy." He sashayed around the counter and sat next to her. The brown leather bag he carried might fit a small laptop. Was he here on business? Maybe a salesperson. Not many bothered to travel to

16

Home At Last

the island. Most of the marketers or salespeople emailed these days.

She straightened her messy bun. "Are you here to convince me to sell your products in my store? I've placed orders for the summer, and I'm already setting up my displays."

Each year she created a spread sheet and tracked her sales, plus a column for suggestions from her employees or requests from customers. Then she used the information to restock or try something new. Several tourists had inquired about ornaments this past summer and since many of them made return trips, she wanted to have a variety available. Her gaze wandered to the shipments Regina had stacked against the wall, and she longed to check out what else had arrived, but she'd have to wait on whatever this guy wanted.

He rested the leather satchel on his lap. "No, I'm not a salesman. I'm here to relax for a while and check out the island. I'm staying at Sadie's cabin. She and her husband seem nice and the cabin is comfortable."

"I helped Sadie paint the cabins. They're wonderful people. Joel is my brother and one of our local police officers." This guy knew how to get people to talk. He was too good looking and charming. She needed to monitor her words before she spilled her life story.

He clasped his hands together on top of the satchel. "I'll come out with it. I'm playing with the idea of buying a business on the island. I want to invest in a place with a unique culture and a tourist venue. Of course, I want to spend a few weeks here and get a feel for the place, but I value your take as a business owner."

Interesting. If he was serious about buying a business, wouldn't he have done due diligence?

"As I said, I've owned the store long enough to say I've had success. In the off season, I have online orders, and I sell items the year-round islanders need. If you want a successful business on the island, you have to consider the ebb and flow of the island life. Year rounders amount to about 150 people, give or take a few. Summer brings in the most traffic, with spring and fall not far behind. We've experienced more tourism in the last two years because more people are traveling closer to home. A lot of people from southern Ohio, Indiana and Michigan are vacationing here. Before you invest your money, you'll want to understand the islanders."

Andrew stood and slung the bag over his shoulder. "Okay. Thanks for chatting. I'll let you get to your business. If you don't mind, I might stop in again."

Lucy clutched the crutches and pulled herself out of the chair. She limped her way to the door with him. "I'm here most of the time." She shut her mouth before she rattled on about her new tiny home and where she lived. After he walked out, she clicked the lock on the door and turned the *at lunch* sign over. A crutch under each arm, she hopped to her office.

At her desk, she gnawed on a carrot and the idea of selling her store. Could God be answering her prayers through this stranger? Something about him didn't ring true with her. His smile appeared phony, and he didn't make consistent eye contact. When she talked about getting to know the island, he left. Other businesses on the island might have his attention. Wouldn't a man with serious interest have researched before he tried to meet the owner?

Home At Last

CHAPTER FOUR

After lunch, Lucy unwrapped the other ornaments and added them to an artificial tree she had purchased at the Nifty Thrift Shop in Sandusky. Decorating a Christmas tree in April muddled her sense of the seasons, but she adored the wooden stars with a nativity scene engraved on them, and the vintage designed baubles in pinks and teals with Abbott Island printed on them. Certain they'd be bestsellers, she ordered a second box of each.

Gray clouds hovered over the town square as Lucy stepped outside. She stood on the porch of the General Store, leaned the crutches against the rail, and wrapped her arms around her middle. A chill breeze slid through the railing and caused a shiver to climb her spine. She inhaled the fresh, sharp scent of the rain to come.

A patrol car rolled along the side of the road and parked in front of her store. Joel and Levi exited the car and climbed the steps to meet her.

"Hey, you guys. How's your day going?" Lucy hugged her brother.

Joel removed his hat and fingered the bill. "Can't complain." He looked at Levi.

"Me neither, but we did stop to talk to you about the holes in your yard. I investigated more on the opposite side of the island. Someone dug three holes the same size as the ones in your yard."

Lucy leaned against the rail. "Why dig holes? It wasn't on park property, was it?"

"No. You don't know if Owen is working on a job over there, do you?"

She shook her head. "I have no idea." She didn't keep track of Owen. Why ask her, and why did her tummy flip at the mention of his name? "Can I fill in the holes yet? I want Owen to do the landscaping."

Levi nodded. "Yeah. We have what little evidence we could gather."

Joel placed a hand on her shoulder. "I installed your light this morning. Make sure you lock your doors and windows at night."

"Thanks, brother. Of course I'll lock the door. It's not like Finn can protect me." She quirked one side of her mouth into a half grin. "By the way, I met the man renting one of Sadie's cabins, Andrew something. He came in the store this morning and asked me questions about owning a business on the island. Know anything about him?"

Joel placed his cap on his head. "I don't interrogate Sadie's

Penny Frost McGinnis, Abbott Island Book 3

customers. I do know he's from somewhere in Pennsylvania and he plans to stay on the island for the next few months. Which is more than I should be telling you. Did his dashing good looks capture your attention?" He laughed.

"Funny, aren't you? No. Well, maybe. But, no. I was curious because when I started talking business, he left." She lifted her palms in the air. "Doesn't matter, anyway."

Her brother eyed her foot. "How's your ankle?"

"Better. I can ditch the crutches tomorrow. At least I hope so." She grabbed the crutches from where they leaned against the railing. "I'm closing and going home before the rain pours."

Levi lifted his gaze to the sky. "The dark clouds tell me it's going to hit us hard. Take care."

The officers drove away and Lucy limped into the store.

She hung a stray ornament on the little tree and stacked the empty box on a pile to recycle later. Rain spit against the window as Lucy turned the *open* sign to *closed,* locked the store, and made her way to the Jeep. Good thing she wasn't walking or riding her bike.

At home, she prepared blueberry tea and two shortbread cookies in her pink kitchen. She hobbled to the tiny living room without crutches, parked her teacup on the end table, and plunked on the couch. One bite into the shortbread and she shut her eyes and let it melt in her mouth. Almost as good as her Scottish grandmother's cookies. She missed Nana, the woman who had baked the best cookies and given the best hugs. She had ventured to America with her parents at five years old and never lost her brogue. Joel swore Lucy inherited her spunk and resilience from Nana. She had survived the loss of her husband and a daughter, yet her faith never wavered and she lived an abundant life. Never one to hide her feelings, everyone knew where she stood on most everything. In other words, Lucy had a big mouth like Nana. Good thing she had friends who understood her. She doubted a man wanted a woman who spoke her mind, but then again, God might send her someone unexpected. She rested her head against the thick, comfortable cushion of the couch, and she shut her eyes.

What's tapping? Lucy pried her eyes open and listened. The tapping grew louder. She pushed herself from the couch, balanced on her good foot, and shuffled to the door. A shadow cast across the slatted blinds. She lifted one and stared into the eyes of Owen. The breath she'd held released, then she opened the door.

"Owen?" She backed away. "Come in."

Dressed in a blue and white plaid flannel shirt and jeans, he stepped inside. "The rain stopped, so I took a minute to check in on you."

"How kind of you. I must have slept through the storm." She glanced at the clock on her wall. Six-fifteen. She'd slept an hour-and-a-half. No wonder her tongue stuck to the roof of her mouth. "I'm going to pour us glasses of sweet tea. Have a seat in the living room."

He rested on the edge of the couch and fiddled with a blue bandanna. Lucy handed him a drink and sat on the opposite end of the couch.

Owen sipped his tea, then leaned in and eyed her foot. "How's your ankle?"

Her hair had escaped the ponytail holder and drooped down her back. She must look terrible. Why did it matter? Owen wasn't interested in her. *He's so quiet and cute.* Handsome in a boyish kind of way. She pulled the band out of the ends of her hair and fluffed it out around her shoulders. "My ankle feels better. I can stop using the crutches tomorrow. I'm moving around the house without them since everything is near enough to grab hold of."

His shoulders dropped, and he leaned against the couch cushion. "Good to hear. I'm glad it wasn't broken."

~~~~~

A bead of sweat rolled along Owen's spine. Flannel wasn't the best choice for today. The warm weather after the rain or being near Lucy heated him. When she let her hair down, the temptation to run his hands through it overwhelmed him. Thank goodness he had the bandanna and tea to keep him occupied. Something about the beautiful blond drew him to her. Even her boisterous personality appealed to him. He'd admired her work ethic ever since he'd known her and appreciated her kind heart. The potent attraction disarmed him. He'd not connected to another human in a romantic sense since his ex-fiancée walked away because his lifestyle no longer matched hers.

Lucy emptied her glass with one last swallow. "I talked to Levi and Joel earlier today and they told me the holes can be filled in. They also said another property on the island had holes dug the same as here. I can't fathom why."

"Aunt Marley and Uncle Jed think it's got something to do with a treasure buried on the island in the late 1800s." He scooted closer to Lucy. "A woman who had mined for gold with her brother in the Klondike carried the nuggets to Ohio and buried them in a box. The story has circulated for years and others have tried to find it. I'm not sure I buy it."

Lucy squinted and stared at Owen. "Are you serious? I'd forgotten about the story of the Klondike treasure. Dad used to tell it to us around the campfire. I'm sure it was his own version." She rested on the back cushions of the couch. "Leave it to me to be part of a treasure hunt."

She faced Owen. "Do you suppose it could be true? Has anyone seen a map? Wouldn't you imagine with all the mining for limestone the islanders did in the early 1900s, they would have uncovered gold?" She

Penny Frost McGinnis, Abbott Island Book 3

paused and tapped her nose. "Of course, they didn't dig for limestone on this side of the island. The quarry is on the west side. What do you think?"

"It's a far-fetched tale people had fun telling. If the culprits who dug in your yard were looking for treasure, wouldn't they have dug deeper holes? And why so many if they had clues or a map?" He crossed his legs. "Probably bored kids waiting for summer."

"A treasure hunt sounds a lot more exciting than ornery kids." She limped to the desk attached to her wall and retrieved a clipboard. "Any who, Levi said they're finished and we can put the yard together. Want to go over the landscape plans again?"

Lucy tucked in beside Owen and unclipped papers from the board and spread them across the narrow cherrywood coffee table. "You said you have the trees for me. I'm glad you haven't planted them yet, because I changed my mind about where to place the dogwoods." She pointed at the circles she'd drawn in red ink. "I want the pink one on the corner, here, and the white one on the other corner, instead of putting them side-by-side."

Her knee touched his and he struggled to keep his thoughts on the drawings instead of the beauty beside him. "Um, trees on both corners will work. What if I dig a flower bed across the front on each side of the porch to give a flow to the design? You wanted lavender and thyme, and those would be pretty with daisies, purple coneflowers, and rosemary. Behind the house, I can plant black-eyed Susans." She moved her knee and he missed the warmth.

"Oh, I love daisies and black-eyed Susans. Will you still plant the redbud and tulip poplar along the tree line beside the house?"

He eased back against the pillows behind him. "Of course. You have a nice grove of oak and maple separating you from your neighbor. The ones you want will work." He scribbled notes on the paper. "I can start tomorrow morning, if that's okay with you. With the delay, I was able to catch up on a few things for Uncle Jed." Owen stood. "I know what to bring, so I'm leaving the papers here. I'll get them from you tomorrow. Thanks for the tea and I'm glad your foot's doing better." He walked out the door.

~~~~~

Still glued to the couch, Lucy stared at the door. If she hadn't shifted her knee away from his, she might have kissed him. Preposterous. What was she thinking? She'd enjoyed his nearness and those gorgeous brown eyes like liquid chocolate, and who didn't love chocolate?

Ugh. What was wrong with her? She didn't have time for romance. She stacked the papers and tapped them on the table to straighten them, then clipped them to the board. She'd see him tomorrow morning, bright and early. Should she make coffee? Buy donuts? No, just coffee. *Take a breath, Lucy.* She placed the clipboard on the desk and stepped outside.

The lack of ache in her ankle gave her a reason to celebrate. She stepped off the porch, and heedful of the uneven surface, she moved with deliberate steps to the sandy beach. On the rift between scraggly grass and sand, she lowered her body to sit on a log. The waves lapped against Lucy's beach. She watched the water move and a few motorboats skidded past. What had the lake and island been like in the 1800s? Would she have been as brave as the sister and brother who traveled to the frozen tundra to find their treasure? Her heart thumped at the thought of dating, let alone taking a train across the country, riding in a ship, and then hiking through freezing weather.

Nope, not this lady. Her biggest adventure had involved a 200-foot-tall Ferris wheel at Navy Pier one summer when she and Joel went with their parents to Chicago. Living on an island in the middle of a great lake gave her plenty of adventure. Her store and spoiling her niece kept her busy. Too much time and effort went into dating. If things didn't go well and both people lived on the island—disaster might follow. Besides, Owen hadn't asked her out. She closed her eyes and let the waves carry her made-up anxiety away. At least for now.

CHAPTER FIVE

Thursday morning, sunlight cut through the slats of Lucy's window shades. She pushed them open and raised the sash on the window facing the lake. The water sloshed in the golden glow of the sunrise. Yesterday, she had relaxed beside the lake for an hour and let her spirit calm. Nothing beat an evening resting in the presence of God's creation. Today, she planned to tackle the latest shipment of boxes at the store and tidy the storage room. She might check the cellar to make sure none of yesterday's rain had poured in.

Whoever had built the General Store, originally a residence, had dug a root cellar. She kept the dirt floor tidy and available in case she required protection in a severe storm. When unpredictable weather stirred the lake, she might be forced to use the dank area. In the meantime, she sometimes stored things there that resisted the dampness. Last time she ventured into the dark hole, she had discovered walnuts, acorns, and pinecones the squirrels had stashed. At least no skunks skulked under the ground.

After she dressed, she made coffee and stirred in creamer, then poured cereal and milk in a bowl. She cut a banana on top, then carried them to the living area. "Good morning, Finn." She put the bowl and cup on the table and lifted the lid on her fish's food. "Here you go, buddy." When she finished feeding him, she gathered her bowl in her hands and munched the crunchy granola.

From her couch, she watched Owen pull into her yard. His truck loaded with trees and tools bumped onto the dirt and sparse grass. She shoved another spoonful of cereal into her mouth, swallowed, then gulped her coffee. On her way to the door, she glanced in the mirror to check her teeth, squinted at her reflection and fluffed her hair, then glared at herself for primping.

When she opened the door, Owen's hand was raised in a fist to knock. "Good morning." Her smile widened as surprise covered his face.

He lowered his hand. "Good morning. I wasn't expecting you to open the door before I knocked."

She giggled like a thirteen-year-old. "I saw you pull into the yard, and I'm ready for you to make this lumpy mess into a beautiful space."

His warm brown eyes lit with enthusiasm. "That's what I want to hear. You're my second landscape job on the island, and I want to create flower gardens people want for their yards. The farm keeps me and Uncle

Jed busy, but I'm afraid the money isn't made from the soil anymore, at least not farming the soil. If I can build a business landscaping, mowing, selling Christmas trees, and someday having events at the farm, I can stay afloat and enjoy my work. Wow, I spilled my dreams out on you. Sorry."

Lucy's insides warmed at the thought of Owen's ambitions. How could she help him reach his goals? *Whoa, girl. Why do you need to help him? You barely know him. At least see how the landscaping goes before you jump in with both feet.*

Marigold would be proud. Lucy slowed herself down and didn't volunteer to jump feet first into something else. Not only did Lucy dive in headfirst most of the time, she put her foot in her mouth more than she cared to think about.

"Let me get the plans we worked out." Lucy set her bowl and cup in the sink, then retrieved the clipboard.

She stepped onto the porch and clicked the door closed. "Here we go. Is there anything else I can get you before I go to work?" Proud of herself for not volunteering to stay home and help, she handed him the plans.

Owen studied the top page. "This looks good. I'll plant the trees today and outline where I'll create the flower beds. I can't plant grass for a while yet, but over the next week, I'll prepare the soil." He pushed a pencil behind his ear. "You still have a chance to make changes in the type of flowers you want or if you want any other flower beds, plus whatever shrubbery you might want. You have a gorgeous view of the water. I hope to make this a showcase for my work."

Lucy's heart thumped faster. Was he doing this because he was fond of her or to promote his business? When she took the love language quiz in Sunday school class, she had discovered she loved when someone performed an act of service for her, like doing the dishes or landscaping her yard. Of course she was paying him, so did it count as a service? *Come back to reality, Lucy.* "I'm excited to see how your work turns out. I trust you to create a place I can hang out in and enjoy, and I hope to have a party after you're finished. Did I ask if you can install twinkle lights? We could insert poles and string lights around the yard. Say from the corners of the porch to a couple of poles."

Owen scribbled on the paper, then eyed the yard. "No, you didn't, but I can add them to the cost. They shouldn't be too much extra. I'll work the changes up for you and give you an estimate. You might consider extending the porch with a wrap-around deck."

She eyed the area around the porch. "Great idea. Do you build decks? I'd love an extension to add more outdoor space."

He pulled a tape measure off his belt and handed the end to Lucy. "Let me stretch this across and decide how big you want to make it." He stretched the tape across the front, then the sides of the porch and determined how big to build the area. "I'll write an estimate for this and the lights and poles. If you agree, I can build it for you. I think you'd appreciate having the extra space. You'll have to secure a construction permit to add the deck. Once you have it, I can get started. In the meantime, I'll plant the trees, then you can decide how you want to handle the flowers and greenery. The deck will help determine what you want where."

Lucy's broad grin stretched across her face and she clapped her hands. "This is going to be amazing."

~~~~~

Later in the day, quiet shadowed the General Store. Lucy flipped on the radio, one her dad had gifted her, to an oldies station. With her ankle improved, she gyrated across the floor to Creedence Clearwater Revival. Her parents had played them, James Taylor, Carole King, and Carly Simon all the time. Mom would grab her by the hand and have spontaneous dance parties. Laughter spilled out the windows on those days. Her mom no longer danced, but her hands clapped to the rhythm. At Joel and Sadie's wedding, Dad had spun her in her wheelchair.

Lucy missed her childhood. She had grown up with two loving parents and a brother she adored on an island they explored together. Would she ever have a daughter to dance with? Even if she didn't, she looked forward to teaching Gracie her moves.

She lowered herself to the floor and opened the last Christmas ornament shipment. A miniature Christmas tree, complete with a star and baubles, winked at her. Each tree's unique color and style enchanted her. A pink tree with silver balls rested in her hand. "This one is going home with me."

A low-pitched voice sounded from the front of the store. "Hello. Is someone here?"

How had she not heard the bell on the door? Lucy rose from the floor and craned her neck to see who entered. "I'm over here." She slipped the pink tree onto the counter. The handsome stranger she had met the other day stepped across the hardwood floor. "Andrew, wasn't it?"

"You remembered me." His white teeth formed a bright smile.

She brushed dust off her jeans. "I try to recall customers if possible." Especially ones who asked a lot of questions. "How can I help you?"

He rubbed his temple with his fingers. "I wanted to apologize for leaving so abruptly the other day. My phone buzzed in my pocket, and I thought it was a call I'd been waiting for."

"Was it?" Lucy tilted her head to the side.

"No, but I'd like to make up for my rudeness by taking you to lunch over at Johnny's Place. We could continue our conversation."

Lucy bit the inside of her lip, then said, "Sure. Did you want to go

Penny Frost McGinnis, Abbott Island Book 3

now?"

A smile spread across his face. "If it's okay. It is noon."

"Give me a minute." Lucy closed the box she'd started to unpack, then picked up the little tree and carried it to her office. She laid the tree on her desk, lifted her purse from the coat rack, then ambled to the front of the store and posted the *out to lunch* sign.

The pit of her stomach quivered at the idea of eating lunch with a man she didn't know. Was this a date or a business lunch? A business lunch, yes, nothing more. Lunch with a man who looked like a Hollywood star made her palms sweat. How silly of her.

~~~~~

The fragrance from Johnny's Place matched any expensive restaurant. His Greek gyros with his homemade tzatziki sauce made her taste buds dance. Lucy's favorite remained the hamburgers he grilled and topped with co-jack pepper cheese, hand-cut dill pickles, and his special sauce. Johnny and Henry's cooking pleased their customers so much, they had an article written about them in the *Lake Erie News*.

The hostess seated Lucy and Andrew at a table in the courtyard, an addition Johnny had made last summer. The sun beamed and warmed the afternoon air. Seventy degrees on a day in April blessed the island folks.

Lucy watched a cloud float across the blue sky. "Today is amazing. We've had a mild spring. I've already seen a few tulip leaves poking through the soil."

Andrew studied her face and squinted. "That's nice. What do you eat here?" He bowed his head over the menu.

He must not be interested in plants. Owen would have told her which variety of tulip bloomed early. She brushed the thought aside. *Doesn't matter.* "All the food is good. I love their hamburgers and the Greek salads are delicious. Johnny makes his own sauces, and Henry creates decadent desserts. If I'm not careful, I'll gain ten pounds in one meal." Lucy's loud laughter rolled across the courtyard.

Andrew jerked his head up and stared at her. "Ten pounds is a lot. I'll try a burger and skip dessert." He folded the menu and leaned away from the table.

Not much sense of humor, she guessed. "A salad sounds good to me."

The waitress took their orders and left them alone.

Andrew's gaze swept the area. His eyes stared at something across the fence as he spoke to Lucy. "How long has Johnny's been in business?"

"More than ten years. Before he bought the restaurant, it had been a fish and chips place with a few rooms to rent upstairs. I think Johnny uses it for storage now. The building has been here since the late 1800s. Of course, it's had several updates and repairs over the years. It started out

Home At Last

as a residence, like many of the businesses in the downtown. My store was a home back in the day. The Russell family bought it in the 1950s and made the downstairs into a store while they lived upstairs."

The waitress set their lunches on the table.

"When did you say you bought it?" Andrew lifted his burger to his mouth.

Lucy mixed the creamy Greek dressing into her salad with her fork. "I've owned the store for five years. I started working there when I was fifteen and never left. I've loved it until..."

"Until?"

She shook her head. "Never mind." She lifted a fork full of salad to her mouth and chewed. "This tastes so good."

Andrew watched her for a moment, then glanced over the fence again. "My sandwich is delicious. Thanks for the recommendation." He sipped his tea. "Does the store have a yard in the back? Like this one?"

Lucy turned her head to see what had caught his attention. Nothing in particular stood out. She faced Andrew. "A small one. There's a residence behind me with a larger yard. I don't know if the yard was an original part of the home or not."

"It's fascinating to learn the history of places. A little island in a big lake could tell many stories." His smile transformed into a leer and his eyes fixed on Lucy. He bit into his burger without taking his eyes off her.

What's he thinking? Best to go on with the conversation. "Are you interested in buying property on the island?" Lucy bit into a fork full of lettuce, cucumber, and olive.

He swallowed his bite and wiped his mouth with his napkin, then cleared his throat. "I'm not sure. I need to see what's available and if it's viable for what I want to do."

"Do you have a business in mind?"

He peered over the fence again. "I'm not ready to discuss it yet. Hope that's okay."

"Sure. No worries." If she sold the store, was Andrew's restlessness the right fit for the island, or was her curiosity running ahead of her at break-neck speed?

CHAPTER SIX

A weathered satchel that smelled of mildew and dirt rested on the desk. After Mother had died, Travis had rummaged through her belongings until he found the relic he had wanted for years. Yes, he missed his mother, but now he clutched the letters his great-great-great-aunt had left behind. Too bad about her brother. An avalanche in the Yukon had swallowed him, along with many other gold miners. Amazed the woman made her way home, Travis respected her and her hand-drawn map of Abbott Island. The details amazed him, but she failed to add an important one — the exact place she had buried the treasure. She hadn't left behind great information, but at least he had a few places to target.

The letters she'd written to her mom read as journal entries. If he figured out the order, maybe the clue to the treasure, if there was still one buried, would come to light. Imagine if he found Klondike gold. He'd buy the island. A snort of arrogance escaped him.

The man scrubbed and dried his hands, pulled on white gloves, and slid each letter from its envelope, one by one. Twelve letters lay before him. He had read them but wanted to study them, with hopes an obvious clue might rise off the page.

He lifted one and held the thin paper to the light. The smeared ink of the date appeared to be June or July 1897.

My Dearest Mother,

I know your heart sorrows without Jonas and me at home to celebrate your birthday. With loving hearts, we send you all the joy you deserve. This might put your mind at ease. After you sent us off on the train, surely some dear angel watched over us. Our journey to Omaha was completed without issue, other than the hard third-class benches we sat on for the trip, but we needed to be careful with our money and not over extend what little we had.

Before we boarded the last train to Omaha, we caught a peek of the first-class dining room and my goodness, the seats were covered in velvet and the tables' legs were decorated with fancy carvings and curlicues. I've never seen anything so elegant. The smells from the kitchen left us drooling, but biscuits and cheese kept us full. We'll soon leave the city and traverse the next leg of the trip. Jonas and I miss you. Maybe we'll ride home in first class after we discover Klondike gold.

Your loving daughter,
Merrilee

Travis placed the letter on the table he'd cleared. He guessed this letter was the first one of the trip, written on the train, then mailed in Omaha. His ancestors rode in third class. Sounded as if they needed the gold, and so did he.

On previous excavations out west, he had dredged up a few treasures, but nothing compared to this one. If this gold cache proved real, he could pay off his and his mother's debts and support his next venture, but it was imperative his minions kept the hunt quiet. No need for anyone else to join the search.

His mother had believed Aunt Merrilee fabricated the whole thing and wrote letters to tell her momma a story. Close examination of the letters might speak otherwise. He unfolded the next one on the pile. She'd recorded nothing but an update on their whereabouts. Six letters more revealed a lot of train travel.

Last year, he had poured his savings into attempting to solve the ciphers of the lost Beale treasure—gold, silver, and jewels discovered by Thomas Beale near the Colorado-New Mexico border and carried to Virginia where Beale buried it. Beale had wanted his treasure passed down to family, so he had created three cyphers for them to follow as a map, but only one was ever solved. Travis had wasted time and money searching for the long-lost treasure. Now, no matter what he had to do, he planned to find the gold his ancestors buried.

He raised the phone and tapped in the number.

"Hello." The man sounded as if he startled him awake.

Travis barked into the phone. "You haven't dug any more holes, have you?"

"No, sir."

"Good. Don't do any more until I call you again. You've made a mess jumping ahead without my input. I'm working out a plan to pinpoint where the item I want to find might be. Remember, when you do find the box I described, do not open it. Call me and wait for me. Don't bungle this and you'll get a nice cut." He clicked off the connection.

Part of Travis's plan included snooping around the island and chatting with people who might provide a clue. Of course he'd be discreet. No one else needed to poke their nose into his treasure hunt.

~~~~~

A little over a week later, temperatures stayed steady in the fifties and sixties. The glassy surface of the lake reflected the sun as a few boaters

Home At Last

navigated the water. Owen carried lumber into Lucy's yard. He stacked the pieces for her deck along the side of the house, then grabbed his tools from his truck. Before he tapped on the door, Lucy stepped outside.

"Good morning." Lucy stretched her arms. "It's a beautiful day."

"Morning." The corner of Owen's mouth lifted. "Be right back." He set the toolbox on the porch and trotted to the truck to retrieve his portable saw. He carried it to the house and set it beside his toolbox.

Lucy wore a light blue sweatshirt with the Abbott Island logo printed in white. The color of the shirt made the blue in her eyes sparkle. Her blond hair hung to one side in a ponytail. Owen's heart beat a bit faster than normal. He had carried the saw, after all. That was what it was, physical exertion, not the beautiful woman standing in front of him. He paused to slow himself.

"Do you have a place I can plug my saw in?"

Lucy turned her head and pointed to the receptacle beside the door. "There's an outlet here. I haven't used it yet." She moved her Adirondack chair to the side. "Is there anything else I can do for you or get you?"

Before he could stop himself, he blurted out, "Want to go to dinner sometime?" What had he said? Must be his aunt's insinuations and suggestions he should date Lucy. Now what?

Lucy smiled and his heartbeat sped up. "I'd love to."

He fumbled with the saw's cord. "Great. How about Saturday night? We can go to the mainland if you want. I have Uncle Jed's boat. I'll pick you up at six." He rushed through his words and heard himself sound like a schoolboy. "In the truck, not the boat."

"Sounds fun. I haven't been over there in a while." She tugged on the hem of her sweatshirt.

Owen adjusted the bill of his Boston Red Sox baseball cap. "Me neither." He'd not been on the mainland or on a date in a long time. What was he thinking?

~~~~~

Lucy stepped inside her home and leaned against the closed door. Owen Bently had asked her to dinner. On the mainland. The two of them. A real date. The last time Lucy had gone on a dinner date with a man ended in disaster. Bart what's-his-name took her to the Abbott Island restaurant and ordered for her. He chattered the entire meal and she nodded and filled her mouth with food. He didn't stop long enough for her to inject any kind of comment, let alone conversation. Lucy had left with a headache and ringing in her ears. When he asked her out again, she had replied with a firm no. Two months later, he moved off the island.

She flitted to the kitchen and dropped a pod in the coffee maker. The aroma of the caramel flavor wafted through the house. Mug in hand, she walked to the front window and watched Owen slice a piece of wood with

33

Penny Frost McGinnis, Abbott Island Book 3

the table saw. His muscular arms lifted the piece with ease. Giddiness skidded through Lucy. She raised her arms as if to cheer, until coffee dripped on her head.

"Good grief, Lucy. Get it together and stop stalking the man through your own window."

An hour later, Lucy stepped outside in her best nonchalant pose. Her hands hung at her sides, and she shook them to flitter away her nerves. The smack of the hammer filled the air. She waited for Owen to pause.

"Hey, I'm heading to work. Do you need anything?" She'd rather stay home and help him build the deck, but the store couldn't prepare itself for the summer rush.

He lifted his safety glasses and removed his ear protection. "No, I'm good. Have a great day." His eyes locked on hers.

"Gotta go." She darted across the yard and mounted her bike. The thought of a date with Owen threw her off kilter. Good thing she had to leave.

At the back of the store, Lucy parked her bicycle, then unlocked the rear entrance. She flipped on the lights and stood as if glued to the floor. Something felt off. Nothing was disturbed in her office, but discomfort draped over her. An odor of evergreen and spice drifted across the room. Not something she sold in the store, like an air freshener. No, it smelled more of aftershave and body odor. She lifted a baseball bat she kept in her office and stepped into the retail area. Other than the creaking of the old building, no other sounds met her ears. She surveyed the store.

A piece of yellowed paper lay on the floor near the counter. Just a corner of what looked like an old newspaper or page from a book. The letters "Klo" were printed near the torn edge of the brittle paper. Regina may have been reading one of her old books. She loved learning about the history of the area, but she didn't stink like a man who ran a marathon and tried to cover it with smelly cologne. Unless Lucy found something out of place, she wouldn't worry about it. Could be some weird odor from outside had drifted in or the last customer yesterday stank. She shrugged and carried the bat to the office. Before she went to set up displays, she worked on the computer and checked shipment dates for a few items she hadn't received.

"Hello. Lucy." Regina's voice called through the office door.

So engrossed in orders, Lucy hadn't heard Regina arrive until she entered the office.

"Good morning. Or is it afternoon?" Lucy checked the time on the computer. "We have another hour of morning."

Regina hung her jacket on the coat rack and sank into Lucy's well-loved flowered chair. "I've been awake since six this morning."

Lucy scrunched her eyebrows and peered at her friend. "Why so

Home At Last

early? Did the kids wake you?"

Regina crossed her legs and arms. "Not the kids or Gio. He's off island for work this week." She swung her crossed leg. "I heard a rumor. One I'm a little concerned about."

"You look tense. Must be a doozy. No one is picking on the kids, are they? I'll help you go after them." Lucy smiled until Regina glared. "Did I do something wrong?"

"Not yet. I just wish you'd told me first." She uncrossed her arms and rested them on the chair.

Lucy stood, walked around her desk, and leaned on the edge. "Told you what?"

Regina lifted herself from the chair and stood nose-to-nose with her boss. "You want to sell the store."

Lucy's spine straightened, and she planted both feet on the floor. Regina moved back a step. "Where did you hear the rumor? I know this island is tiny, but I only told my brother I was thinking about it."

Regina's shoulders relaxed. "I saw Levi the other day, and I guess he thought I knew. He mentioned it in passing. He said, 'when Lucy sells, I wonder who will buy the store.' I didn't let on I didn't know, but you can imagine my shock. I love this job and I don't want to lose it."

Lucy rubbed her forehead. "He must have overheard me tell Joel, or my dear brother told him. I did tell Joel I wanted to sell. I've been praying about it for a few months." She leaned against the desk. "I'm ready for bed by eight o'clock, most nights. It's hard to fall asleep, because my mind runs through the tasks for the next day. When summer traffic picks up, I ride a crazy roller coaster. I've loved owning my business, but I'm not sure how long I can keep at it. There's no time to have a life."

Regina patted Lucy on the shoulder. "I'm sorry. I should have approached you in a kinder manner."

"No. I should have told you. I haven't talked with a realtor yet, but I think I will soon. The timing isn't great, but if it sells during the busy season, the person will already be ahead. There has been an inquiry, but I don't know if he's serious. A man is staying at Sadie's who is interested in buying a business on the island. He may or may not be interested in this one, but I'd talk to him about it after I speak with a realtor.

"Whatever you do, you know I'll help you, whether I have a job in the end or not. You have to do what's best for you." She gave Lucy a quick hug.

"You are so sweet. Thank you."

Now to figure out how not to feel guilty if Regina found herself out of a job.

Home At Last

CHAPTER SEVEN

Saturday morning, Lucy rolled over in bed and checked the clock for the fourth time since midnight, then stared at the slanted walls above her bed. Sunlight shined through the small window, onto the peak of her ceiling and decorated her wall with rays of morning cheer. Eight o'clock and the hammering outside drew her to a lower window in her loft. She knelt on her mattress and peered outside.

Owen's blond hair glimmered in the light. He hauled a long board across the deck and laid it in place. The man still used a hammer and nails. He had told her he didn't do enough carpentry to own a nail gun or many other tools and his uncle worked the old-school way, so he worked the old-fashioned way, too. His healthy physique showed his years of...what? Lucy had no idea where Owen had worked during the years he stayed away from the island. After college, his trips to visit his aunt and uncle had been few. Now, he worked in her yard, and she'd be on a date with him tonight.

With no idea where he wanted to take her, she descended the narrow stairs to the bottom floor of the tiny house. Her dressier clothes hid in a small closet under the staircase. She rummaged through her collection of outdated—or vintage, as she called them—clothes and found a pair of navy-blue wide leg, pleated front trousers. Yes, she had considered donating them, but they fit so well she'd kept them. The flowery peasant blouse with blue and violet pansies still looked good. With her bangle bracelets and hoop earrings, she'd at least have fun playing dress up.

After breakfast, she planned to avoid Owen. He might cancel on her, or worse yet, try to talk to her and the oatmeal in her stomach would churn. She hurried out the rear door, hopped on her bike and sailed to Sadie and Joel's for a little chill time with her sister-in-law and sweet little Gracie.

Sadie rocked on the porch with her baby in her lap. "Lucy. What brings you out this morning? Shouldn't you be working?"

Lucy parked her bike beside the house, then ascended the steps and sat in the rocker beside Sadie. "I wanted to see my favorite niece, and Regina has the store covered. We've been switching every other Saturday during the slow season."

Sadie passed Gracie to her aunt. The little one gurgled and cooed.

"Hello, sweet girl. I've missed you." She planted a kiss on her chubby cheek. "She's grown again, hasn't she?"

Sadie folded the burp cloth she'd had on her shoulder. "Each day she changes. The doctor said she's healthy and her rate of growth is on target. She has so many facial expressions now. I love watching her."

Lucy played with the little bit of hair on her head. "You'll be making her a ponytail before long."

"Let's not get in a hurry. I want to enjoy all the moments of baby time before they're gone." Sadie eyed Lucy. "Tell me why you're really here."

Wind chimes on the porch tinkled a joyful tune. "How do you always know?"

"We've been friends way too long for you to be out on a Saturday morning, your day off, and me not wonder what's going on." Sadie's eyebrows raised.

"Fair enough." She lifted Gracie up and down with a gentle bounce. "I've got a couple of things on my mind. Did Joel tell you I want to sell the General Store?"

Sadie's eyes widened. "No. Was he supposed to?"

"No. I thought he might have. I guess Levi overheard me tell Joel, and he mentioned it to Regina. Not on purpose. More like in conversation and it slipped. She confronted me, but we smoothed out the issue. I'm tired of the constant strain on my time. I've worked there for years, and island traffic has increased the last few summers. Keeping track of sales trends and supplying what might sell keeps me awake at night. Summers aren't fun anymore, and if I want to date Owen, I don't know if I'll have time."

Sadie pressed her hands against the arms of the rocker, sat straighter, and stared at Lucy. "Wait, what? Date Owen? When did this happen?"

She'd blabbed too much again. "Owen asked me out. He wants to take me to the mainland and eat dinner."

"Ooh-la-la." Sadie wiggled her shoulders up and down. "I assume you said yes."

Lucy rested Gracie on her shoulder and rocked. "I did. He's a great guy, a hard worker, and he's kind-hearted. I'm happy he asked, but I'm worried it could ruin a good friendship. There aren't many folks our age on the island, and I don't want to isolate anybody. We'll be losing Levi at the end of summer when he marries Charlotte and moves to Vermilion. I'm sure he'll visit and bring her too, but we lose one younger person."

Sadie moved her chair in rhythm with Lucy's. "The guy renting one of my cottages may decide to live here. He's talked about how much he loves the peace and quiet."

"You mean Andrew?" The lake's waves splashed the shore and reminded Lucy not to take the springtime serenity of their community for granted. "He might change his mind when the summer crowd arrives."

"I mentioned the summer tourists to him, and he said he wanted to own a business and make money off the visitors. I'm not sure it's a good reason to buy a store or any other business." She readjusted her long, brown ponytail. "He might be interested in the General Store. Would you sell to him?"

Lucy stood and walked Gracie across the porch and back. "He stopped in and asked me questions. I think I was the only business owner willing to give him the time. I suppose I could ask him what he's interested in, but I don't want the store to go to any old buyer. I hope whoever invests in it keeps the island vibe and cares about the customers."

Sadie rose, placed her hands on her hips, and faced her friend. "He may not appear the best choice, but you know you can't control what a buyer does with the store after they purchase it. I updated Gram's cottages and changed her rental practices. If God shows you the opportunity to sell, trust Him. Pray about it, Lucy. I've learned the hard way to take my worries to God and not try to control everything."

"I know, and I'm talking to God about it. Thanks for the reminder."

Gracie released a wail into Lucy's ear, and she glanced at Sadie. "Time to eat?"

"Sure is." She turned to the door. "Let's go inside."

They settled in the living room. Lucy sat cross-legged on the over-sized red leather couch her sister-in-law had inherited from her grandfather, while Sadie nursed Gracie in the recliner.

"Have you picked an outfit for tonight?" Sadie wiggled her foot.

Lucy straightened her legs and crossed them at the ankle. "Yes. When I moved into the tiny house, I downsized everything, including my wardrobe. I wear jeans and t-shirts for work, but I kept a couple of my favorite dressy clothes. They're out of style, but I don't care. I have my navy wide-leg pants and the peasant blouse I wore to Johnny's party last year. I'm adding a wide leather belt and chunky jewelry. It's out-of-style or the little black dress I wear to everything else."

"Same here. I live in jeans and t-shirts. Since we wear jeans to church now, I don't wear dresses or dress pants. Although our favorite matchmakers, Miss Aggie, Miss Flossie, and Miss Hildy, don't favor the jeans." She sat Gracie upright on her lap and patted her back. "If those three find out you and Owen went on a date, they'll pester the stuffing out of you." Sadie leaned into the recliner and released a laugh.

"Not funny."

"Sorry. Anyway, your outfit sounds cute. Try to relax and have fun. A night out with dinner sounds wonderful."

Gracie let out a burp.

Lucy rose from the couch and lifted her niece out of Sadie's arms. "Any time you and Joel want to go to dinner, let me know. I'll be happy to babysit this sweet girl." She eyed Sadie and her lips pressed together. "I wasn't nervous about the actual date until you mentioned relaxing. Thanks a lot." She paced across the room, stared out the window, and listened to the lake.

~~~~~

Owen kicked up dust in his aunt and uncle's driveway around four o'clock. No point unloading the tools from the truck bed, but he needed to clean the front seat for Lucy. Sheep baaed in the field and a breeze blew Aunt Marley's wind chimes. He lifted a dirty work jacket and the wrapper from his favorite candy bar from the seat. At least he had thrown most of the trash away yesterday.

In the barn, he wet a clean rag at the utility sink, then carried it to the truck. With vigorous motions, he scrubbed the seat, then used a broom to sweep debris from the floor. Good enough. Although Lucy deserved better. Better than a broken-down baseball player. He doubted she had followed his short time in the major leagues. If she had, she'd know he had failed. He rubbed his shoulder and tried to alleviate the pain. The rotator cuff never fully recovered from the surgery. The doctor had tried to fix him, but the therapy failed to bring his arm back to full strength. At least the surgery had allowed him to have a working arm.

What was he thinking, asking a beautiful woman out on a date? The words had fallen out of his mouth before he could stop them. She'd said yes. A shock to him.

He trekked into the farmhouse. Aunt Marley and Uncle Jed relaxed at the kitchen table with mugs of tea and a plate of peanut butter cookies.

"Would you like tea and a cookie?" Aunt Marley stood.

"No thanks. Sit and relax. I'm good." Owen scrubbed his hands at the kitchen sink.

When he turned to the table, the older woman munched a bite of cookie, swallowed, then sipped her tea. "I'm about to start fixing supper. Anything you want in particular?"

Oh, boy. He'd not hear the end of this now. He cleared his throat. "No thanks. I won't be here to eat."

Uncle Jed stirred his tea and clinked the mug. "Where are you going off to?"

Owen lowered himself into a chair and his gaze moved from his aunt to his uncle. "I'm going on a date." As soon as the words left his mouth, he lowered his head and stared at the table. No one said a word. He raised his gaze and his aunt's face said it all.

Her smirk lifted into a grin. "I'll be. It's about time. Are you taking the pretty Grayson girl out?" She carried the mugs and empty plate to the sink, then leaned against the counter. "Are you?"

His eyes pleaded with Uncle Jed.

Home At Last

"Don't look at me, son," the older man said. "You best answer her."

"Yes, I'm taking Lucy to the mainland for dinner. If it's okay, can I take the boat instead of taking the ferry tonight?"

His uncle tapped his fist on the table. "Fine by me. It's filled with gas and ready to go."

Aunt Marley sashayed to the table and sat. She folded her hands under her chin. "Where you taking her?"

He drew in a breath. His aunt and uncle meant well, but their nosiness pushed an uncomfortable button. He shoved his frustration away and answered. "I'm taking her to the Bayside Waterfront Restaurant. I met some of my past teammates there for dinner a few times and the food is good."

"Sounds kind of romantic, too."

Aunt Marley batted her eyelashes, and it about undid him.

"Please don't make this bigger than it is. It's just a date. Two people going out together to share a meal." He glared at his aunt. "Since when are you a romantic?"

Uncle Jed leaned in and kissed her on the cheek. "You might be surprised." He wiggled his eyebrows.

Before they added more to an already uncomfortable conversation, Owen left the table and bounded out the door. In his cabin, he stared at his closet. A pair of jeans and a dress shirt made sense. However, going on a date with a beautiful woman didn't. After his disastrous relationship with Rebecca had ended, he had vowed no more dates. So, why go on this one?

Home At Last

CHAPTER EIGHT

Dim light filtered through the window. Travis flicked on the lamp on the small desk to allow himself enough light to study the letters and a surprise he'd discovered in the old satchel. Pages wrapped in quilted cloth appeared to be a journal of sorts. With a sandwich from Johnny's Place, he settled in the desk chair to inspect this latest find.

The stitching sewn to keep the yellowed pages together had disintegrated in places. A few threads clung together enough to keep the pages in order. He turned the papers and found scribbled notes on the days his great-whatever aunt and uncle journeyed to the Yukon.

Day 39
We got off the train in San Francisco, tired and dirty. Stayed the night in a hotel and prepared to board a ship to Seattle. Light on money, we took a freighter to Skagway.

Day 41
Seasick for two days. Stomach settled enough to go on deck. Saw a black and white whale, somebody called it a killer whale. Don't want to see one again. Their size scared me.

Day 43
Mountains are taller than any we've ever seen. Glaciers reached from the peaks to the waterline. The freighter dodged multiple islands and icebergs. Seasick again.

Travis rubbed his eyes. They ached from squinting at his aunt's penmanship and the lack of an overhead light in the crummy cabin, but he wanted to read their whole story. He might miss something if he didn't take his time on each page. The letters she had sent home to her mother had scratched the surface, but he mined little information about the gold or where she might have buried it. He laid the journal on the desk and lifted the sandwich. He'd eat, then read more of what appeared to be about one hundred pages. In his earnest search for clues, he hoped to connect enough dots not to destroy more of the island. He'd reprimanded the knuckleheads who forged ahead and dug holes without his permission. Then, he drilled into them the need to avoid attention from the police. Once he found the link and the possible hiding place, he'd

43

befriend the person who lived there or owned the property and find his treasure. In the meantime, he'd slink around and observe the layout of the town. If he failed, he'd lose his mom's house and what little security he had, and if he discovered the gold, he'd do whatever he wanted.

~~~~~

The yellow siding and white trim on Lucy's tiny home stood showcased against evergreen pines and maple trees. Even with the deck half-finished, the place beckoned Owen to sit and chat. Just like Lucy. Her home gave off a friendly vibe, from the pink kitchen to the teal living area.

Owen pulled the truck into the gravel along the edge of the yard. He considered installing a stone walkway for her from the pull-off to the deck, but she might not have it in her budget. If he carried flat rocks from his uncle's creek, he'd save her money.

Get out of your head, Owen. She's not your project or your girlfriend. Go on the date, enjoy a good meal, and let it go.

At the door, he knocked and waited. When the door popped open, he held his jaw closed. Talk about stunning. She had made some sort of twist in her hair and curls fell to her shoulders. The blue in her top made her eyes sparkle. *Wow! She's gorgeous.*

He untangled his tongue. "Hi, Lucy. You look amazing." His lips widened into a smile. "Are you ready?"

Her cheeks pinked. "Thank you." She stepped out the door and twisted the knob. "It's locked. I'm all set."

Aunt Marley would be proud he offered his arm. Lucy slipped her hand in and walked beside him.

"Sure glad I didn't find you in a hole when I got here." A nervous chuckle spilled out of him.

Lucy tilted her head. "What? Oh. Yeah. I'm upright tonight. Not a hole in the yard since you filled them in. By the way, the deck looks great. I know it's halfway finished, but I'm getting the feel for how it will wrap around the porch."

At the truck, he opened the door. "I'm sorry the cab's not super clean."

"No worries. I'm sure it's fine." With a small grunt, she raised herself to the seat and scooted in.

Inside the cab, Owen started the engine and drove to the boat.

"Did I grunt? I'm sorry. Not very ladylike." She pressed her fingers to her forehead, then laughed out loud.

Owen joined her and they guffawed. "It's okay, Lucy. If you're as nervous as I am, I understand. I would have been louder than you."

"Thank you. I've been nervous all day. Silly isn't it? We're two friends going to dinner."

The tightness in his shoulders released. "Exactly what I told Aunt

Home At Last

Marley and Uncle Jed."

At the dock in town, Lucy climbed into Uncle Jed's boat. Owen's eyes caught sight of her shoes. Smart and practical, she wore white tennis shoes tied with navy blue ribbons. Rebecca always wore spiky heels. He had never understood how women walked in them. From Lucy's sweet smile to her sensible shoes, this woman could snag his heart.

~~~~~

On the fifteen-minute boat trip to Sandusky, Lucy appreciated how Owen took his time, but she got chilled from the night air, and chided herself for not bringing a jacket. At least her hair stayed in place. The windshield and hardtop protected them from the wind and water.

"Your uncle's boat is cool. Is it an antique?" Lucy tugged the sleeves on her peasant blouse over her shoulders.

Owen turned from the steering wheel. "It's a Skiff Craft Hardtop. Uncle Jed has babied it since he bought it in the 1970s. I'm surprised he lets me use it, but he says he's too old anymore, and he wants me to keep it running. It's a beauty. One of the few wooden ones still on the water around here. We delivered it to the town's dock a few days ago and went over the engine. The old dock he had near the farm bit the dust last year, and he found it more practical to keep the boat in town, for now. He plans to build a new deck this summer." He placed his hands on the steering wheel, and she moved to stand beside him.

"I love being on the water. Joel has Dad's boat and we take it out once in a while. Not as much since he married Sadie, but I'm guessing we'll get on the lake with Gracie."

"Sounds fun. I'm sure Gracie will grow up with a love of water and island life. It would be nice to see more families stay on Abbott."

"I agree." Lucy pointed across the water. "A sailboat. Have you ever ridden in one?"

He pursed his lips. "A few times, when I lived in Boston. I went with... a friend." He slowed and steered the skiff into the dock area.

A friend, huh? What kind of friend? The sour frown on his face before he answered gave her something to chew on, but his past wasn't her business.

After he secured the ropes, Owen took Lucy's hand and helped her out of the boat. A spark sailed from Lucy's hand to her shoulder. His work-worn palm fit into hers, and she didn't want to let go, but she wanted to give him a good impression. Rather than appear as a clingy date, she released her hold and walked near him. Her tennis shoes made the two-block walk to the restaurant easy.

The building's warm, welcoming feel opened to brick walls painted a shade of aqua, wooden benches, chairs, and tables, well-placed greenery and a deck over the water. Grilled steak flavored the air. The hostess

Penny Frost McGinnis, Abbott Island Book 3

guided Owen and Lucy to a table on the edge of the deck.

Owen pulled her chair out for her and goosebumps rose on Lucy's arms. Not from the chill in the air, but because she found herself in the presence of a man with a kind heart and gentle manner. The times she had allowed herself the luxury of considering what type of man she might want to marry, she had dreamed of someone tall, dark-haired, with a strong personality who might help tone down her personality. Owen had the tall part. Why she thought someone should rein her in, she didn't know. Marigold had said time and again, "Be yourself, Lucy. We love you for who you are."

Once she had accepted her friend's wisdom, she no longer wanted someone to bridle her energy. A few years ago, she had learned from her sister-in-law to find someone who complimented her personality, not extinguished it.

The waiter delivered a carafe of sparkling water flavored with lemons and the menus.

"Thank you." Owen viewed the list of foods. "What do you like, Lucy? They have excellent walleye, and their steak is delicious." He lifted his eyes from the menu and watched Lucy check out the offerings. "I didn't ask. Are you a vegetarian?"

Her gaze rose to his, and she shook her head. "No. I enjoy the burgers at Johnny's. How about you? What do you like?"

"I'll eat about anything, especially if someone else cooks. My skills in the kitchen are few."

The waiter arrived, ready to take their order. "What can I get you this evening?"

Both ordered steak, baked potatoes, and salad.

"Sounds like we both like the same thing." Lucy unfolded her napkin and rested it on her lap. "I'm with you. If someone else cooks, I'm happy. I can cook, but I seldom take the time since I'm by myself."

"Aunt Marley fixes breakfast and dinner. She says she loves to make meals that make people happy. I'm not going to argue with her. Her dinners make me happy. When I was in the minor leagues, I had to fix my own meals or eat out. Since I didn't make much money, I ate a lot of grilled cheeses and canned soup." He sipped his water.

"What? You played professional baseball? How did I not know?" Lucy tilted her head and scrunched her eyebrows.

He dabbed his napkin to his lips. "Um. I didn't make a big deal of it when I came back to the island."

Both hands on the table, Lucy leaned toward Owen. "Who did you play for?"

"In minor leagues, I played for the Sea Dogs, an affiliate of the Red Sox based in Maine. Then they called me to the majors, and I pitched for

Home At Last

one season." He flipped his fork over.

"You were a major league pitcher? I'm impressed." Lucy loved baseball. She watched all the Cleveland Guardians' games, but she didn't know Owen had played. Every spring and summer for the last ten years, she had organized a mixed softball league on the island. Why hadn't Owen joined them?

"Don't be. I lasted one season due to injury."

The waiter placed their salads on the table. Lucy shared a sweet smile and thanked him.

She stabbed a tomato with her fork and the juice squirted across the table and landed on Owen's cheek. "Oh my goodness. I'm so sorry." Despite her embarrassment, a giggle erupted from her. "I didn't mean to squirt you."

Owen lifted his napkin and wiped away the juice. A smile spread across his face. "It's okay. I had no idea I was so hilarious."

"Sorry. I tend to burst out laughing when I do something stupid." She covered her mouth with her hand to calm herself.

"You didn't do anything stupid. You poked a tomato. Could have happened to me." He stuffed a forkful of lettuce into his mouth.

"Thank you." Lucy imagined her cheeks glowed as pink as her kitchen. Owen's sweet response to her embarrassment warmed her heart. Some men might get mad or laugh at her, but not him. He wanted her to feel comfortable.

By the time the steak and potatoes arrived, Lucy's nerves had settled. She sliced a bite of ribeye and savored the tender bite. "Delicious."

Owen nodded in agreement. "The garlic sour cream on the potatoes tastes amazing, too. I've eaten here with some of the guys I played ball with. They came out to the farm and stayed a weekend, then we came over here on their way home."

"You mean we had professional ball players on the island?"

He cut a piece of steak. "Last summer, when the island was swarming with people, I picked them up from the dock here, and we landed at Uncle Jed's boat dock before it fell apart. If I'd known you were a crazy baseball fan, I would have introduced you."

Wait a minute. Lucy sat across from a major league baseball player. A handsome former player. Her insides quivered. Owen had pitched on a professional team, yet he remained humble. The man treated her with respect and bought her great food. Before she lost control of her fangirling, she breathed, sipped her water, then stuffed a bite of potato into her mouth.

Home At Last

CHAPTER NINE

Moonlight shimmered across the lake, and the fragrance of grilled steak colored the air along the dock. After dinner, Lucy and Owen strolled along the nearby streets and scouted for the three-foot, artsy lighthouses showcased throughout the city. Sold to raise money for Sandusky's Merry-Go-Round Museum, several businesses had bought and displayed them. Tourists often drove or walked around the city to find the quaint decorations.

One painted with a lake and fish caught Owen's attention. "The artist captured the lake scene pretty well."

Lucy bent and admired the detail. "They sure did. There's a small lighthouse here on the shore above the water. I remember when they sold the lighthouses at auction. *Lake Erie Press* ran an article on them. The artists had donated their time to the project."

Owen twined his fingers with Lucy's. "I'm glad we did this. I haven't been on a date in a long time. You're a lot of fun, Lucy."

Rebecca's selfish, money-hungry ways had tainted his desire to get close to another woman. Why offer his heart and take the risk of someone ripping it in two? Yet, he held Lucy's hand and hoped she found comfort in his.

Lucy ambled beside him. "I haven't dated in years."

He stopped, dropped her hand, and faced her. "Seriously?"

"Yep. It's been at least three years. Running the store takes all my time. Plus, taking care of Mom and Dad's house, which I don't have to do anymore. I'm hoping the tiny home helps me relax. I can sit on the porch and watch the water, and I want to sell the store." She started walking.

He caught up to her. "Why do you want to sell, if you don't mind sharing?"

"I don't mind." She moved her hands as she spoke. "I'm tired of retail. Something the pastor shared a few months ago struck me. He preached about storing our treasures in heaven instead of on earth, and it hit me. I spend my days trying to get people to spend money on things they don't need. I'd rather find something to do to help people. I have a couple of dreams I've not shared with anyone, because I'm not sure how feasible they are."

They headed to the boat. "I'm happy to listen if you want to share."

She shrugged. "I've considered installing more tiny homes for people

Penny Frost McGinnis, Abbott Island Book 3

on small budgets, but don't see it happening. My other idea seems out of reach too. When I figure out if it might work, I'll talk about it."

"No worries. I understand about dreams. Mine ended sooner than I expected, but I'm thankful I had the opportunity to try."

At the boat, Owen helped Lucy board the vessel. "Are you cold? I have a blanket I can get you. I didn't consider how chilly a boat ride in April might be." He gathered a soft knit afghan from a cupboard below the steering wheel.

The splash of the lake against the boat beat in a calm rhythm. "Thank you. I forgot to bring a jacket." She snuggled into the warmth of the crocheted yarn. "I love being on the water at night. It's magical. When we were teenagers, Joel, Sadie, and I spent many evenings on the water."

He steered the boat to the island. "Sadie and Joel met when they were teenagers?"

She stood next to him and inhaled his woodsy scent. "Yes. Sadie visited her grandparents in the summer. The cottages she rents and the home she and Joel live in belonged to them."

The island came into view. He slowed the boat's speed and faced Lucy. "Kind of like me. I spent a lot of time with my aunt and uncle, but I didn't mix with the locals. Uncle Jed kept me busy." He tucked a strand of Lucy's hair behind her ear. "I wish I'd paid more attention to the locals." Before he allowed himself to get carried away, he gripped the steering wheel.

Slow yourself down. Now isn't the time to get tangled in a relationship. Creating a way for the farm to bring in money and not be a burden to Aunt Marley and Uncle Jed required his full focus. Although they pushed him to spend time with Lucy, he needed to give attention to his landscape business.

Once off the boat, he drove her home and walked her to the door. "Night, Lucy."

She unlocked her door, then met his gaze. "Night. Thank you for a lovely evening. I enjoyed getting to know you. I feel like I should grab a baseball and get your autograph."

"Um, I don't think we need to share my story on the island. Your enthusiasm is appreciated, but that part of my life is behind me."

"I'm sorry."

"No need to be sorry. I'm glad I told you, but I can't go back." He studied her face. "You're an amazing woman, and I hope we can always be friends." He emphasized friends even though he longed for more. By the time he pulled himself together and found the best way to save the farm, she'd be dating someone else.

Lucy clasped her hands in front of her. "Friends sounds good. Speaking of friends, a group of us on the island play softball. I hope you'll

50

Home At Last

join us. We enjoy old-fashioned rivalry between the teams. Sign-ups start soon."

"Sounds fun. See you tomorrow at church."

Lucy smiled, then went inside.

Discontent gnawed at his insides. Why not date an amazing woman like Lucy? Beautiful, smart, hard-working, and not after his money. His heart sank to his toes, but he had to focus and not lose sight of what was important for his family. Besides, why chance another broken heart?

~~~~~

The small pink refrigerator hummed and the smell of the cherry candle Lucy had burned earlier lingered. She untied the blue ribbons on her tennis shoes, kicked them off, then padded to Finn's fishbowl.

"Here you go, buddy." She sprinkled food in the water. He swam to the top and gobbled the bits. "You're the only male I've had a relationship with that lasted longer than three minutes. I'm glad Owen wants to be friends, but I thought we clicked. He held my hand, and we laughed. Oh, well. Time for bed."

She changed for bed, then climbed to the loft. Before she flipped the bedside wall sconce on, she perched on the edge of her bed and peered out the window. Waves lapped the beach and seagulls squatted in the sand, but her attention focused on the man standing on her beach. He turned, and she swore his eyes met hers, but the darkness erased any chance of recognition. She watched him walk away. Was he carrying a satchel or briefcase? Certain he'd left her property, she closed the blinds, crawled into bed, and pulled the covers to her chin.

~~~~~

Sunday morning, Lucy rolled out of bed and tromped downstairs. A hot shower, her prettiest dress, and a breakfast of oatmeal and blueberries readied her for the day.

"Finn, watch the place while I'm at church." She locked the door, then stepped off the porch. Before she walked to church, she wandered to the beach and searched for clues about who stood there last night. Any footprints had washed away. No holes — good. A few branches and bushes appeared trampled. Under a scrub pine, Lucy spied a piece of paper. A crude drawing of Abbott Island spread across the page. The paper appeared reprinted on a copier, but the original lines of the drawing looked old. Someone may have sketched it with a fountain pen, and the handwriting and spelling were hard to read. She recognized Division Street where an X marked a spot and another X marked a place along the shore on the northeast side of the island. Curious but late for church, Lucy folded the paper and stuffed it in her Bible.

In the sanctuary, she hustled inside and sat by Joel and Sadie. She nudged her brother. "Pass me your sweet baby, please."

Penny Frost McGinnis, Abbott Island Book 3

She wrapped Gracie in a hug and sang hymns to her as the congregation worshiped. Gracie napped in her arms during the sermon. The baby's fresh scent filled Lucy with calm. When the service ended, Sadie lifted her from her sister-in-law's arms.

"She's a joy. Thanks for letting me hold her." Lucy rose and nudged her brother. "I have something to show you."

Joel followed her outside to a bench.

"What's with the mystery? Did you find a long-lost treasure?" He parked himself beside her.

She retrieved the paper from her Bible and handed it to him. "I'm not sure."

He unfolded the paper. "Is this a map of the island? Where'd you find it?"

"Last night, after I got home from my date, I saw someone walking on my beach. This morning, I found this under a tree. The paper looks new, but the map appears old."

The corners of Joel's lips rose into an ornery grin. "How was your date with Owen?"

Lucy raised her eyebrows and heaved a sigh. "Our date was nice. Now, what do you think of the map?"

He studied the page for a minute. "It could be a copy of an old map. Some kids may have found it and were playing by the water and dropped it. Or your mystery man last night may have thought he found something. From the looks of it, he was mixed up. You're on the east side of the island and the X here is northeast of you. I'm not sure if these other blots are Xes. I'm leaning toward kids playing. The man on the beach may have been on a walk and stumbled onto your property by accident. Do you want this back?"

"Of course I do." She snatched the paper from him and her mind lit with curiosity.

"You're going to try to figure it out, aren't you? I see the wheels turning."

"Perhaps." She pursed her lips to keep from talking.

Joel got to his feet. "Be careful. You don't know who's behind this. Remember what happened to Sadie? Her ex stalked her, and Levi and I arrived in time to get him before he nabbed her."

"I remember. I don't have past boyfriends who cared enough about me to hunt me down." Nor a current boyfriend who seemed to want to seek her out. She planted her fists on her hips. "So no worries, brother."

Lucy walked to the church steps as Owen descended. His aunt and uncle followed. Turn and go the other way or smile and say hello? What to do? Lucy chose the latter. She donned a grin and waved hello.

Aunt Marley sprinted to her. No matter her age, she moved like a

52

Home At Last

deer. "It's so good to see you, dear. I wondered if you'd join us for Sunday dinner. Jed and I would love to have you."

From the corner of her eye, Lucy saw Owen lean his head into his hand. He had no idea of Marley's intention to invite Lucy over. Dinner sounded wonderful, and Owen bragged on Marley's cooking, but she feared embarrassing him.

Marley waved Jed and Owen to her side. "Gentlemen, wouldn't you enjoy company for dinner today? Lucy, how about it?"

Owen raised his eyebrows as if to say, 'up to you,' and Jed nodded.

Lucy fingered the edge of her Bible. "Sure. What time do you want me to come?"

Marley rested her hand on Lucy's arm. "We eat at two, but you can come before. Owen can show you around the farm. He can share his new ideas he has to help us stay in business."

"What can I bring?"

"Bring your appetite, sweet girl." Marley tilted her head, smiled, and sighed.

On the church steps, Miss Aggie, Miss Flossie, and Miss Hildy each held a hand over their hearts and Cheshire Cat grins brightened their faces. Aunt Marley turned toward them and nodded and winked.

Lucy rolled her eyes, then searched for Marigold. She approached her friend and waited for her to finish a conversation with another parishioner. "Hi, Mari."

Her older friend wrapped her in a hug. "Hey, girl. How was your date last night? Sadie told me."

"Of course she did. We had a great time, but Owen assured me he wants to be friends." She shrugged.

"Okay. Maybe he isn't interested in anything serious right now. Friends is good, right? Johnny and I were friends for a long time before we realized we loved each other."

Lucy wrapped her fingers around Marigold's arm. "I understand. I have no problem with being friends, but his aunt invited me to dinner today, and I picked up a vibe of discomfort from Owen. I didn't want to offend Marley, so I said yes. Now I'm a little panicked."

Marigold patted Lucy's shoulder. "I'm sure Owen will be fine. He's a smart young man, and he'll handle dinner with finesse. Relax and enjoy yourself."

Easy for her to say. The word *relax* didn't exist in Lucy's vocabulary.

Home At Last

CHAPTER TEN

The rays of sun Travis awakened to Sunday morning did not brighten his mood. On his walk along the east side of the island last night, he had lost the copy of the map. This morning, he growled at himself in the mirror.

Yesterday, he had discovered a crumpled, yellowed paper crammed between the last two pages of his great-great-whatever aunt's diary. He unfolded it with care and stared at the hand-drawn map for an hour. Later, at the library, he had printed two copies. Good thing he could access the printer himself, since those nosy volunteers asked so many questions. The fellow with the thinning hair and wire frames offered to copy the paper for him, but he insisted he do it himself. At least with his back to them, he had blocked their view of the map, but their glares pierced his back.

What if someone else found the copy he lost? The lady in the tiny house had peeked out the window, but she moved away before he recognized her. She left him alone, so she must not have cared he walked on her property, or fear kept her at bay. Either way, she didn't matter.

He pulled on his jeans and a clean shirt, then inhaled the coffee he brewed. Good old, strong-as-he-could-make-it, caffeine to awaken the brain. He poured a mug full and parked it on the desk, then he scrounged in his satchel and plucked the other copy of the map from his folder. When he first laid eyes on the drawing, he had turned it every possible way to determine the layout. Once he deciphered the line that appeared to be Division Street, he determined the approximate locations of the Xes, although some appeared to be smears of ink. One sat on a property once owned by someone named Becker, the other one a person named Hamilton. Not much detail, but the crude rendering of the island gave him a glimmer of hope. If his aunt had buried the gold in one of those places, and he found the nuggets, he'd live as a rich man.

In the cramped kitchenette, he peeled a banana and heated a muffin in the microwave. He carried his meager breakfast and added it to the desk. He flopped into the chair in the corner. While he ate, he reread the description of the box Merrilee claimed to have buried the treasure in. "A bentwood box, made of cedar decorated with a Tlingit tribe design."

He opened the browser on his phone and typed in Tlingit designs. Images of animal faces carved in wood with thick black lines popped up.

55

Penny Frost McGinnis, Abbott Island Book 3

Some carvings featured reds and greens with feathers, fins, and eyes. Could the box be valuable? Depended on the shape the wood was in, if he found it. No. *When* he found it. Before he sent his minions to dig again, he would research the island and find out who these properties belonged to now.

Tomorrow, he'd pay somebody to pilot him in their boat to Sandusky, to the county recorder's office. They kept maps of the area and he'd study the older ones and compare them to the island today. He kissed the end of his fingers and waved a salute to great-great-great-aunt Merrilee. Crazy old coot should have kept her gold to herself. Lucky for him, she'd buried it. *Somewhere.*

~~~~~

Lucy latched her door and stepped outside. The water sparkled as if diamonds reflected sunshine on the calm lake, while her heart thumped. Why had she agreed to go to the Millers' for dinner? Sure, Marley was a hard to resist personality and Jed's sweet smile reeled her in, but Owen made her hesitate. He wanted friendship, so he may not want to spend his free time with her. Sure, friends hung out, but not with an aunt and uncle in tow. Unless said aunt and uncle wanted their nephew to date her. The two of them wouldn't scheme, would they? Aunt Marley had winked at the church ladies. Were they in cahoots? Whether they tried to manipulate Owen's future or not, she had promised to eat dinner with them.

She breathed in the faint smell of fish in the lake air, shook her arms and hands at her sides, and forced her feet to walk to her pink Jeep Wrangler, one of her few treasures. She seldom drove, but today she needed the confidence she gained from maneuvering the Wrangler around the island. In the tall seat, above the road with clear vision, and over her collection of rubber ducks, she ruled. *Just kidding.* Her tummy twisted for no good reason. She'd known the Millers most of her life, and they gave her nerves no reason to quiver, except for Owen.

By the time she settled herself, the gravel in their long driveway crunched under the tires. A well-cared-for two-story farmhouse rose from the ground. The wrap-around porch offered hospitality and comfort. Four rockers invited folks to sit a while and a bed of tulips brightened the scene with reds and yellows. As far as she remembered, the Millers had lived on the island all their lives. Mom knew Mr. Miller's mother and father when she was a girl. Lucy hadn't visited the farm in years. The last time, at least sixteen years ago, her mother had sent her for eggs.

Jed and Marley kept to themselves most of the time, and Owen, too. He came and went with little notice. Unlike Lucy, who drew attention from her loud laugh and chatter.

Lucy knocked on the front door and waited. Uncle Jed answered the door. "Marley should have told you friends and family come to the back.

56

Home At Last

This old front door is for those pesky folks trying to sell us their junk. Come on in."

Lucy ran her fingers over the top of her dress's flowered skirt to press out an imaginary wrinkle. "Thank you, Mr. Miller. I'm not selling a thing today."

He welcomed her with a wave to enter. "Call me Jed, please. I appreciate manners, but you're an adult now. We can use first names." A grin split the older gentleman's face. "I remember when your momma sent you for eggs as a child. Those blond curls of yours bounced as you ran. You always smiled." He walked her to the living room. "How are your mom and dad? I haven't visited with them in a long time."

Drawn to the fireplace, Lucy glanced at the photos of Owen as a boy. "They're both doing well. Dad's been busy with his woodworking and Mom's been making lap quilts for a VA project. They send them to soldiers or veterans in homes and hospitals." A clock on the wall clicked to two o'clock. "Your home is lovely."

Jed made his way to a cabinet in the corner and lifted a plastic box from a shelf. "I want you to see something before Owen gets in here." The box held a baseball. "This is the first major league ball Owen pitched. He signed it for me and gave it to me to keep. I think he misses the game, but I'm sure grateful he came to stay with us to start over. That girl Rebecca..."

"Uncle Jed?" Owen stood in the doorway. "Please put the ball away. It's an old game ball I pitched. I know it's important to you, but I doubt Lucy wants to hear about it."

~~~~~

Sun streamed through the picture window and the light lit Lucy's blond locks. Owen's breath hitched. Uncle Jed returned the baseball to the shelf, then he excused himself to the kitchen.

"I'm sorry, Lucy. I'm not sure why Uncle Jed is obsessed with my baseball." He shoved his hands in the pockets of his jeans. "It's just an old ball."

"I'm guessing he's proud of you, and the ball reminds him of your accomplishment." She crossed her arms over her chest. "Playing on a major league team is a big deal."

"Yeah, I'm sure for him it was. He used to play catch with me when I'd come in the summer, and he and Aunt Marley watched the Cleveland Indians, before they became the Guardians, for years. I guess I forget how involved they were in my time on the field. They helped pay for my college, too. Since they never raised kids, they treated me like their own." He gestured to the couch. "Want to sit until dinner is ready? Aunt Marley's about finished. I set the table while she mashed the potatoes."

They sat on opposite ends of the couch.

"I don't mean to be nosy, although I've been told I am, but your uncle

Penny Frost McGinnis, Abbott Island Book 3

didn't seem too fond of Rebecca. He kind of spit her name out." A slight smile lifted the corners of her mouth.

He ran a hand over his hair. "Yeah. Uncle Jed and Aunt Marley met her a couple of times, and they didn't click. When she broke up with me, they said they were relieved and I deserved better. I wasn't as sure, but they thought she wanted me for the money I'd signed for in the majors. When she found out my baseball career ended, she freaked out. Her family came from old money. They pushed her to marry someone in their circle. I found out a year later she did. My aunt and uncle knew what they were talking about."

Lucy opened her mouth as if to respond, but Aunt Marley marched into the room. "Time for dinner, you two. Let's eat." She led them to the dining room. "Lucy, you and our nephew can sit on this side of the table. My honey and I will sit over here." The older lady pointed to the opposite side of the table.

Subtle, Aunt Marley. Not the matchmaker the three church ladies attempted to be, but a bit pushy. Owen pulled Lucy's chair out at the same time Uncle Jed showed his gentleman side to Aunt Marley. At least he'd learned a few lessons from them. Their kindness and generosity had poured into him since he was a boy. They had decorated a room for him when he turned ten. Baseball posters hung on the wall, and Aunt Marley pieced him a baseball themed quilt. Every summer after, he had spent time on the farm. They taught him how to work hard and when to rest. Both life lessons had proved valuable in his seasons of baseball in college, the minors, and the professional level. Then they opened their arms to him and invited him home to lick his wounds and start fresh.

"Owen, want to say the blessing?" Aunt Marley patted his hand.

"Sure."

After brief words of gratitude, Uncle Jed passed pork chops, peas, and mashed potatoes, followed by homemade yeast rolls.

Lucy spooned peas on her plate. "These look delicious."

Aunt Marley straightened her back and sat tall. "Those are from our spring garden. I shelled them after church."

"Impressive. I'm not sure I've eaten fresh peas since my Nana grew them." She took a bite. "Yummy."

Owen cut into his pork chop. "Aunt Marley could give Johnny a run on his cooking. His dishes are fancier, but hers are made with lots of love and flavor."

"Compliments will get you everywhere." His aunt buttered a roll. "I enjoy making food to feed the people I love, including you, Lucy."

Lucy's cheeks pinked. "Thank you. You two have been a staple on this island. I remember when Mom had her accident, and you stopped by with food and sat with her for hours. Your kindness meant so much to my

Home At Last

family."

"We love you all. How's your brother and his wife and their sweet Gracie? I saw her at church this morning, and my she's growing." Aunt Marley's eyes lit with delight.

Lucy bubbled over with enthusiasm. "She stole my heart the minute I met her. Joel and Sadie are well, and little Gracie is pure joy. I love spoiling her."

What would it be like to have a family with Lucy? She was so energetic and loving. He pictured kids with golden hair. A brown-eyed girl and a blue-eyed boy. The four of them on the farm, building a life together.

"Owen, where's your mind at?" Aunt Marley tapped his hand. "Seems you left us for a minute."

He lifted his napkin from his lap, dabbed his lips, and shut down the wandering thoughts. "I was enjoying this delicious pork. Uncle Jed, how do you stay slim eating Aunt Marley's cooking every day?" He stuffed the meat in his mouth and chastised himself for daydreaming about the woman next to him.

Home At Last

CHAPTER ELEVEN

Monday morning, Travis grasped the boat's seat as choppy water rocked the dory and ominous gray clouds threatened more rain. The smell of fish offended his nose and queasiness rolled through his stomach. He appreciated the local fisherman's offer of a trip to the mainland for a small fee, but the waves tilted his stomach. His gaze focused on the shoreline, and he counted to ten several times to keep from tossing his breakfast over the side.

When he stepped onto the soil of the mainland, he thanked the man and scheduled a pickup time. His stomach settled as he hailed an Uber to the public library.

Outside the limestone building, Travis admired the turrets of the old structure. He climbed the steps and walked into the entry. At the circulation desk, he approached the librarian. "Morning."

"Good morning, sir." A young woman, mid-twenties with her hair in two buns and tattoos on her arms, greeted him.

Travis squinted at the woman. He'd expected gray hair and glasses, not pink hair and tats. "I'm needing to check out, no not check out. Look through your maps of Abbott Island. I'm trying to figure out where a couple of plots of land are located." He kept his map in his leather bag for fear of tipping someone off to the whereabouts of the treasure.

"I can help you." She led him to the reference area where the library held local information. "Here are a couple of our maps of the area and books on the history of the homes on the island. Is there anything else I can do for you?"

Leave, so he could peruse the stack of books and the rolled maps. "This is great. Thanks."

As soon as she walked away, he opened his satchel, retrieved the map, and unfolded it. He unrolled a current assessor's map with plots of land numbered. He ran his finger along Division Street and located the X on his aunt's map. Then, he studied the modern map and discovered two or three possibilities for matches. Since the old map was drawn, he doubted he'd find an exact location, but at least he had an idea of where to search and dig. The other X proved a bit more difficult since the land ran into the water. He thumbed through a book on historic homes and found a few of the addresses that now housed businesses, including the General Store, but his family name wasn't listed. Just in case he missed a clue, he studied the other marks and pinpointed the possibilities.

He snapped photos of the information he wanted with his phone, then packed his map into his satchel. At the circulation desk, he thanked the young lady.

Outside, he cued the GPS to check how far a walk there was to the county recorder's office. On the six-minute hike, he considered his approach to discovering the treasure. He had to find the gold. Without the treasure, life veered toward misery. Tired of the monotonous data entry job his buddy hired him for, he longed to live an independent life, apart from his mother's lower class. The few treasure hunts he'd endured left him with less money than ever, except for the jewels he'd taken, but those dollars dwindled in a few months. Now, he planned to play out every possible scenario that might reveal the box of gold his aunt had buried.

~~~~~

Four o'clock Monday afternoon, a rainbow whispered across the sky. Lucy spritzed a vinegar-based cleaner on the windows of the store and applied paper towels to remove the grime. Her elbow grease gave way to a clear view. If only insight on the sale of the business and what to expect in the future appeared as crystal clear to her.

After dinner with the Millers yesterday, she and Owen had toured the farm. His animated description of what he hoped for the farm had impressed her. Later at home, she had dragged an old notebook out of a box she had stored in the outdoor storage space at the end of her house. She loved how a tiny home held storage in the most unexpected places.

She mulled over the scribbles and pictures she'd pasted into her notebook as she rubbed the glass clean. Not certain she'd earn enough money to live on if she chased her dream, she planned to find out. An undemanding day job might allow her time to explore.

A wave of fear followed a spurt of excitement, as the what ifs ticked through her mind.

As her mind flitted through possibilities, a face filled the window she'd scrubbed clean. She jumped and dropped the paper towels and cleaner. Her hand flew to her neck, and a squeak escaped her mouth.

When Andrew entered the store, he held his arms in the air. "I'm so sorry. I didn't mean to scare you. I guess I have a habit of making you jump."

Lucy lifted the vinegar bottle and towels from the floor and placed them on the counter. "No worries. I was daydreaming."

"Anything interesting?"

She tilted her head and gave him a questioning look.

He stuffed his hands into the pockets of his jeans. "Was your daydream interesting?"

"Kind of, but not to anyone else." She crossed her arms in front of her. Her dreams remained her secret. Lucy stepped behind the counter. "What can I do for you?"

Andrew peered across the room, then turned to Lucy. "What time do you close?"

Lucy tucked her supplies in the cabinet under the counter, then checked her watch. "In about fifteen minutes. Give or take. This time of year, I let the customers dictate the hours. If no one comes in the last hour, I shutter the doors early. We won't get busy for a few weeks, yet. By busy, I mean islanders will come in to check out the new shirts and souvenirs before Memorial Day weekend.

"Want to get dinner with me after you close?" Smugness crossed Andrew's face.

Lucy leaned on the wooden counter and spread her hands. "Um. Sure. Where do you want to meet? I need to go home and change." She wrinkled her nose. "I smell like vinegar."

He chuckled. "Not your new perfume, huh?"

"Afraid not. I don't usually go out smelling like a pickle." A funny sensation rolled through her stomach. Nerves or anticipation?

"I'd pick you up, but I don't have a car here."

"No worries." She preferred to meet him since she knew little to nothing about him. After their other business date, she planned to leave when she chose.

"Let's meet at the Abbott Island Restaurant at six o'clock. Pizza sounds good tonight." He rubbed his hands together, turned and left the store.

No dates in years and now two in one week. The world might end soon.

~~~~~

At home, Lucy rolled her bicycle onto her property, as Owen hammered the last boards on the deck with a steady pounding. The smell of freshly cut wood met Lucy's nose, and she inhaled a deep breath. "I love the fragrance of cut wood. It reminds me of Dad when he's in his workshop."

Owen lifted his hammer and let it smack one more nail. "It reminds me of the Louisville Slugger bat factory. Have you ever been there?"

"No, but I'd love to go sometime." She ran her fingers over a wooden plank. "Thanks for finding this repurposed wood. I'm happy Habitat's restore had enough to complete the deck. Plus, you saved me money, and we can paint it right away.

"You're welcome. It was your decision." Owen bent and touched the nail. "Last one. Other than paint, it's finished. What do you think?"

"It's perfect. The added outdoor space makes my living space bigger. When the builders added a porch large enough for two chairs, I loved it,

Penny Frost McGinnis, Abbott Island Book 3

but now the porch plus the deck's square footage may be as big as the house." She clapped.

"I can't wait to host a picnic on the deck. I should be able to paint it over the weekend. White matches the porch, but I'm not sure. I'd have to be vigilant to keep a white deck clean. Maybe I'll go with a stain." She sat on the step. "What if I went with a blue to accent the yellow?"

Owen studied the decking. "I've seen blue stain. It shows less dirt. You can get samples and try them on a piece of leftover board." He rubbed his chin. "I can take you to Sandusky and check out paint and stains, if you want."

"Yes, please. You have a great eye for design. At least from what you've shown me. I hadn't realized how I'd love the deck. The shape and size work perfect with my house." Before she stopped herself, she threw her arms around his neck and hugged him. She stepped away, and her face heated. "Thank you." She scrunched her nose, then covered her eyes.

Owen touched her arm. "It's okay, Lucy. I'm glad you like it."

She uncovered her eyes and gave him her best smile. "Good. I've got to get going. I need to change and meet Andrew for dinner at the Abbott Island Restaurant. We're having pizza."

Why go into a description of the date? No, not a date, the meeting. Yes, a meeting to talk about the store.

"Who's Andrew?" Owen grasped the handle of his hammer.

"He's the guy who is renting one of Sadie's cabins. He's been in the store a few times, and he might be interested in buying my business. At least, I hope he is." She twirled the ends of her hair around her fingers.

He spun the hammer in his hand. "Be careful, Lucy. I'd hate for you to get hurt by a person you don't know. Some men see a woman in a vulnerable position and take advantage. If he thinks you want to get out of retail too quickly, he could low ball you."

"I'll be careful, but thanks for the advice. I've not considered myself vulnerable, but I get how someone might assume I'm a push-over instead of a level-headed business woman." She shrugged. "I gotta go. We'll talk soon and plan a trip to the mainland for paint." She wiggled her fingers in a goodbye wave.

She had no plans to be taken advantage of since she had run a successful business and planned to continue her success whether she sold the store or not.

~~~~~

The sun warmed his back as Owen carried his tools to his truck. The deck project complete, other than paint, left him with less connection to Lucy. When he warned her about Andrew, alarm bells sounded in his head. *You care about Lucy more than you want to admit.* Not ready to let himself care for another woman, he shoved the idea aside and climbed

64

into the driver's seat.

Without forethought, he steered the truck to the downtown area and cruised by Abbott Island Restaurant. Sure enough, one of those good-looking male movie-star types with stylish clothes sat on a bench outside the place. A green dart of jealousy shot through him. First, the need to protect Lucy made him spout off to her about vulnerability. Now envy and jealousy pricked his heart. Nope. He hit the brakes on his emotions and his truck. Like a fool, he stopped in the middle of the road. His eyes met the man's. Owen hit the accelerator and gunned his truck. Thank goodness no one else looked his way as he sped off.

On the road to his aunt and uncle's, he slowed the truck and pulled to the side. He bowed his head. "God, I'm an idiot. Please save me from myself. If I'm supposed to get involved with Lucy, can you give me a sign? How about a kick in the pants? I'm at a loss. She's a great person, and I'd like to get to know her better. Help me."

He raised his head. A vivid reel of Lucy on his boat played in his mind. She'd laughed and talked with him as if they'd known each other for decades. She beamed with joy and gave off the most comfortable vibe. He'd be crazy not to pursue her and get to know her better. He wanted to kick himself for giving her the impression he wanted no more than friendship.

On the trip to Sandusky, he might address the issue and check her reaction. If he volunteered to help organize the spring softball teams with her, he'd spend more time with her, but playing ball again meant picking up a bat. His shoulder ached from time to time, but he could still play softball. Underhand pitching didn't hurt nearly as much as overhand. An urge to drive to Lucy's pulled at him, but she was on a date with Andrew. She hadn't called it a date, but he assumed Andrew thought it was.

Tomorrow he'd stop by the General Store and find out when she planned to buy paint. His heart flipped when he considered time with Lucy. He was in big trouble.

Home At Last

CHAPTER TWELVE

By the time Lucy biked downtown, streaks of pink painted the sky around a bright yellow-orange orb. She parked her bike beside the restaurant and trekked around to the front.

Andrew stared at his cell phone while he waited on a bench. His dark hair waved across his forehead and a day's scruff of beard darkened his face. When she drew near, he glanced up and smiled, then punched a few keys on his phone and slid it into his pocket.

He rose to greet her. "Thanks for meeting me. You look beautiful." He offered her his arm.

Lucy's cheeks warmed at the compliment as she clutched her purse and ignored the offer. "I appreciate you asking me. Pizza sounds wonderful." Not her best conversation opener, but she knew little about him, and she didn't want to compliment him and give him the wrong idea. Although his blue Henley shirt set off his eyes and stretched across his muscled chest, she stopped herself from any mention of his physique.

Inside, the hostess seated them at a table beside the window. Not many people haunted the downtown on a Monday evening. A stray yellow cat darted across the street and a couple of senior citizens took a brisk walk. The same pair Lucy saw from her store window most days in the summer. Soon tourists would fill the streets, and she'd be buried in business. Not a bad problem, but an exhausting one.

Andrew ran his finger down the list of ingredients on the menu, then raised his eyes to meet hers. "What do you eat on your pizza? Or would you prefer something else?"

Lucy straightened the collar on her pink flowered shirt. "I enjoy their salads and their deluxe pizza. How about a small salad with our pizza?"

"Sounds good."

The waitress took their order and hustled to the kitchen.

Andrew fiddled with his napkin. "Sounds like we have similar taste. I always order pepperoni and mushroom. My friend says I'm eating fungus." The waitress delivered their drinks and bowls of lettuce topped with tomatoes, olives, cheese, and croutons. "I tell him it's because I'm a fungi. Get it. Fun guy, fungi." His laughter echoed through the restaurant.

Lucy sipped her Pepsi as he spouted his joke. She covered her mouth to keep herself from spitting her drink on him when she laughed. Corny but cute.

"I eat about anything on pizza. As a matter of fact, I eat about anything." She forked a bite of salad.

After she swallowed, she rested her fork on her bowl. "You've been on the island a while. What do you think of our beautiful home?"

He glanced out the window, then at Lucy. "I've enjoyed the quiet, but I understand tourists arrive soon."

"Have you hiked to the alvar? Even when the vacationers are here, it's still quiet on the trails." She ate a bite of lettuce and olives with French dressing.

"What's an alvar?" He scrunched his forehead.

"It's limestone on the shore of the lake covered with a thin layer of soil. It's fascinating because plants grow in the barely-there dirt. A few rare plants grow on ours and it's an interesting sight. The balsam-squaw weed, a pretty little yellow flower, pops up every year. I love the small cliffs around it too." Lucy closed her mouth before she yammered on about all the trails on the island. From Andrew's bored expression he didn't share her fascination with the natural world.

He stared at her. "Never heard of an alvar. Sounds interesting."

Lucy squirmed in her seat. His intense stare pierced through her. She pushed her hair behind her ears and glanced away. "The pizza is coming."

A spicy aroma, along with steam, rose from the pepperonis. "Looks delicious." He served each of them a slice. When should she bring up the store? She warred with herself, and her appetite faded.

Andrew swiped his napkin across his mouth. "So, tell me about your store. How long have you owned it and why sell?"

His question jolted her from her distraction. "Sure. I started working at the General Store when I was fifteen, and I loved it. Meeting the tourists and the teens who worked here was fun. I met Sadie when she joined the crew. Then in my mid-twenties, the opportunity presented itself for me to buy the business. The former owner retired, and my nana had passed and left me money. So I made the down payment and bought the store."

"You were young to take on a business." He bit into a piece of pizza and sauce dripped onto his chin.

A giggle escaped Lucy. "Sorry." She covered her mouth.

He dabbed the sauce off. "No worries. I'm a little messy."

"Anyway. I've run the store since then, and I'm ready to let it go and move on to something more satisfying. Don't get me wrong, I've enjoyed what I do, but it's time for a change." Should she reveal her dream to him? She hadn't shared with Owen, whose words came to mind. *Some see a woman in a vulnerable position and take advantage.* She felt confident with Owen, but she wasn't acquainted with Andrew enough to establish trust.

He laid his fork on the table. "I'm guessing you don't have time for much else."

"True. The store takes most of my time." She sipped her pop.

Home At Last

"I bet." Andrew pushed his plate aside. "The pizza was delicious. Want to take a walk?"

"Sounds good."

Andrew paid the bill.

"Thank you, but I planned on paying my half."

"Nonsense," he said as he pulled Lucy's chair out for her. "I can't let a lovely lady pay her way. Let's go."

Perplexed, Lucy followed him out.

They strolled along Division Street. "The island is a beautiful place to live this time of year, but how are the winters?"

Lucy rubbed her arms. "Cold, but I love the snow. The lake sends oodles of it our way. We close streets and sled ride and have hot chocolate. Getting groceries can be a challenge. Between the General Store where I sell snow shovels, salt, and outdoor equipment and the grocery, we take care of everyone. I don't sell as much merchandise in the winter, but I do okay with the sales of household supplies."

They crossed the street and walked to the General Store, then climbed the steps and sat on the bench.

"The store was originally a residence, built in 1880 before the village was established. The main room inside was part of the original structure, much smaller than what you see today. The owners before me remodeled and added on, but kept the charm. They built on from here over and added the porch." She pointed to the addition. "I've re-stained the outside once and added fresh paint to the inside when I bought it and again two years ago."

Andrew moved to the sidewalk and stood back and took in the structure. "Mind if we walk around the building?"

"No. Not at all." She trailed behind him.

In the back, Lucy pointed to two large doors covering an opening in the ground. "Here's the original cellar. They built it to store their root vegetables and anything else that required a cool place. I don't go in there often, except to check and make sure it isn't caving in. I've stored a few things there from time to time, but I don't enjoy the thought of spiders creeping around me." She laughed. "I'm told this grassy area was where the chicken coop stood. I believe it. The grass grows so fast we have to mow it every five days. Of course, most of the original yard is taken up by buildings now."

Andrew ran his hand over the siding of the old building. "You've kept it in great shape, and I love a building with history. Have you learned anything about the family who built the house?"

"I've read what I could find, but there isn't much available. I believe a family from the mainland built it as a summer cabin. As I said, it was a lot smaller. They lived on the mainland and visited the island in the

Penny Frost McGinnis, Abbott Island Book 3

summer. It was common for mom and kids to stay here and the dad to travel back and forth on the weekends. The book I read referred to a mom, son, and daughter who stayed here." She pulled a weed along the foundation. "The library has several books on the island's history. You should check them out."

"Thanks for sharing with me, Lucy. I'm searching for something to invest in, and if you're serious about selling, I might take a closer look. Of course, I need to crunch some numbers. We'll talk later."

"Oh, okay." She hoped to talk sooner than later. "I better go home. Thank you for dinner. I enjoyed the pizza."

He walked her to her bicycle, then leaned in to her and planted a kiss on her cheek. "We need to do this again soon."

"Thanks, Andrew."

Lucy straddled her bike, then pedaled away. An uneasy tumble in her stomach sent a squeamish vibe through her. She turned on Marigold's street and hoped her friend wasn't busy.

The stars, like jewels, sparkled overhead, and a cool breeze gave Lucy a shiver. Marigold's light in the living room window invited her to stop. Before she pushed down the kickstand, her friend swung the door open.

Lucy climbed onto the porch and plopped into the swing. She patted the seat, and Marigold joined her.

"What's going on tonight?" Her friend squeezed her hand, then let go. "I saw you from the window."

Lucy gathered her shoulder length hair into a hairband and pulled it into a ponytail. "I had dinner with Andrew at Abbott Island Restaurant, and now I'm confused. He seems nice enough, but something about him is off."

Marigold tapped a finger to her mouth. "I've met him a couple of times, but don't know much about him. Sadie told me he came to the island to relax, although he works online, too. He's polite and handsome."

"He's good looking, all right."

A laugh escaped Marigold. "Yes, that's a real problem."

"Stop. Appearance isn't everything, but it helps." Lucy swung her legs.

"Didn't you go out with Owen the other day?" Marigold pumped the swing.

"Yeah. I mean, neither date was a date. Okay, Owen's was. At least he called it a date, but then told me he wanted to be friends." She made air quotes. "Andrew didn't call it a date but kissed me on the cheek when it ended." She placed her hands on her legs. "I've not dated anyone in so long, I'm rusty at this whole boy-girl thing. Plus, Andrew might be a potential buyer for the store. I can't mix business with pleasure."

Lucy and Marigold pumped the swing together and listened to the

70

Home At Last

crickets fill the night air. The peace of the island hugged Lucy and her shoulders relaxed. She had caught herself overthinking more often than not. When she ordered for the store, arranged a section of t-shirts, decorated her tiny home, she drove herself crazy. No wonder no one asked her on a date.

Marigold stopped the swing and looked at Lucy. "Have you prayed about these two gentlemen who have come into your life? God knows your future and you can consult Him."

"I was thinking about how I overthink everything. I overreact, too. Remember when I caused issues with you and Johnny when I thought you said you were getting married, and you weren't?" She shook her head. "You're right, and I'm embarrassed I haven't prayed yet." She tapped her forehead with the palm of her hand. "Will you pray for me too?"

"No worries about me and Johnny. You got ahead of us. We're happily married now, and of course I'll pray for you. Let's pray about the sale of your store too. I want the best person for the job in your place." She put her arm around Lucy's shoulders. "I'm confident God's plans for you are good ones."

Lucy rested her head on her friend's shoulder, while Marigold bent God's ear. After the amen, Lucy wiped a tear from her cheek. "Talking with you makes me feel better."

"I've gotten wiser with my age, and I'm happy to help. I love you, friend."

"Love you, too." She hugged Marigold, then trotted off the porch.

On her bike ride home, Lucy poured her heart out to God. Whatever the future held, she'd be ready.

CHAPTER THIRTEEN

By Saturday morning, Lucy's confusion evolved into anticipation of what the future might bring. She sipped her coffee, laced with sweet cream, and flipped through paint colors on her phone. A knock on the door startled her, and she splashed coffee on her tiny table.

"Just a minute." She grabbed tissues and sopped the mess before she answered.

The front door's window framed Owen's silhouette. At the sight of him, a tingle started at her toes and zipped to her heart. Was this a response to her prayers or her hormones? She hoped in time she'd know.

She tugged the door open. "Good morning." She bit her tongue to stop the word *handsome* from rolling off. Even though the endearment described him well.

"Hey, Lucy." A smile as sweet as a chocolate drop crossed his lips.

"Come in for a minute. I need to feed Finn." She waved to the tiny room she called her living space. "Have a seat on the couch."

She sprinkled food for her fish into his water. "He gets hangry if I don't feed him on time."

Owen perched on the edge of the couch. "How do you know a fish is hangry?"

She pointed to an artificial plant in the bowl. "See the greenery? If you look here, there are bite marks. He chewed a piece off the other day when I hurried out of the house without feeding him. He can be a vicious little fellow, but I love him."

Finn swam around and pecked at his food.

"I get the attraction. Less work than a dog, no attitude like a cat, and as long as he's fed, he behaves." Owen watched him swim. "I've had a couple of dogs, but never a fish."

Lucy went to the kitchen and washed her hands. Back in the living room, she parked in her cozy reading chair. "I'd love to have a dog. I adore Sadie's dog, Rosie, but I'm too busy with the store, and there's not much room here. If I ever get a dog, I'll rescue a big dog. Little ones are cute, but I've always loved Goldens and Labs."

"My last dog, Jersey, was a Chocolate Lab. I had her for thirteen years. Once I joined the minors, I couldn't keep a dog. A couple, who took in mature dogs, adopted her. They let me know when she passed. Maybe Aunt Marley and Uncle Jed would want one on the farm. Their last one, a collie, has been gone for a long time." He stood and moved to the door. "You ready to go?"

Lucy fetched her purse from the closet. "All set."

Outside, he opened the door on his truck. "We'll take the boat again. It's quicker than the ferry and less expensive."

"Of course." She zipped her lightweight jacket then buckled her seatbelt. Her stomach quivered, so she dug through her bag and found a peppermint to suck. The minty flavor calmed her. Frustrated that her nerves reacted to a simple trip to the paint store, she wrung her hands. She had prayed last night for today to be a fun day with no tension. Not happening, at least not yet. She closed her eyes and asked God to calm her.

"You okay, Lucy?" Owen's voice sent a shiver along her spine.

She nodded. "I'm fine. Considering what color paint to buy."

He pulled into a parking place beside the dock. "I brought a piece of wood for you to test the colors on."

Was he always so thoughtful? "Thank you. I appreciate your help."

"No worries. I'm happy to make life easier for you."

What a kindhearted man. Could he be "the one"? Did she believe in "the one"?

~~~~

The lake's easy ripples gave way to a smooth trip. The sun glinted on the water and sparkled like a million stars. Owen docked the boat, and he and Lucy climbed to shore.

"The store is on the other side of town. I'll call an Uber for us." He used an app to call the driving service. Ten minutes later, a compact sedan picked them up. "I never dreamed we'd have Uber and Doordash around here. I had both in Boston, but it's a bigger city."

"When you were a big deal baseball player?" she teased.

He lowered his head. "Yeah, then."

She touched his arm. "Hey. I was kidding. It's wonderful you had a chance at the big leagues. I'm sorry if I upset you."

He placed his hand over hers. "I'm not upset with you. I struggled for a long time after I injured my shoulder and the surgery failed to help me enough to get back into pitching. Life is better now. Time at the farm has helped and so has time with you." There, he said it. He wanted her to know she made him a better person, but he might have overstepped.

The Uber stopped in front of the paint store, and they stepped onto the sidewalk. He reached for his wallet, but Lucy touched his hand. "I'll get this. I'm the one we're here for."

He stepped away from the driver's door and let her pay. "I plan to buy lunch before we leave town, and there's a place I want to take you that I hope you'll enjoy."

Home At Last

"Sounds good."

He opened the door for her and followed her inside. The odor of paint permeated the store, and a rainbow of color decorated every rack of samples.

She turned to him with a furrowed brow. "I'm not sure where to check first."

"The outdoor paint is over here. They have paint and stains, so you can compare them and decide what's best. I took a photo of your house, so we'd have it as a reminder of the colors we're working with."

He'd used the word *we*. Did he mean more than the two of them picking out paint? His heart said yes. Her joy and zest for life encouraged him to embrace every day and enjoy her company.

Lucy fingered the swatches as she picked through them. "Here's a pretty blue, but more of a teal-blue might work. Where is the blue you mentioned?"

Owen found sky-blue in paint and stain and a lighter teal in both. "Let's paint samples of these on the wood."

At the counter, a young man of about twenty found the samples for them and offered them disposable brushes.

"Thanks." Lucy carried the small containers to a table. Owen laid the wood in front of her.

He opened the jars and handed her one at a time. She brushed with the grain of the wood. "You're right. The sky-blue paint will complement the yellow and white. I can't wait to paint. Let's buy brushes or rollers or whatever will work best." She jumped from her seat and hugged him again, then moved away from him.

"I did it again. I'm sorry. I get so excited and can't stop myself."

He grinned. "I'm okay with hugs." *Especially yours.*

They gathered the supplies and mixed paint, then headed outside. "We should call for a ride and stash this on the boat before we eat lunch or go anywhere else."

Once they dropped off the paint, the car driver took them to Pasquel's.

"They have the best Reuben in town, or if you eat fish, they make a great walleye sandwich. Want to try an appetizer or two?"

"Sounds good. I didn't have breakfast. Not only do I forget to feed Finn, I forget to feed myself."

He laughed at her silly joke and it felt good.

"Are you getting hangry?"

"I might be. There's a green leafed plant in the corner I could nibble on." She giggled.

Owen laughed with her. "Don't pull a Finn on me."

Not long after they ordered, the waiter delivered a plate of fried

Penny Frost McGinnis, Abbott Island Book 3

green tomatoes and three homemade meatballs in marinara sauce.

"These smell yummy. I hope I have room for my sandwich." Lucy cut a piece of tomato and dipped it in the house-made sauce. "Oh, wow. The best I've eaten, but don't tell my mom. Hers are good, but these tomatoes are better."

"I won't tell your mom if you don't tell Aunt Marley. She makes them, and hers are never crisp enough."

The appetizers disappeared by the time the sandwiches arrived.

"This was a great choice, Owen. You sure know where to find the best food." She pulled the toothpick from one half of her sandwich.

"What can I say? I love to eat."

"Me, too. I'm concerned if I sell the store I'll gain weight. I lift and move heavy merchandise and boxes in my day to day." She bit into the toasted rye bread and corned beef with Swiss cheese, and Thousand Island dressing and sauerkraut oozed out.

She's cute when she's messy. He blinked to clear his head. "The farm keeps me moving, and it's a good thing since most of Aunt Marley's food is carb heavy."

"Maybe I could cook with her and improve my skills in the kitchen. Mom tried, but I never stayed still long enough for the lessons to stick." She gave up on holding the sandwich and sliced a bite off.

"Sounds good to me. I mean, yeah, you should learn. If you want to." He ate a kettle chip.

She smiled at him. "Are you volunteering to be my guinea pig?"

"I guess I am."

After lunch, Owen placed Lucy's hand in the crook of his arm and led her along the street.

Her grip tightened when her foot caught on a crack in the cement. Before she hit the sidewalk, he wrapped an arm around her and pulled her to him.

She steadied, and he let go. "I'm such a klutz."

"Anyone might trip on this old sidewalk. The city needs to pour new ones." He snugged her to him and continued to walk.

"Where are we going? You haven't told me." Her eyes pleaded for information.

"It's a surprise, if that's okay. You may have been here before and it won't be a big deal, but I thought you'd enjoy this place."

They rounded a corner and the Merry-Go-Round Museum came into view.

"I love this place. I haven't been here since I was a kid." Lucy bounced on her toes.

Her childlike enthusiasm renewed Owen's hope in life. After baseball, he had lost his career, his fiancée, and his purpose. He'd

Home At Last

struggled through the days after surgery. While he built his strength, he asked God to open his heart to the next thing, then Aunt Marley and Uncle Jed had asked him to live with them for a while, which turned into a permanent solution. He had built a small cabin on their farm and rediscovered his love of farm life. The ability to grow his own food, plant flowers and trees, and create a cleaner environment set his wheels in motion.

"Are we going in?" Lucy waited for a response.

"Let's go." He wrapped his hand around hers, and they entered into the magic of childhood.

Lucy stood at his side as he paid admission. Her face filled with joy and a huge smile.

"You ready to explore, or do you want to ride the carousel first?" he asked.

"Let's explore." She held his hand and led him to a display of carved horses in the process of being painted.

A woman dressed in jeans, a t-shirt, and an art apron stepped from behind one of the horses. "Hello. I'm Catrina, one of the restoration crew members. Want a mini-tour of what we do to restore the carousel animals?"

"Yes." Lucy and Owen answered in unison.

"Wonderful. Follow me." In a room off the main part of the museum, Catrina stopped in front of a bench. The odor of paint and wood drifted around the room. "This is where the magic happens. We build new menagerie animals and horses or repair antique ones. A lot of folks believe the animals are carved from one block of wood, but they aren't. After we design the piece on paper, we cut patterns and work on the body, head, legs, and tail separately." She explained the process from start to finish. "Any questions?"

Lucy touched the mane of the horse Catrina had carved. "These are amazing. I had no idea how you created these beautiful creatures. Thanks for showing us what you do."

Owen thanked her too, and they walked to the carousel. "Want to ride?"

"You know I do. I'm afraid I'm childlike when it comes to things like this."

One of the things Owen appreciated about Lucy was her innocence when it came to fun. Rebecca never relaxed enough to enjoy herself. She worried about her appearance and how others viewed her. Lucy embraced the joy of life and took chances. As far as looks, her natural beauty shone. If he kept company with her too often, she'd capture his heart.

She hurried to the large amusement ride. "I can't imagine how they got the idea to set this up here."

"Here's a bit of history." He pointed to a metal sign beside the ride. "It coincides with when the postal service created stamps with carousel animals. This building was a post office."

He handed the attendant their ride tokens and they climbed on. Lucy straddled an ostrich, and Owen mounted a black stallion beside her. The carousel rotated, calliope music played, and the buttery scent of popcorn filled the air.

Lucy's complexion glowed. "This is so much fun. Thank you for surprising me."

His hands wrapped around the pole, and he soaked in the moment and the charming blond by his side. He had never met a woman quite like Lucy.

Home At Last

CHAPTER FOURTEEN

Waves washed over the sand on Lucy's beach. Saturday evening, Lucy wandered along the shore and gazed at sailboats as they cruised across the lake. She bent and gathered a few cone-shaped shells, no longer than a paper clip. A band of off-white wrapped around the golden, gray, or brown snail shells and created whorls. They reminded her of candy cane stripes. She pocketed her treasures to add to her collection of lake ephemera.

"Lucy." Sadie's voice cut through the air.

Lucy turned from the water to see her sister-in-law amble across the yard to the beach. Little Gracie snugged to her momma in a baby wrap carrier. "Hey, Sadie. How's my sweet little girl?"

She met Sadie and her niece at the edge of the sand, then the women moved to a set of beach chairs Lucy had arranged under an oak tree by the beach.

Sadie released Gracie from the carrier and offered her to Lucy. "My doll baby is growing so fast. I'm afraid I'll blink, and she'll be a teenager."

Gracie cooed and grinned at her aunt. "Hello, sweet girl." Lucy kissed her on the cheek. "Don't grow up too fast."

Sadie folded the wrap and smoothed it on her lap. "I heard you had a date with Owen again."

"Who told you?"

"You sound defensive." Sadie snickered. "Joel saw you get in his boat with him. He sent me to see if it was a date. Of course, I'm a little nosy, too."

Lucy bounced Gracie on her knee. "Brothers. Sheesh. There's no privacy on this island." Gracie grinned. "We took the boat to Sandusky, and it didn't start out as a date. He took me to buy paint for the deck. Then we ate lunch, and he had a surprise for me."

"Tell me." Sadie scooted to the edge of her chair.

Lucy cuddled Gracie on her shoulder. "We visited the Merry-Go-Round Museum. We did a tour and rode the carousel."

Sadie's mouth formed an O. "No way. Did he know you've wanted to go visit there again since you were young? You talked about it all the time when we were teenagers."

"No. Unless someone told him, but I doubt it. I'm not sure why I haven't gone on my own. I guess I was waiting for someone to share the experience with." A motorboat sped past. "We had so much fun. I like Owen a lot, but I'm not sure if he's as fond of me. Plus, I went to dinner with Andrew. He's interesting, but something about him bothers me." She turned to Sadie. "I don't expect either one to ask me out again, but if they do, do I go?"

"Why wouldn't you go? You aren't committed to either one. If you don't spend time with them, how will you be sure which one might be a good friend or a good fit for you?"

Gracie reached for her momma.

Lucy passed her to Sadie. "You have a good point. I've embarrassed myself in front of Owen. I spontaneously hugged him, not once, but twice. Why do I let myself behave like a crazy woman?"

"You aren't crazy. You're passionate. I'm sure he didn't mind a hug or two." Sadie's mouth bent into a smile. "I'm praying for you. Listen for God's lead. He's not going to guide you in the wrong direction. Look at Joel and me."

A seagull landed in front of Lucy. "I'm not a good listener, but I'll try."

"All you can do is try." Sadie rose from her chair, passed Gracie to Lucy and attached the wrap, then tucked Gracie in. "I need to get this little one ready for bed. I love you." She hugged Lucy and left.

Lucy wrapped her arms around herself and lifted her eyes to the sky. "God, I'm not good at this. I mean, I pray, just not with eloquence. According to our preacher, it's okay to talk to You the same way I talk to my friends. So here goes. There are these two guys and I like them both. One more than the other, and I believe You will help me discern between the two. I'll do my best to listen and be alert to Your guidance. You may need to kick me in the pants. I hope it's okay to say that. Thanks for listening. Amen." She peered to her left and right to make sure no one had heard her.

~~~~~

Eleven o'clock, Saturday night, a light breeze washed over the island and a thumbnail moon hung overhead. Without a full moon, darkness shadowed the streets. Travis pulled an Indiana Jones style fedora low on his forehead and meandered along Division Street. His leather jacket kept the coolness of the evening away as his boots clicked along the sidewalk. Other than security lights in the businesses and a few streetlights, the town rested under the dark sky. From what he had learned from his time on the island, most people went to bed early to prepare for Sunday morning church. Good thing he had never gotten into the habit. He preferred late nights and sleeping in.

The sound of an engine hummed behind him. He stepped between buildings and waited. A police cruiser drove by and parked in front of the station. Travis regarded the younger police officer who exited the car, stretched his legs and climbed two steps at a time, then entered the building. If he wanted to check behind the buildings, he needed to watch his back.

He grasped the penlight in his coat pocket, flicked it on, then shined its bare light on his great-blah-blah aunt's map. Couldn't the lady have drawn a better outline of the island and the gold's location? Why so many Xes? She must have been afraid someone else would find her map. He stuffed both into his pocket and stepped behind the school. The map showed this stretch as the one with an X. One of these properties might hold his future wealth. If he discovered the gold, he had to keep it quiet, extract it from the ground, and leave the island. The law could prove to be a problem, since ownership fell to the owner of the property for anything found there, and he couldn't bear to lose his fortune to a stranger.

In the school yard, he poked around the building. Logic told him since the school was built in more recent years, the excavators or builders would have unearthed the box. Next door, the town had renovated an old home into the library. This ground held more potential. One of these buildings had been built by his family, but which one? The police station, built of limestone, had stood on the island for a long time, but not long enough.

He peered across the yards at the General Store. A powerful tug in his gut told him to search the grounds. Before he moved across the police station's yard, someone stepped onto a small stoop from the back door of the station. The cop he saw earlier shined a flashlight and glanced around the area.

Time to duck and run. Travis slid between buildings and waited for him to leave. When the flashlight flicked off, he hustled away from downtown and raced to the cabin.

Inside, he settled at the wobbly desk his host provided, and he brought out the letters Merrilee had written to her mom. He sorted them and lifted one to read.

Dearest Mother,

I hope you received my last letter where I told you Jonas died. Your heart must be filled with sorrow, like mine. I'm halfway home on this train. I used a nugget to buy passage in a better car than the trip out. I'm keeping the box in the bag I'm holding on my lap. It doesn't pay to trust anyone. When I get home, I'm going to the island first and hide the box. I hope the key to the summer house is still in the secret place. If not, you'll see me sooner than later. I'll keep a few nuggets out for you. Until I'm with you.

Penny Frost McGinnis, Abbott Island Book 3

> *Your daughter,*
> *Merrilee*

~~~~~

A light breeze washed the scent of lilacs across the island Sunday morning. The sun shone on the church's lawn when Owen and Lucy stepped outside after the service ended. Her fingers brushed his as they descended the steps. Warmth crawled along his arm as he longed to take her hand, but he shifted to self-control mode. A public display of any affection in front of Miss Aggie, Miss Flossie, and Miss Hildy meant a visit to the gossip train. No way he'd give them fuel to talk about him or Lucy. He respected Lucy too much.

From the bottom of the steps, they strode to their cars. Owen opened the door on Lucy's Jeep for her. "What are you doing this afternoon?" He had chores to do, but once he finished, he hoped to spend time with her.

Lucy buckled her seatbelt. "After lunch, I'm going to tackle painting the deck. I want to take advantage of the beautiful weather today. Tomorrow, I've got to finish the inventory at the store and clean out the storage area. We have more items coming in."

He knew how to paint. "Do you mind if I help paint? I'm pretty good with a paintbrush."

A smile spread across her face. "I'd appreciate your help. It's not a huge deck, but I'd love to finish it today."

"Great. I can get there about two o'clock. Aunt Marley will want me to eat lunch with them after I finish a few farm chores."

"Two sounds good. I'll have everything ready." She started her car, and he closed her door. With a wave, she drove away.

~~~~~

Before lunch, Owen fed the cows and sheep and added water to the trough. He checked his to do list for the week. The fir trees he had ordered were due to arrive on the ferry Tuesday. He'd requested six trees to better understand what it took to raise Christmas trees. As soon as they arrived, he planned to plant them. He had prepped the soil for his experiment in hopes of mature trees in six to seven years. If the trees grew the first year and he learned the trade, he'd plant more each year until he had a small rotating crop. Once the process started, he would be committed to the island life. Thankful Uncle Jed offered him a chance to try his ideas, he stopped daydreaming and finished his work.

At two o'clock, he parked his truck in front of Lucy's property. He climbed out and saw her spread a tarp in the yard. Her blond ponytail shimmered in the sun. Dressed in jeans and a paint shirt, she radiated beauty. If he planned to spend the afternoon with her, he needed to rein

Home At Last

in his attraction.

"Hey, Owen." Lucy brushed a stray hair from her face. "I think I have what we need." She moved her hand in a fan motion to the paint and brushes.

He delivered a tin of cookies to her. "Aunt Marley baked chocolate chip cookies for us. Her idea of nourishment."

Lucy carried the tin to the porch and rested it on a small table. "These will taste good later with iced tea, and Owen, thanks for spending the day with me."

At the tarp, they each poured paint into a tray. "The blue was the perfect choice. Thanks for suggesting it."

Owen dipped his roller in the paint and covered a large area with a coat. "When I lived in Boston, I saw several homes painted in a variety of blues and yellows. I admired the landscapes, but the homes caught my eye too. My mom loved the design magazines when I was a kid, and she'd point out homes she thought were pretty whenever we were driving through town."

Lucy used a brush to cover the edges. "I enjoy looking at houses and interesting buildings. There are some beautiful ones on the island and in Port Clinton. How long did you live in Boston?"

"One year when I played for the Red Sox. It's an interesting town with the American heritage woven into its history, but it wasn't good to me." He filled his pan again. "When I played baseball there..."

The crunch of gravel interrupted Owen's train of thought.

A tall man with dark hair rolled a bicycle over the parking area and let it drop on the grass. "Hello, Lucy."

She set her brush in the pan, then shaded her eyes to block the sun as she watched him saunter toward them. "Andrew. What are you doing this afternoon? Have you met Owen?" She waved toward him.

Andrew held his hand out and Owen shook it. "I don't believe I have. Nice to meet you."

"You, too." Owen let go as fast as he could. *What does he want with Lucy, now?* Why were his protective instincts out like claws? Lucy was a grown woman, and she was allowed to talk to whomever she wanted.

"Can I chat with you a minute?" Andrew motioned with his head to move away from Owen.

Lucy glanced from one man to the other. "I guess." She tagged behind Andrew to the side of the house, but still close enough for Owen to hear.

Hands in his pockets, Andrew rocked from the balls of his feet to the heels. "I wondered if you had time this evening to go with me to South Bass Island?"

Owen dropped a roller filled with paint on his shoe.

CHAPTER FIFTEEN

The waves on the lake swished like Lucy's stomach. She and Owen planned to finish painting the porch this afternoon, then she hoped they'd have dinner together. Now, Andrew's eyes bored into her and he waited for her answer. Her heart longed to say no, but what if Owen planned to go home when they finished and had no intentions for the evening? A dart of selfishness pricked her conscience.

Middle school anxiety roared in her mind. Rowen Roberts, the most popular boy in school, had asked her to hang with him in the park on a Saturday. She had dressed in her cutest outfit and hoped to go to the outdoor movie with him later, if he asked. Logan Janson had approached her the day before and asked her to watch the movie with him. She had said no, and Rowen never asked her. At the movie, she spotted him with Kelley Connors and Logan had sat with his buddies.

She shook the memory away. "I appreciate you asking, but I want to finish painting my porch."

He hung his head. "I understand. Guess I'll see you later."

"Sure. Talk to you soon."

He skulked away.

Weird, she had no remorse for saying no, but she imagined he'd ask her again. Then what? She had hoped to meet and date someone special but had no idea she'd be caught between two guys at the same time. Who was she kidding? Only one of them held her attention, and he currently cleaned paint off his shoe. Owen appealed to her, inside and out. His warm brown eyes, honey-colored hair, muscular body, and air of confidence stirred a desire to hug him again, and snatch a kiss. The kindness of his heart, his courtesy toward others, and his faith impressed her. Rebecca had hurt him and his baseball career ended on a sour note, but he had moved forward.

What had she learned about Andrew? Not much, unless his movie star handsomeness counted. He appeared polite enough, but an edginess emerged on occasion, and he didn't make eye contact half of the time. She'd stay on his good side, just in case. Plus, his interest in purchasing the store might open her life to new experiences.

The fresh paint smell tickled her nose as she dipped her brush in and made strokes along the edge of the deck. She peeked at Owen.

He straightened and rested the roller's handle across the pan. "Your

Penny Frost McGinnis, Abbott Island Book 3

friend left in a hurry."

"Yeah. He wanted me to go to South Bass Island with him this evening." A dab of blue dropped on her pants and she rubbed it.

Owen's mouth drooped into a frown. "What time do we need to wrap up for you to get ready?"

"We don't. I mean, I want to finish, but not at a particular time. I'm not going." She stretched.

A smile tugged at the corners of Owen's mouth. His response hinted he was happy she stayed.

He rolled more paint. "Want to have dinner with me? You said you ate at the Abbott Island Restaurant the other day, but we could order food from there and take it to the park, if you don't mind. It's warm enough to eat outside."

Lucy tamped her enthusiasm and took a breath before she answered. "Yes. I'd love to."

They stepped back and surveyed the deck. "I love it. Ready for cookies and tea?"

"Sounds good."

Lucy took a step toward the deck and stopped, foot in midair. "Since this isn't dry yet, I better go to the other door." She chuckled and hustled to the other side of the tiny house.

Inside, she ducked into the bathroom and washed her hands. She glanced in the mirror at her messy self. Blue freckles dotted her face and hair. Her smurfy looks hadn't kept Owen from asking her to dinner. With a washcloth, she scrubbed away the flecks, then went to the kitchen and poured drinks.

~~~~~

In the cabin, a low light glowed on the desk. Travis's arms crossed his chest, and his legs stretched in front of him. He tapped his foot against the leg of the desk. The excursion in town Saturday provided few clues to where Merrilee had buried the treasure. For all he knew, the gold didn't exist, but he had the letters. Merrilee's life had ended not long after she arrived home, which probably meant she never unearthed the box. Her mother died a few months after her. The gold had to be buried on the island. Mom knew the story from her great-uncle who had said his great-grandfather had heard the tale from Merrilee's mother before she had died. She had told family and friends the gold had killed her daughter, and she hoped no one ever found it.

Abbott Island residents had spread rumors of the gold. He had heard the older folks had passed the story to their children. If someone had discovered the nuggets, the newspapers would have reported it, unless the finder never told anyone. Nonsense, they'd have to cash it in.

He stood and paced across the room, annoyed by the squeak of every

Home At Last

step. What to do next? He dropped onto the bed and rubbed his hand over his hair. Tonight he planned to check out the X near the water on the east side of the island, further north than when he tromped through the woods the other night. He'd send his goons to dig once he decided on the spot.

After ten o'clock, he donned his black jeans and hoodie and packed his satchel with a water bottle, the map, and a candy bar. He tied his hiking boots and walked outside. A grown man dressed in black riding a bike through the streets might draw unwanted attention. The area he had scoped out sat about three-and-a-half miles from where he stayed.

He ditched the bike idea and took off on foot. A calm covered the island on the warm May evening, and the walk might help him think.

Half an hour later, he inched along the beach beside the tiny home. No one appeared at the window. He crept past, then jogged along a stretch of beach. He reached the area the X appeared to mark. A barn loomed ahead and an old farmhouse stood in the distance. When he had researched the property, a man named Redmon had owned the land years ago. Several yards away from the farmhouse, lights glowed from a small log cabin hidden in a wooded area. A group of pine trees grew in a field and cows gathered around the barn.

How would he find the treasure on a farm? He pressed the button on his penlight and shined it on the copy of the map. The X appeared about halfway between the barn and house. He'd call his minions and meet them here late tomorrow night and dig a few holes. If they found nothing, he'd employ more aggressive tactics.

~~~~~

The sun hid Monday morning, but Lucy's spirit glowed. After a shower, she fed Finn, then she walked to town. The brisk walk warmed her against the cool May morning. She whistled a hymn as she surveyed the downtown.

"Morning, Johnny." She waved at Marigold's husband, who owned Johnny's Place across the street from the General Store and created delicious Greek dishes. "I'll be in to buy lunch today."

"Sounds good. See you then." The bald fifty-something chef waved and hurried into the restaurant.

On the porch of her store, Lucy twisted the key and unlocked the door. Inside, she flipped on lights.

"Hello, Lucy." Regina's voice called out behind her.

She spun around to greet her manager.

"Morning." Lucy dropped her purse under the counter. "How was your weekend?"

Regina stashed her bag beside Lucy's. "Wonderful. My family cleaned the house for me and cooked dinner on Saturday. The girls are growing too fast, but I love the help. Gio cleared junk out of the garage

Penny Frost McGinnis, Abbott Island Book 3

and he found my grandpa's old wooden toolbox. You'll never guess what I found inside, besides the antique tools.

Lucy tapped her finger to her mouth. "I have no idea."

Regina reached into her pocket and pulled out a yellowed piece of paper. She unfolded an eleven-by-fourteen-inch sheet. With her hands, she smoothed out the folds. "This is a map."

A pencil drawing of the island covered the page. A few Xes marked spots on the east side of the island, one along the main street and a few others. The artist had scripted the initial M in the corner with a flourish.

Lucy lifted the map and stared. "I've seen the M in the corner before."

She riffled through her purse until she located the copy of the map she had found on the beach by her house. "Look at this." Regina leaned her head near Lucy's and considered the paper.

"The handwriting appears the same and the lines defining the town match. How many Xes are on yours?" Regina and Lucy each counted the Xes on their maps.

"This one has three or four. This smudge might be an X, but these are on Division Street with two near the northeast side of the island." Lucy pointed to them.

"Mine has five. Three, the same as yours, and one near where Marigold's kayak stand sits and one near Sadie's house. Weird, the person who drew the map marked so many spots with X." The manager flattened her paper on the counter and leaned over it. "The real question is, why did my grandpa have a map? What's it for?"

"I'm not sure, but remember the holes dug in my yard?" She tapped her finger on the paper. "These have something to do with those. Owen's aunt and uncle told him about a supposed treasure buried on the island after the Yukon gold rush. He told me local people discovered gold and buried it here. Whoever drew the map may have added extra Xes to throw people off."

Regina rested her hand on Lucy's arm. "Sounds far-fetched to me. Wouldn't gold have been found by the workers at the limestone quarry?"

"Not necessarily. These Xes aren't near the quarry." Lucy sat on a bench behind the counter. "I showed my map to Joel, but he thought it was kids playing around. I'm not so sure now."

"I asked my mom if Dad told her anything about this, and he hadn't. The paper is pretty old and fragile."

The bell over the door jingled. Andrew brushed his hand through his hair as he entered. "Hello, ladies."

"Hi. How can I help you?" Lucy folded her map and stuck it in her pocket.

Regina snatched her bag, map, and Lucy's purse. "I'll put these in the cabinet." She made her way to the office.

88

Home At Last

"She's in a hurry." Andrew pointed his thumb at Regina.

Lucy shook her head. "Not really. She's getting ready for the day." Her heart beat faster than normal. Not because of the man in front of her, but because the paper in her pocket left her with questions. Lots of questions. Did whoever dug the holes in her yard know there might be gold buried? Or was it a prankster bored after winter? She sucked in a slow breath. "Are you shopping for anything in particular today?"

Andrew stepped closer to Lucy, right into her personal space. "I'm hoping a certain lady will have dinner with me tonight on South Bass Island. I want to talk more about your store and island life." His stare riveted to her face.

Heat rose to Lucy's neck. Discomfort twisted her gut. "Um... I'm busy with the store and my home. Marigold is coming by to help me make pillows for my porch later. Maybe another time."

Two men asking her out seemed fun at first, but not anymore. She swallowed hard. Owen's kindness spilled over on her, and comfort and peace filled her. Andrew's nearness made her shudder. He'd not treated her with malice, but something about him bothered her. He never held her gaze unless he asked a pointed question. The one time she had met him for dinner, he had hijacked the conversation. If she sold the store, she might consider him as a buyer, but she hesitated.

Regina carried a box to the counter. "This is the last box to unpack before this weekend when the locals wander in to check out what's new." She glanced from Lucy to Andrew. "Am I interrupting?"

"No." Lucy hopped off the stool and sliced the lid with a box cutter. "I can't wait to display the bathing suits we ordered for babies. One goes to Gracie."

"Of course it does." Regina lifted a plastic bag filled with pastel shades of pink, blue, green, and lavender.

Andrew cleared his throat. "Another time then."

"We'll see what we can work out." Lucy gave him a wave.

After Andrew exited the store, Lucy leaned on the counter.

Regina placed a fist on her hip. "What did he want?"

"He wanted me to go to dinner with him tonight."

"Are you going?"

"I'm not. I don't care for his edginess, and he keeps asking me about selling the store, but doesn't listen when I answer questions."

"Okay. Can I ask you a couple of questions about selling?" Regina twisted her mouth.

"Sure. What do you want to know?"

"If a person isn't hearing you when you share information about the store, are you sure you want to sell to them?" Regina sorted the bathing suits.

Lucy lifted a pink one with a flamingo on the front. "I'm not sure." She raised her eyebrows and scrunched her nose. "I can't do this much longer. I want to have a life. If it wasn't for you, I'd never have time off. So, yes, I plan to sell and explore other things to do, but I want the best person or people in place who understand the island life and the tourists. I'm not sure Andrew is the one."

"Would it hurt you to talk to him one more time?" Regina lifted a pair of green baby-boy swim trunks from the pile.

"I guess not." Lucy folded a pair of blue trunks. "The other time I ate dinner with him, he kissed me on the cheek. I felt uncomfortable." She wrinkled her nose, then gave her friend a nod. "I'll call him and tell him I changed my mind. After we eat, I'll keep my distance."

"You have his number?"

"Yeah. From the other time I had dinner with him. I don't want to go to South Bass, though. I'll ask if he wants to meet me at Johnny's. He opens with full-time hours tomorrow."

CHAPTER SIXTEEN

Clouds hung low in the sky and cast a shadow over the early evening. Lucy carried a light-weight jacket for the chilly walk home. At Johnny's, she swung open the wooden door and entered the Greek styled restaurant she and her friends had helped paint after last year's fire. The chef served American fare, but his Greek dishes brought in the crowds.

The smell of garlic braided with oregano and basil filled the restaurant. Lucy searched the tables for Andrew. He waved to her from a corner booth. As she made her way to him, she heard her name called.

"Lucy." Owen sat at a table with Levi. The one across from Andrew.

She paused beside him. Great, now he'd see her with Andrew again. "Um. Hi." She stuttered out the greeting. She was happy Owen and Levi had become friends and spent time together, but why tonight?

He stood and motioned to a seat. "Want to join us?" His smile invited her to sit with him and the police officer.

She pursed her lips, then noticed movement beside her.

"Sorry, man. She's with me tonight." An ugly expression of smugness crossed Andrew's face.

Owen lifted his chin and sank into the chair.

Andrew tugged on Lucy's sleeve. She jerked away from him and bent over Owen's shoulder. "We're meeting about the store. He's interested in buying it." Her voice escaped in a whisper to keep the rest of the patrons from hearing.

His eyes met hers. "No worries. You don't owe me an explanation, but if you need me, I'm here."

"Thank you." She patted his back and nodded to Levi before she sat in Andrew's booth.

After they gave their orders to the waitress, Andrew leaned across the table. "Can I ask you a personal question?"

Lucy squared her shoulders. "You can, but I may not answer."

He folded his hands together in front of him. "Is Owen your boyfriend?"

Her eyes widened. She hadn't expected that question. "We've spent time together, but nothing is official. We're friends." Did she say the right thing? Did Owen hear the conversation? She hoped not. Talk about awkward.

"I wondered. He seems to be wherever you are."

Penny Frost McGinnis, Abbott Island Book 3

The waitress delivered waters and an appetizer of pita bread and tzatziki dip.

Lucy placed a saucer in front of her and spooned dip on her plate. She drenched the bread, then stuffed it in her mouth. If she ate, she wasn't tempted to babble or prattle, words Marigold used for excessive talk.

Andrew's Hollywood appeal paled in comparison to Owen's handsomeness and his kind heart. Of course, Owen's muscular build didn't hurt anything, either, especially when he helped her with her deck. Did she deserve a man like Owen? He outshined all the men she'd met over the years, and none of them wanted her. She was too much, they'd said. Yes, her personality exploded with emotion at times. Over the top, another one told her. She laughed so loud and made too many jokes. If she let herself babble to Andrew, then he might leave her alone.

"Lucy?"

"I'm sorry. What?"

"I asked you another question."

"Want to ask again?"

He sipped his drink.

"I wondered how your sales numbers were last year. Do you have it written down?" He ate a piece of pita bread sans dip.

She dug in her purse and pulled out a sheet of paper. The copy of the map fell out at the same time. Andrew reached for it, but she snagged it and stuffed it in her bag.

"Here you go." She unfolded the page of numbers. "I printed this in case you wanted the sales for the previous year."

He studied the sheet. "These look great. You must have a lot of tourist traffic. People who buy souvenirs."

She pointed to a couple of different lines on the paper. "We have many who come and stay for the summer, and they purchase items to take to family and friends. They buy those in August most summers. Plus, the ones who come for weekends and the summer people buy supplies. I carry things like bug spray, sunscreen, and essentials for outdoor activities. It's not all about kitsch and t-shirts."

"I hadn't thought about the variety of items you sell."

The server placed a plate of moussaka in front of Andrew and a platter with a burger and fries in front of Lucy.

"No Greek food tonight?"

"I love Johnny's burgers. They're the best anywhere. I enjoy his Greek food, too, but I can't resist his burger and fries. I haven't had them since, hmm… last week." Her laughter rang through the restaurant.

Andrew's face registered surprise.

She covered her mouth with her napkin, then lowered the white cloth. "Sorry. I can be loud sometimes."

92

Home At Last

Johnny approached the table. "I thought I heard you out here. How's the food?"

"Amazing as always." Lucy bit into a fry.

"Are you the chef Lucy has raved about?" Andrew asked.

"I am." Johnny nodded.

"I'm Andrew. I'm staying on the island for a while."

Johnny tapped the table. "I've seen you here a few times. It's nice to meet you. I better get to the kitchen. I'm sure Henry misses me."

Lucy watched Johnny walk to the kitchen. Marigold had found her match. He not only cooked, he treated her as if she were a queen.

Andrew had eaten half his meal. "I'm going to take the rest of this home for tomorrow. It's delicious, but there's too much for one meal. When you finish, can we take a walk and talk about the store?"

Not sure she wanted to be alone with him, Lucy took the last bite of her burger. Her stomach quivered and goosebumps covered her arms. A sure sign of discomfort reminded Lucy to step with caution, even though she didn't understand why.

She swallowed, then wiped her mouth with the napkin. A walk sounded good, but she found comfort in Owen's presence nearby. Levi had left ten minutes ago. Maybe Owen wanted to go, yet he hung around for her.

"I'd rather stay here. Besides, you'd have to carry your leftovers. Plus, my feet hurt, and I have to walk home later." Why had she told him she had to walk home?

He waved his hand in front of him. "No worries." The waitress brought a box for him and he filled it with leftovers. "When are you planning to sell?"

Lucy's shoulders relaxed and her stomach calmed. "I want to sell at the end of summer. I'm ready for a change. I enjoyed the store and meeting the tourists, but I'm ready to let it go and move on to something else." She had written a price on an index card. "I have the price I want if you'd like to see it. The number includes the inventory, the building, and the property it sits on. It's a prime location on the busiest street on the island."

"I'd like to do a walk-through of the property before we talk about price. When can we go through the property?" He fiddled with his napkin.

Of course he'd want to go through the entire building and around the grounds. What was she thinking? She'd have Regina with her to answer questions about inventory and shipments. "Any day this week. Regina and I work every day." If he wanted the property sooner than the end of summer, she'd negotiate.

Andrew narrowed his eyes. "Why does Regina need to be there?"

Lucy placed both her hands on the table. "She's my manager, and she's quite knowledgeable about the ins and outs of what sells and what

Penny Frost McGinnis, Abbott Island Book 3

doesn't. She's an amazing lady. If you buy the store, you may want to keep her as an employee."

He held both hands in front of him. "I meant no offense."

Lucy scrunched her forehead. "None taken." *What's his deal with Regina?*

~~~~~

Frank Sinatra crooned about a river. The sweet taste of baklava melted on Owen's tongue. He waited for Lucy to finish her dinner with Andrew. At least his seat faced away from them. Something about the man caused Owen's neck hair to prickle. His imagination worked overtime as Lucy's laughter and the murmurs of conversation tempted him to peek over his shoulder.

A shuffle sounded behind him and he sensed movement. From the corner of his eye, he glimpsed the red of Lucy's shirt. He gave his head a slight turn and saw the two of them stand. Before he allowed his mind to overthink his movements, he rose from his seat. Thank goodness he had already paid his bill.

He angled to meet her in the aisle. "How was your dinner?" Did she want him to accompany her outside?

"Great." Lucy moved ahead of him.

Did he imagine the rescue-me-please look in her eyes?

Andrew, Lucy, and Owen spilled onto the sidewalk outside the restaurant. An awkward moment left Owen without words, much like his high school days. He had hoped his experience on the baseball team had helped him overcome his shyness, but not today.

One glance from Lucy shook him out of his silence. "Do you want a ride home, Lucy?"

Andrew stepped between them. "I had planned to walk her home."

Lucy cleared her throat and stepped closer to Owen. "I told Andrew my feet hurt. I'm going to take you up on your offer." She turned to Andrew. "Thank you so much for dinner." She shrugged into her jacket. "Stop by the store later this week. Bring your questions, and Regina and I will give you the tour."

Andrew grunted and plodded away.

In the truck, Owen said, "I didn't mean to interfere with your date."

"It wasn't a date. We met to talk about the store, but he paid for my dinner."

Owen steered the truck onto the road. "Is he going to buy the store? Has he had retail experience?"

"Good question."

"Which one?" Owen drove along the lake.

Lucy snuggled into the seat. "Both, I guess. He wants to walk through the store and the grounds before seeing the amount I want for it. I'd have

94

Home At Last

thought he'd want the price to make sure he wasn't wasting his time." She tapped her fingers on her knee. "I'll ask when he stops by about the retail. I don't want someone to buy the store who doesn't know how to run it. I realize a new owner will make changes, but I hope they understand the needs of the island folks and the tourists. Plus, if he gives off an unfriendly vibe, the island people won't tolerate him, and something about him is off-putting to me."

"I get what you mean. He sure doesn't like me." He stopped the truck in front of Lucy's home.

Lucy undid her seatbelt. "Do you want to come in?"

Of course he wanted to, but should he? The more time he spent with Lucy, the more he enjoyed her company, but he'd promised himself not to get caught in a romance again, at least not yet. The logical part of his brain said go home, but the other said sure, why not? The other side won.

Owen slid out of the truck and went to the passenger door and opened it. Then he held her hand and helped her out. His mom insisted a true gentleman treated a lady with respect. He took every opportunity to honor his mom.

"You are one of the last gentlemen left on the planet." Lucy laughed. "Most guys don't think I'd want them to open the door, but I do. I realize I come across as a strong independent woman, but I'm also a bit of a romantic. Plus, having a man show kindness warms my heart. Thank you."

They walked to the front door, she unlocked it, and let him in.

"Let me feed Finn, then I'll make us decaf tea. If you'd drink some?" Lucy sprinkled fish food in the beta's bowl.

"Tea sounds good. Aunt Marley and I share a pot once in a while." Owen settled on Lucy's small couch. He observed the tiny living space Lucy called home, a one-person domain. The colors and decor reflected her cheerful demeanor. His life could use a dose of brightening.

Lucy handed him a mug of tea with a slight citrus smell. "I hope you don't mind Earl Grey. It's my favorite with a touch of honey."

He sipped the tea. "Tastes good to me."

She closed her eyes and appeared to inhale the scent.

"Lucy?"

Her eyes flew open.

"I looked around your property when I built the deck. You had mentioned you might want to install a few more homes here and sell them as part of a tiny home park. Would that work here? On the island, I mean." He rested the mug on a small end table.

Lucy cupped her hand around her mug of tea. "No. I don't have the money to make it happen. Plus, I'm not sure the homes would draw people, and I'd rather not take on the responsibility of landlord. I have my mind set on another idea I've wanted to do since I was fourteen, but I'm weighing the possibilities."

This woman intrigued Owen.

CHAPTER SEVENTEEN

Darkness shrouded the road on Owen's drive home. Lake water splashed in the distance and the odor of fish washed across the island. On his drive into the farm, all three sheep bleated.

He parked in the barn lot, then climbed out of the truck and walked to the barn to check on the animals. His aunt loved her milk cows. The two of them mooed at him every morning. About halfway along his walk on the path, a shadow swept along the edge of the barn. Uncertain if he saw a person or an animal, Owen circled the building, but didn't see anyone or anything.

Inside the barn, he flipped on the outside light. He'd be sure to leave it on through the night. No one came around the farm most of the time, except to buy eggs or vegetables, and they didn't drop by at night. His aunt and uncle lived a quiet life despite being near town.

The cows stood in their stalls and chewed their cuds, but the sheep baaed at each other. He filled the trough with water and poured extra food in their buckets. Outside, he secured the gate then headed to the house. In the middle of the barnyard, three holes about two feet wide glared at him. The depth of the first two reached about three feet, but the third one barely dented the earth. What now? Whoever dug these dove deeper than the ones in Lucy's yard. No wonder the sheep cried. If only they could talk.

In the house, Owen called the police station, and Joel assured him he was on the way.

Uncle Jed stepped into the kitchen. "What's going on? I heard you on the phone."

"Someone dug holes in the barnyard. Bigger than the ones in Lucy's yard. Why would they dig in our yard or anywhere on the island?" Tires crunched over gravel in the driveway. "There's Joel. Want to come with me, or fill Aunt Marley in?"

"I best let your aunt know, then I'll be out."

Outside, the barn's security light brightened the barnyard. Joel held a flashlight over the indentations.

"I can't figure out why anyone wants to dig on the island at random properties. This is the third location and none of the holes are the same size or depth. I'm going to check for tire tracks."

Owen shook his head. "They may have walked from the road. When I got here, I saw a shadow dart past the barn. They ran through the field.

I hope they stepped in a cow patty."

A laugh rolled from Joel. "I hope so too. I'll head to the field and search for clues." He carried bags with him and wore gloves. "I'll watch my step."

"Mind if I go with you?" Determined to discover a clue to the mystery, he matched the policeman's stride.

"A second set of eyes might help."

The men wandered through the field where Owen had spotted the intruder. The sliver of moon cast a faint illumination on the ground. A glint bounced off the ground. Joel squatted and lifted the end of a piece of metal with his pen. "Someone dropped one of those fancy mechanical pencils with the metal clasp. I'll bag it." He lifted the pencil from the ground and placed it in an evidence bag. "Do you use this type of pencil?"

"Sure don't. I use a good old-fashioned number two pencil I have to sharpen. Pretty sure Uncle Jed and Aunt Marley don't either." When he'd rummaged through the kitchen drawer for a pencil, he had found plastic Bic pens and yellow school pencils.

"I'll take it in and check for fingerprints. I don't guarantee we'll find any, and it will take several days." Joel waved his flashlight across the grass.

"At least you found something."

"I'll send Levi in the morning to check in the daylight. I'll be on Gracie duty tomorrow." A smile crossed the new dad's face.

"Sounds good. I'll fill in my aunt and uncle."

Joel pulled out of the driveway and Owen sauntered into the house. Uncle Jed met him at the door as rain broke loose.

Inside, he sat at the kitchen table with his aunt and uncle. "Joel found a mechanical pencil. He'll check for fingerprints and whether any match. Levi will be back in the morning. There are three good sized holes, but I must have interrupted them on the third one. It's not as deep." Owen tapped his fingers on the table. "Did you two hear anything?"

Aunt Marley touched her husband's hand. "Not a thing. We had the television on in the front room, and it drowned out any other sounds."

His gaze turned to his uncle. "Do you have any history on the farm? Who lived here in the 1800s?"

"I might could look into it. I'll go through some of my papers and see what I can find." Uncle Jed tapped the table.

Aunt Marley stood from her chair. "I'll help you tomorrow. I'm going to bed now."

"Me too." Uncle Jed left Owen at the table.

Was eleven too late to call Lucy? He stepped onto the front porch and dialed her number.

~~~~~

In pajamas, Lucy climbed the steep stairs to her loft and the soft bed and memory foam mattress she had purchased for her home. She set her alarm for six in the morning and crawled under the covers. A romantic suspense waited for her on her e-reader. As she flipped the switch on her reader, her phone chimed. Owen's name popped on the screen. *Late for a call.*

"Hello. Is everything okay? Are your aunt and uncle all right?" She stopped herself before she babbled.

A chuckle scrambled through the phone. "We're fine, but we had an incident. I hope I caught you before bedtime."

She leaned on her pillows. "I climbed into bed about five minutes ago, but I'm not asleep. I planned to read before I turned in. What's up?" She inhaled the lavender scent of the sachet under her pillow.

Owen shared about the holes and Joel coming by to search the property. "He's sending Levi in the morning to take a closer look."

Lucy tugged her blanket to her chin as if she might protect herself from whatever craziness was happening on the island. "Why on earth is someone digging? What are they searching for? Do you think it's a local or a person from the mainland?"

"My best guess is a visitor, if you want to call them that."

"The story about the treasure reminds me of when Joel and I were young, and I tried to find pretty rocks in the dirt and sand, and I remember Dad employing a metal detector to find coins and stuff after the tourists left. He found a Rolex watch one time, but we found the owner. I've not heard of random holes appearing on the island. Could it have something to do with the legend of the Klondike gold? It makes for a good story, but who's silly enough to believe it's still here, if it ever was in the first place?" She took a breath. "Sorry, I talk a lot when I'm nervous."

"You're fine. Makes me nervous, too. Have you noticed any visitors besides Andrew?"

"I've had a few couples come into the store on the weekends, and a family or two. Andrew was at the restaurant with us, so I doubt it was him." She reached for the cord to close her blinds, then shuttered them.

"True. He left when we did. I don't understand what's going on, but I want to find out. My aunt or uncle could have broken their leg if they'd tripped in a hole the way you did." His anger poured out with his words. "I'm glad I found the holes before Aunt Marley went out tomorrow morning to feed the chickens. Joel helped me place sawhorses around them so they wouldn't be a tripping hazard."

Lucy pondered her response instead of blurting something out. "I'm sorry, Owen. I'm glad you kept your aunt and uncle from getting hurt." The memory of the pain with her sprained ankle brought on a faux ache. "I'd hate to see either one of them hurt. Too bad you didn't get a better

Penny Frost McGinnis, Abbott Island Book 3

look at the person who ran."

"Since I've had time to think about it, there may have been more than one. When I drove into the lane, I thought I saw deer, but it may have been a person."

Lucy checked the time on her pink digital clock. "Do you mind if I stop by in the morning on my way to work? I want to compare the holes to the ones in my yard." She let go of a giggle. "I'm sorry, but whoever imagined we'd be talking about holes in the yard? Seems ridiculous, you know?"

Owen chuckled. "Yeah, you're right. I'd rather talk about something else. How about going to dinner with me Friday night? I'd like to take you to a new restaurant in Vermilion."

His invitation gave Lucy tingles from her grin to her toes. After she clicked her phone off, she snuggled into her covers and fell asleep with a handsome man on her mind.

~~~~~

Rain doused the island and thunder rumbled. At eleven o'clock on Wednesday evening, Travis wore a navy-blue rain slicker. He paced across the abandoned picnic shelter's floor. Hidden by shrubs and trees, he waited for his minions. A rustle sounded from behind the shelter. Two men trudged onto the concrete. Hair flattened and clothing drenched, they collapsed on a bench.

"It's about time." Travis stood over them with his arms crossed. "Find anything?" His rough voice scratched across the air. "I've been here for an hour. Did you figure out if the treasure is buried on the farm?"

The skinnier man wrung out the tail of his shirt. "The farm's not small. There's a big area to cover."

"So, you're saying you didn't find anything?" Travis stepped in front of him. "I'm paying you to find what I'm hunting for, not play in the dirt."

The man with a beard rose and shook out his leather hat. "We dug holes in the barnyard but didn't find nothing. The metal detector dinged a few times, but we only found a couple of coins and a bottle opener."

"You didn't find anything worthwhile." He smacked his fist on a picnic table.

"That's what I said."

A foul smell attacked Travis's nose. "Did you step in something besides mud?" He retreated from the men and waved his hand in front of his face.

At the edge of the shelter he inhaled fresh air, then strode to the table. "Can you tell me the exact area where you dug?" He pulled a map from his pocket. "Draw on here where you dug." He gave the bearded man the paper.

He leaned over the table and flattened the map on the surface. "Let

100

Home At Last

me get my pencil." He checked his shirt pocket, then his pants pocket. "Man, I lost my mechanical pencil, the one Gramps gave me for Christmas last year."

Skinny stood beside him. "Your granddad gave you a pencil for Christmas?" He guffawed.

"Shut your mouth. It was a fancy one made out of metal. Worked awful good." He rummaged through his pockets.

"You two need to stop your whining. Use this." Travis handed his bearded friend a red pen. "Mark where you searched, before I fire both of you."

"Boss, I believe we dug right here." He circled the area near the Xes on the farm lot. "On here, it looks like the Xes are right in the middle of the barnyard. Course if they moved the barn or house, it might not be right. Do you reckon they moved anything?" The rain slowed to a drizzle.

Travis controlled his temper. He longed to smack the back of this guy's head but knew it wouldn't do any good. Plus, he wasn't the bad guy they assumed he was. He just wanted the gold from his family. Tomorrow he'd research if the house or barn had been rebuilt or moved. Probably not, but it had been several decades since Merrilee buried the treasure.

"I can't believe I lost my pencil." The bearded man fussed with his pockets and searched the ground around the shelter.

"Would you stop?" Travis grabbed his arm and set him on the bench. "You're sure you didn't find any clues?"

"Not a thing." The skinnier one shrugged. "We dug pretty deep holes and about the time we started on the third one, here came a truck. Probably the guy who lives there with the old people. I ran through the field and he had to hide until he could get gone. The police officer showed up, too. We didn't get to fill the holes in either." He nudged his friend in the side. "I bet they found your pencil."

"I sure hope not." He dropped his head and stared at his feet.

"You two go."

The skinny one scrubbed his hair away from his face. "You mean go to our tent in the woods or leave?"

"I mean, don't let anybody see you on the island. I'll be in touch."

Travis watched them disappear into the bushes. He lowered himself to the bench and rested his arms on his knees and folded his hands. He used to pray with his mom this way. When had he moved so far away from God? His insatiable taste for money had overshadowed his desire to follow God. He had disappointed his mom before she died. He moved his hand as if to brush the memories away. *Focus on the gold, you fool. You need the money.* He rose from the bench, strode through the woods, and left any thoughts of reconciliation with God behind.

Home At Last

CHAPTER EIGHTEEN

Dew spotted slender leaves of grass the next morning, and fog danced on the water. Fifty-five degrees on a May morning reminded Lucy she lived in Ohio. Dressed in her boots, jeans, and a sweatshirt, she wiped the moisture of last night's rain from her bike. She mounted the leather seat and rode to Owen's farm. The mystery behind the holes ate at her insides. What motivated a person to dig on other people's property?

She parked her bike by the farmhouse. Aunt Marley's lilac bushes perfumed the air. Owen pushed the kitchen door open and stepped outside. "Saw you coming up the drive."

His handsome face caught Lucy off guard. The green plaid shirt he wore complimented his brown eyes and blond hair. *What a good-looking guy.* She stopped a sigh before she embarrassed herself. "Morning."

"Levi is on his way. He called a few minutes ago. With the rain last night, I'm not sure he'll find anything useful." They walked to the sawhorses and peered at the holes. "Joel found the pencil and a few useful footprints. He said he spotted two different shoe treads."

"If anyone can figure this out, it will be Joel and Levi. They don't give up easily." Lucy squatted beside a hole, where the smell of wet dirt accosted her nose. "They're bigger and deeper than the ones in my yard." She pointed to the smaller one. "You may have interrupted them."

"I may have. I think I saw one running away." He grasped Lucy's hand and helped her stand.

Lucy held on and didn't want to let go. Warmth moved from his hand and traveled along her arm. The wait for their Friday date might undo her. She already fretted over what to wear and whether she'd put her foot in her mouth or fall. She might spill her dinner on herself or worse yet, on Owen. Every day she worked with customers or salespeople, and she ran a profitable business, yet she worried over a simple dinner with a friend. Was he more than a friend? The question unnerved her and sent her into an anxious spin. She needed to talk to Sadie and Marigold. They'd help her calm down.

The sound of a car driving on the gravel pulled her out of her ramblings. Good thing Owen couldn't read her mind. Levi parked, exited the patrol car, and jogged toward them.

"Good morning." He shook their hands. "Joel said the hole digger struck again."

Owen pointed behind him. "Here's where they dug, and I say they because there may have been two of them." He reported to Levi what he had witnessed.

Aunt Marley and Uncle Jed stepped out the door. "Morning, Levi." Uncle Jed nodded. "Lucy, good to see you."

Lucy waved. "Good to see you too."

Levi jotted notes on his pad, then examined the area. "With the rain, it's hard to make out footprints or trampled grass. Did you notice anything else? Joel said he found a pencil and took photos of the footprints."

"We didn't hear a thing." Uncle Jed shrugged.

Aunt Marley leaned over one of the holes and pointed. "What's the shiny thing I'm looking at?"

Levi squatted and shined a flashlight on the spot she pointed to. "Be right back." He trotted to the cruiser, then returned with a small shovel and a plastic bag.

With a few pokes and prods, he loosened the dirt and discovered a rock with the appearance of a gold nugget. "I'll take this in and see what we can find out about it. It's the color of gold but may be a rock. I'll let you know as soon as I find out. It might take a few weeks or more." He bagged the piece. "If you don't care, could you leave the holes until we get results for the fingerprints off the mechanical pencil and find out what this hunk of rock is?"

Uncle Jed nodded. "No problem, Officer Levi. We'll leave the sawhorses so we don't fall in." He patted Levi on the back. "Much obliged you fellas are looking into this. I've never had a lick of trouble here, and I don't want to start now."

"Thanks, folks." Levi left the farm.

Uncle Jed turned to Owen. "Your aunt and I want to talk to you when you get a chance. We'll be inside." The screen door slapped shut after the older couple entered the house.

"I need to get to the store. Thanks for letting me stop by." Lucy shoved a rock across the dirt with the toe of her shoe.

"You're welcome here anytime. Have a good day at work. I'm going to finish around your place today. Make sure the porch is good and plant a few flowers on the side." He tucked a loose curl behind her ear. "I'm looking forward to Friday night. Dress casual. The restaurant isn't fancy, but the food is excellent."

She smiled. "I can't wait." On a whim, she kissed his cheek, then hurried to her bicycle and pedaled away.

~~~~~

Aunt Marley's confused rooster crowed at nine in the morning, after Levi and Lucy departed.

Owen shook his head at the crazy bird. "Must be retired." He entered

Home At Last

the kitchen of the eighty-year-old farmhouse. Uncle Jed had said the original house had burned to the ground, and the owners had rebuilt it in the same spot.

Owen seated himself at the table. "You wanted to talk?"

Uncle Jed wrapped his hand around Aunt Marley's. "We've been thinking and praying for a bit, and we have an idea we hope you'll agree with."

Owen studied his aunt and uncle. They appeared happy, even content. "What idea do you have?"

Aunt Marley let go of Jed and rested her hand on Owen's. "We've lived here a mighty long time and we love it on the island, but it's getting harder and harder to take care of this big, old house. Jed has you to help with the farm, and you have lots of ideas to keep the place running."

"You aren't moving away, are you?" Owen clasped his aunt's hand.

"No. We aren't leaving the island. I imagine you'll carry me off this farm in a box. What we want to do is trade houses with you. You built your little cabin with a bedroom, kitchen, and bath, and that's all we need for the rest of our time. We're hoping you might want to live in the farmhouse, especially if you marry and have a family." Jed paused. "What do you think?"

Before he answered, Aunt Marley jumped from her seat and set a kettle for tea. "Let the news sink in a minute, while I fix tea for us."

Owen's gaze followed the beam on the ceiling. He had loved the farmhouse as a boy, then as a teen when he visited. His home offered him comfort and sat far enough away from the house for privacy. If they switched beds and a few pieces of the furniture he had purchased, he'd be comfortable. Plus, they'd kept up on repairs. He pictured the three bedrooms and the big living room and kitchen filled with family.

He glanced from his aunt to his uncle. They had aged in the last few years, but if something happened to one of them, would the other one be okay in the cabin? If not, he'd bring them to the house. Plans of marriage seemed way off. He enjoyed Lucy's company, but he wanted to get better acquainted with her. Okay, he cared for her more than a little, but he still wanted time.

Aunt Marley passed out teacups and poured tea. They each sugared their drinks and stirred in rhythm with spoons. Jed cleared his throat. "You've had a few minutes to consider our proposal, not enough time I'm sure, but what's your first impression?"

Owen sipped his tea, then placed the cup on the table. He tapped his finger on the edge of the cup. "I believe we could make it work. Whenever you're ready, tell me, and we'll switch a few things around, but if you ever change your mind or need to move in with me, I'm okay with it. You should come to the cabin again to make sure it's what you want. I'll pave

Penny Frost McGinnis, Abbott Island Book 3

a smooth stone path from here to there so you have less chance to stumble. I had planned to add a walkway." He shook hands with his uncle. "Want to tour my place now, before I leave to finish Lucy's yard?"

"We thought you got her yard done." Aunt Marley winked at Owen.

"Pretty much. I want to double check."

"Of course you do." She carried the cups to the sink. "Let's go."

~~~~~

The sun crept from behind the clouds and beamed sunshine through the window of the General Store. Regina dusted shelves and Lucy sorted a shipment of inexpensive and colorful bracelets she hoped parents and grandparents would buy as souvenirs for kids and grandchildren.

Lucy tucked her hair behind her ear. "Thanks for coming in today to get ready for next week. We always have early birds before Memorial Day."

"No problem, but I beat you here this morning. Did you have a late night last night?" Regina laughed.

Lucy finished counting the bracelets. "Actually, I had an early morning. I went to Owen's farm to check out the latest holes dug on the island."

Regina stopped dusting. "No way. More holes?"

"Yep, three. Two pretty deep ones, and one not finished. Joel and Levi found a few clues and Owen may have seen two people, but not well enough to get a description. Crazy, isn't it?" She hung the bracelets on a rack. "Why not say there's something on your land we want to search for and then ask permission?"

Regina propped her fists on her hips. "How many crooks do you know who ask permission?"

"What if they aren't crooks and just want to find what they've lost?"

"No. Something seems off to me." Regina dropped the cloth in a pile of dirty cleaning rags Lucy wanted to take home and wash.

Dust tickled Lucy's nose. She let go of a sneeze, then blew her nose.

"Bless you."

"Thanks."

"I appreciate your attitude when you try to focus on the positive, but sometimes bad is bad." She bagged the laundry and carried it to the office.

Lucy grabbed her bottle of water and followed her.

Regina tapped her chin. "I've been meaning to ask you. Would you show me the cellar? I've not been in it and wondered what it looked like."

Lucy scrunched her eyebrows into a V. "I guess. It's not much. The walls and floor are dirt and there are a few shelves, but sure, why not?" She grabbed her keys from her desk and led the way outside.

"There's a padlock on the door, and I have the only key." She worked the key, and the lock popped open. "The doors are heavy." She lugged

Home At Last

one to the side and exposed the dark entry.

"There's no light, so we have to use the flashlights on our phones." They descended into the opening. "Thankfully, there aren't many steps." She waved her light from side-to-side. "Not much here. I've used it for storage a few times, mostly plastic bins with Christmas decorations."

"This is similar to my granny's cellar. She kept canned goods and potatoes and such in hers." Regina shined her light in a corner. "What's over there?"

The light reflected on a small garden shovel. Lucy picked the tool off the floor. "I have no idea why this is here." She examined the corner. "Has somebody started digging? Unbelievable."

Regina bent over and ran her hand across the ground. "Not so much digging as poking. How odd."

"Let's get out of here and call Joel."

Before either woman climbed out, the doors closed.

"No!" Lucy's light flashed to the door. "Who is out there?" She raised her voice. "Let us out."

She and Regina pushed and hammered on the doors, but they didn't budge.

"Now what?" Lucy checked the signal on her phone. "No bars. I guess we pray and wait."

Regina bowed her head.

Lucy grabbed the shovel and pounded on the doors every few minutes.

A half an hour later, the door opened. The ladies sprinted through the opening to thank their rescuer. Andrew stood in the yard.

"Andrew, what are you doing here?" Lucy clutched her hands to her chest.

"I stopped in the store. When I didn't see you, I came out the back door and heard the pounding. The lock was laced through the hasp and staple, um... the loop but wasn't latched, so I pulled it off and opened the doors." Andrew turned his hands up in an I-don't-know gesture.

"Thank you. I was afraid we'd be stuck. Did you see anyone?" Lucy stared at the man.

Andrew pointed to the corner of the building. "I think someone ran around there when I stepped outside, but I'm not sure. Looked like a man."

"Thanks."

Andrew fidgeted with a pen he had pulled from his pocket. "When I walked through your office, it looked like someone wrecked it.."

Lucy slapped the cellar doors closed, then pushed the u-shaped shackle into the padlock. With her hands in fists, she marched to the back door of the store.

Inside the building, Lucy rushed into the office, Regina on her heels. The store owner sucked in her breath. "Whoever locked us in ransacked my office. What a mess."

She dialed the police station and Levi answered.

"Can you come to the store? Come in the back door. We've had a break-in."

Lucy wanted to fall into her overstuffed chair but knew not to touch anything. Instead, she leaned on the door post and waited.

Andrew stepped past her and surveyed the room. "Wow, somebody wanted something."

Regina wrapped an arm around Lucy's shoulders. "I'm so sorry I asked you to take me to the cellar. This wouldn't have happened if I hadn't."

"No worries. You didn't know." At least Lucy hoped her friend hadn't set her up. *Surely not.*

CHAPTER NINETEEN

Tears threatened to spill from Lucy's eyes. A man-made tornado had destroyed her organized office. File drawers hung open, papers lay scattered across her desk and floor, and her collection of baseball bobble-heads had toppled to the floor. Her favorite one, Cleveland Guardian Jose Ramirez, lay upside down on her chair. She reached to lift him but stopped herself.

Lucy rubbed her forehead. "This is too much." She frowned. "We need to check the rest of the store. The front was locked, but..."

Regina walked to the front and Lucy trudged to the back, while Andrew waited by the outside door.

"Nothing has been bothered here, Lucy."

"Here either."

They hurried to the office, where Levi entered the back door.

"Wow. What a mess. Has anything else been disturbed?" he asked.

"I don't think so. This is enough." Lucy hovered in the doorway with Regina behind her.

Levi extracted a camera from his bag and shot photos. Then he prepared to dust for fingerprints. Being part of the island police crew meant performing every job themselves. "Was the door unlocked?"

"Yes. Regina asked me to show her the cellar. I assumed we'd only be gone a few minutes, but the cellar door slammed shut, and we couldn't open it. We found a shovel and some holes poked in the ground, when we went in. I think whoever it was put the lock on after we climbed in, but didn't lock it, then they destroyed my office and left." Lucy stared out the door. "We didn't see anyone when we climbed out, except Andrew, and he opened the doors for us."

The officer jotted notes. "I'll need you all to write your statements while I finish in here. I'm going to look around outside too. Is there a reason someone would search your office?"

Lucy shrugged. "Could it have something to do with hole diggers? I found a map on my property someone dropped. It looked like a treasure map. Maybe they knew I found it."

"Okay. After I finish, I want you to clean up and tell me if anything is missing."

Lucy and Regina moved to the counter at the front of the store and filled out their statements. Andrew stayed in the office with Levi. Regina placed a hand on Lucy's shoulder. "I'm so sorry I asked you to take me to the cellar. This is my fault."

"No. It's not. I should have locked the front and back doors, but then they may have broken in here anyway. If they picked the cellar's lock to poke around with a shovel, they could have broken in to the store too. I'll straighten the mess, take inventory of the office, and open the store tomorrow. For today, we're closed." She tapped her pen on the counter. "Let's get this done. Once Levi lets me straighten the office, I can go home."

"I want to stay and help, if that's okay."

Lucy hugged Regina. "Of course. Thanks."

An hour later, Levi and Andrew left and Lucy and Regina entered the office.

Lucy rescued Jose Ramirez from the chair he'd fallen into. "At least his bat isn't broken. I got this at a game and he signed the bottom for me. I'd be sad if anything happened to this."

She arranged the bobble-heads on the shelf above her desk. "Do you want to put the file cabinet in order?"

"Yes." Regina sat on the floor and sorted papers and placed them in the proper files.

Lucy straightened her desk. "Something is missing." She studied the papers and office supplies. "I had a book about the history of the island on my desk. One of the local authors wrote it and asked if I'd sell it in the store. I had tucked the map I found inside the book. That stinks." She plopped into her desk chair. "I better tell Levi. Do you mind if I walk to the station?"

"You go. I'll finish this and wait for you."

"Thank you." She stepped outside.

At the police station, Lucy relayed the information about the missing book. "I had stuck the map inside because I had hoped the history in the book might help me figure out the purpose of the Xes." She grabbed her phone from her pocket. "I took a picture of the map when I found it. Here it is." She held her phone to Levi. He examined the photo.

"Hmm... can you send it to me?"

She texted the map to his phone. "There you go. I showed it to Joel when I found it."

"Okay, I'll talk to him, and we'll see what we find."

~~~~~

Mid-afternoon, Lucy and Regina locked the doors on the store. The May day warmed and clouds floated in the sky as if nothing had upset the morning. A bluebird flitted by and Lucy and Regina leaned on the porch rail.

Lucy adjusted her bag on her shoulder. "We've had quite the

Home At Last

morning."

"Sure have. I can't wait to go home and rest before the kiddos get home from school." She hugged Lucy. "I hope tomorrow goes better, and we can get the rest of the boxes unpacked. There are five or six, full of trinkets."

What would Lucy do without Regina, the calm in the storm? "Thank you for helping me today." A wave of guilt rose in her for the moment of distrust in the cellar.

~~~~~

Travis watched from the shadows. Blondie and her sidekick flipped the closed sign on the store. It had felt good to rip through Blondie's office. He patted the pocket that held the bonus he'd found. No cash, but this little item proved more important. The copy of the map he had dropped in the woods found its way home.

Last thing he wanted was some novice treasure hunter looking for what belonged to him.

He'd keep her in his sights and make sure she didn't interfere. Whatever it took, he'd find the gold.

~~~~~

Lucy mounted her bike and pedaled along Main Street. In front of the historical society, she glimpsed something in the shallow ditch. She parked her bike and bent to examine the object. In front of her lay the book she'd had on her desk. She lifted the tattered book and flipped through the pages. Sure enough, the book had been autographed to her, but no map or anything else fell out. Why did someone want the map? The page may have been a copy of an old map with the corner ripped off. At least they didn't take anything else. She dropped the book into her basket and turned the bike to ride to the police station.

She walked into the stone building. "Levi?"

"I'll be right out." His voice traveled from the back room.

He strode to his desk. "Hey, Lucy. Did you find anything else?"

She held the book out to him. "Sure did. This was on the ground in front of the historical society building."

"Is this the one from your desk?" He bagged it as evidence.

"Yep, but no map or anything inside." She crossed her arms over her chest. "A week or so ago, I found a piece of paper in the store. It may have been a corner torn from the original map, if there is one. The air in the store smelled funny too." She waved a hand in the air. "Maybe I'm imagining things. Thanks for all you're doing. I'm heading home."

When Lucy pulled the bike into her yard, she noticed Owen's truck. She rolled the bike to the end of the house and tiptoed around to the front. The man bent over her flower bed.

Lucy paused by the corner of the house. "Owen."

111

Penny Frost McGinnis, Abbott Island Book 3

He turned and stood. "Just finishing here. I had a few more flowers to plant and wanted to get them in before May got away from me. What do you think?"

Lucy rushed at Owen and wrapped her arms around his middle.

He pulled her to him. "I know you like flowers, but..."

A nervous chuckle sounded in Lucy's ear. She pulled away. "I'm sorry. Yes, I love the flowers, but I needed a hug. I've had a rough morning."

"Want to talk about it?"

She nodded. He dropped his gloves on the ground, then grasped her hand and led her to the beach. She held on as if he had cast her a lifeline.

They settled on a log on the sand and Lucy spilled. "Being locked in the cellar about did me in. I hate tight spaces, and when they're dark, they're worse. Thank goodness Regina was with me."

He put his arm around her and tugged her to him. "I don't like tight spaces either. When I had an MRI on my shoulder, I prayed for God to get me out as soon as possible."

Lucy leaned into him. "What happened to your shoulder?"

"Long story."

She tilted her face to his. "I'd love to listen. It would take my mind off of today's turmoil."

"Okay. I'd been a first draft pick and played with the Greenville Drive, Portland Seadogs, then the Red Sox. I had a good signing bonus and earned my dream job and pitched for the Boston Red Sox for a season. Then I tore my rotator cuff. It was a dark time for me. I came to the island to heal. Had to go to the mainland for therapy. While I recovered, my baseball career had ended, and Rebecca gave me an ultimatum. Her father had a job for me in his company, but I couldn't stomach working in an office. She called off the engagement, and I stayed here. At least the injury had a silver lining. I didn't end up with the wrong woman." He squeezed her shoulder.

"I won't hold it against you for playing on the wrong team." She elbowed him. "How is your shoulder now? You lift and move heavy stuff."

He moved his arm away from her and shrugged. "It aches at times but works okay. The constant rotation of pitching was the issue." He watched the lake.

"It's beautiful here, isn't it? Most of the time, the days are peaceful, but these days not so much." She leaned her head on his shoulder.

The comfort he gave her warmed her heart. More than a friend, but not a boyfriend. Without too much hoopla, she hoped they'd get to know each other better. So many questions rippled through her mind. Would she and Owen continue to date? Who might buy the store? Who was the

Home At Last

crazy hole digger? Could she start over and achieve her dream? When would she have time to organize the spring softball teams?

"The softball teams. I forgot about them." She rose from the log and paced in front of Owen.

He stood and moved in front of her and held her hands. "What are you talking about?"

Her mouth changed from a frown to a grin. "The softball teams. You played baseball. Can you help me?"

"I guess. What needs to be done?"

"I have a list of folks on the island who play each year. We need to contact them and tell them when we practice and the date and time of the first game. It's the Wednesday evening before Memorial Day. We let off steam before the crowds arrive. It's a blast."

"How about you give me half the list to contact? Would that help?"

"Yes." She hugged him again.

"What else can I do to get another one of your enthusiastic hugs?"

"You'll have to wait and see."

Did she just flirt with Owen? So many years had passed since she found a man worth flirting with. She had forgotten how. Her heart thumped with every hug, so he was good for her cardio. Nice bonus. He loved baseball and created a beautiful landscape around her home, plus he loved Jesus. She might swoon.

Owen took Lucy's hands again. "I'm praying this mess with the holes and maps is resolved soon. Please be careful. I'm sorry you were trapped, and it scared you. Text me the list you want me to call for softball." He touched her face and embraced her cheek with his palm. "I'm guessing you don't feel like going to Vermilion tonight. Can I take you on a picnic tomorrow instead?"

"Yes. I need to work part of the day, but I'd love to go with you." She put on what she hoped was a dazzling smile. "I'll be home a few minutes after four."

"I'll pick you up then." He dropped his hand and leaned in and kissed her cheek. They meandered to the house where he gathered his gardening tools. "See you tomorrow."

She touched her fingers to her face. *Swoony, yes.* Eyes closed, she stood on her porch and listened to his truck pull away. When she opened her eyes, Joel stepped into her yard with Gracie.

"Hey, big brother."

He carried his little one to the steps. "I heard you had a rough morning."

"I did. Levi shouldn't have told you. You're off work today." She reached for Gracie and cuddled her.

Joel crossed his arms. "You're right. You should have told me yourself."

"Let's sit on the porch." She led them to the chairs, where they each took a seat.

Joel leaned forward, arms on his knees, hands folded. "He said the map you found is missing. Seems strange. Whoever destroyed your office did it for a copy of an old map."

"I know. Weird things are happening, and no one understands why." She held Gracie and lifted her away from her, then drew her toward her. The little girl giggled.

"There aren't many people on the island now, except the locals. Andrew is still in Sadie's cabin and I've seen a few people fishing. Mostly families or couples. I'll chat with folks tomorrow and find out if anyone has seen anything."

"Sounds good to me." She balanced Gracie on her knee with one hand and patted the baby's back with the other.

"In the meantime, pay attention to your surroundings. This doesn't seem dangerous, but you never know." He took Gracie. "I need to get back to Sadie."

"Thanks for the advice and for looking into this."

"Doing my job." He grinned, then left.

Lucy relaxed in her chair and watched the waves wash over the sand. Her emotions swirled like an eddy in the water from her excitement at spending more time with Owen, fear of being targeted, confusion over the holes dug, and curiosity about the map. Someone searched for something important and didn't want anyone else to know what it was. Should she question people herself?

CHAPTER TWENTY

Saturday morning, sunbeams played hide and seek with billowing white clouds. A soft breeze kissed the new leaves on the maple trees and rang the chimes on the porch of the General Store. Lucy's hand shook when she unlocked the front door and entered. She flipped on the lights and strode the aisles front to back.

Everything in its place. Her satisfaction gave way to appreciation. She trekked to her office and found the room intact. The breath she'd been holding released. Her bobble-heads stood in salute to her. Did Owen have a bobble-head? His would be the most handsome one. A shiver ran up her spine. She shook it off and tucked her bag into her desk. From the floor, she lifted a box and made her way to the front counter.

After Lucy split the box open and peeled back the flaps, Regina opened the door and trooped inside.

"Good morning."

"Hi, boss." Regina scoped the interior of the store. "Any overnight disturbance?"

"No. Thank goodness."

Lucy's manager set a plate of homemade cookies on the counter. "I went home and baked yesterday. A great stress reliever for me."

"You were going home to rest." Lucy untangled plastic cords attached to vibrant colored whistles.

"I decided baking would help more. Chocolate chip oatmeal is my favorite. I thought, why not make enough to share? The hubby and kids were happy."

Lucy plucked one from the plate. "These smell amazing." She took a bite. "And taste delicious. Wow! Thanks for baking."

The bell on the door jingled and interrupted the cookie fest.

Andrew carried a long tube. "Ladies."

"Hello." Regina and Lucy spoke at the same time.

"How can we help you?" Regina stood between Andrew and the counter.

His eyes roamed across the merchandise. "I thought I'd see if you're both okay after yesterday, and I wanted to talk to Lucy about the store."

Regina set her hands on her hips. "We're both fine. You can't just pop in when you want and expect Lucy to have time for you." She covered her mouth with her hand, then dropped her hand to her side. "I'm sorry."

Lucy stared at her friend and employee. Yesterday must have shaken her. "Regina, it's okay. I told him to stop by when he had time, and he could talk to us. If you want, you can finish unboxing these." She pointed at the items.

Andrew followed Lucy to her office. She offered him a seat, then lowered into her desk chair. "What's in the tube?"

"I discovered a plat of Abbott Island."

She scrunched her forehead and frowned.

He perched on the edge of her flowered chair. "I wanted to show it to you to make sure it's correct."

She breathed a heavy sigh. "Okay."

He stood and spread the plat on her desk. "I found the layout of the town interesting. Here's Johnny's and there's Sadie's cabins. Your store sits here." He pointed at her property.

Lucy studied the map. "Correct." What was his point? She was aware of the location of her store.

He pointed at a spot near Owen's farm. "Do you know who lives here?"

She stood. "I do. Why?" Her hackles rose as if she were ready to defend a kingdom.

"Curious. I'm trying to get a handle on the island is all." He aimed a smile at her, which didn't quite reach his eyes.

"You can go to the town council building and talk to them. I'm not the one you need to ask. Weren't you stopping in to see the store?" She sucked in a deep breath. "By the way, if you are interested in buying my business, I need your decision by the end of the month. If not, I'll be listing it with a realtor. Have a good day." She dismissed him with a back-handed wave to the door. He may have rescued them yesterday, but today he stretched her last nerve.

"Do you mind if I go out the back and look around?"

"Yes, I mind. Leave out the front."

Andrew rolled the map and shoved it into the tube and stomped out. A moment later the bell rang, and the front door slammed. She sat in her chair and rested her head in her hands. Every day grew crazier. Her calm, peaceful island had turned upside down.

A soft knock on the door drew Lucy's attention. She raised her head to her friend. "I'm sorry if you overheard our rude conversation."

Regina sank into the chair.

Lucy pushed her chair back from the desk. "He has some nerve coming in and asking me questions about the island. I thought he was interested in buying the store, but he's simply nosy."

"Speaking of buying the store, I might know someone else who is interested."

"Who?"

Regina stood and leaned on the desk. "My husband and I were talking, and I'd love to own the store. We need to go to the bank and find out what we can do, and I'd need a price from you. That's why I wanted to take a peek at the cellar, but didn't want to get your hopes up."

Lucy rounded the desk and squeezed Regina in a hug. She stepped back and gave her a high five. "Answer to prayer."

Regina laughed. "I hope so, but we need to make sure it works financially."

"Let's storm the gates of heaven and see what happens." Lucy pumped her arm in a cheer move.

~~~~~

At four o'clock Lucy pedaled home, excited about the evening picnic with Owen. She rounded the curve to her house and saw his truck parked next to her pink Jeep. A thousand fireflies flitted in her belly.

She parked her bike and tapped on the window of his truck.

He opened the door and stepped out. "I hope I'm not too early."

Lucy fiddled with the hem of her shirt. "Not at all. Let me freshen up, and I'll be ready. Want to sit on the porch?"

"Sounds good."

Lucy hustled inside. She washed her face and brushed her hair, then switched her store t-shirt for her favorite blue top. The color complimented her hair and matched her eyes.

Outside, they climbed into the truck.

"I thought we'd go to the church camp. There aren't any campers there yet, and I have the access code. I'm landscaping for them, and they told me I could come by anytime to hike or fish." He drove the winding road to the farthest northern point on the island.

At the gate, he punched in numbers on the security keypad, then steered them to a grassy area surrounded by oak trees, near the water.

They unloaded a blanket and basket of food and settled on the sandy grass.

Lucy's appreciation for Owen grew as he placed each item on the blanket with care.

"Your plate and silverware, madam." He bowed to her.

"You're funny. Shouldn't you say plasticware?" Lucy waved her fork in the air.

Owen chuckled. "Aunt Marley cooked her usual feast. Fried chicken, potato salad, carrot sticks, and her famous melt-in-your-mouth brownies."

Lucy's mouth watered. "Sounds delicious. I don't cook much, so this is a treat."

The two of them filled their plates and ate to the sound of the waves

Penny Frost McGinnis, Abbott Island Book 3

as they swished over the sand. A great blue heron perched on a rock near the shore, dipped her head, and captured a fish.

Lucy pointed. "I guess we're all eating dinner." She dabbed her mouth with a napkin. "I'll have to eat my brownie later. I'm full."

"Me too." Owen packed the basket with the remnants of dinner and placed the brownies at the top. "I'll be right back."

He carried the basket to the truck, then he propped a radio on the edge of the bed.

Lucy stood. "What have you got there?"

"It's a battery-operated radio, CD player. CDs are out of date, but I still use this when I'm working in the barn. I thought you might enjoy some music and maybe..." red colored his cheeks. "... a dance."

"I'd love to dance with you."

He clicked on the player, and John Michael Montgomery crooned *I Swear*. Owen held his hand out to Lucy, and she wove her fingers through his. He placed his other hand on her back as she stepped toward him.

Lucy rested her head on his shoulder and let him lead. His woodsy, masculine scent filled her senses as he moved her through the grass. His solid form gave her confidence. For the first time in a long time, she didn't feel alone. What if she and Owen found the love she longed for? Could she find contentment with him? She had daydreamed about him throughout the afternoon.

The music changed to Edwin McCain's *I'll Be*, and Lucy closed her eyes and let the song pour over her. She opened them and leaned her head back. "Did you make a play list from the nineties?"

His brown eyes sparkled. "I did. I figured we heard a lot of those songs on the radio growing up."

"Thank you."

He leaned in and captured her lips with his. For a moment, time stopped. Her heart sped, and she imagined a life with Owen. When he pulled away, she read the contentment on his face.

"Want to take a walk?" Owen kept her hand in his. With his other hand, he plucked the blanket from the ground.

The two of them wound their way around the camp to the northernmost point of the island, the furthest spot from downtown. He spread the blanket near the water. They sat and watched the waves and the seagulls for a few minutes.

He held her hand. "Tell me about your day."

"It was good and weird. Regina wants to buy the store if the money works out. Andrew came in and asked questions about who owned your farm."

Owen stared at her and squinted. "What did you tell him?"

"I told him to leave and go ask the town council."

Home At Last

His arm slid around her shoulders. "Good answer. I wonder what his deal is. He asks questions and doesn't do anything while he's here."

Lucy leaned into him. "The man is rude and drives me crazy."

"Do I drive you crazy?" Owen kissed her cheek.

Lucy laughed. "In a different way. Your kiss back there, wow." She covered her mouth with her hand.

Owen pulled her hand away, then leaned in and stole another kiss. "You like those, huh?"

"Yep. I do, and I like you."

He kissed the tip of her nose. "I like your laugh and the way you get excited and give hugs. I hope we can spend more time together."

Lucy scooted around, crisscrossed her legs, and faced Owen. "Can I ask you something?"

"Sure." He held her hands.

"Are you staying on the island, like long-term?" She pursed her lips.

He pushed his hair off of his forehead. "I am. Aunt Marley and Uncle Jed want to switch houses. My plans to make the farm viable are moving forward, and I love the island." His eyes held hers. "What are you going to do if you sell the store?"

She'd not shared her true dream with anyone yet. Her trust in Owen grew every day. He'd understand a dream, since he had experienced his own with baseball. "I've wanted to try event planning since I was a teenager. I created a whole notebook full of ideas, and I'd love to help people celebrate life on a low budget. There's so much sadness and darkness in the world, I'd like to help bring the good to light." She paused and searched his face for approval. "What do you think?"

He captured her cheek in his palm. "Your idea is genius." He rubbed her cheekbone. "Do you have a place to hold events?"

She inhaled, then released a breath. "Not really. I'd have to rent or buy something, which might keep me from hosting events on the island." The wind off of the water tousled her curls. "People would come to the island to get married and celebrate anniversaries and birthdays. They do now, but most of the events are at the hotel or on the beach somewhere. If I found the right space, I hope to give them an island experience without the enormous cost."

He grabbed her hands. "We have a barn we don't use much. The building has a concrete floor, heat, and water. If we cleaned it and refreshed the interior, it might be what you're looking for. If Uncle Jed and Aunt Marley agree, I'm sure we can work out arrangements."

Lucy placed a hand on each side of his face and pulled him to her. Her lips met his to seal the deal. She leaned back. "I'm so excited."

"Obviously." He chuckled. "Let's see what God has to say about it. I've learned the hard way to seek His guidance first."

They clasped hands and Owen bent God's ear and asked for clarity for both of them. After his amen, he stood and pulled Lucy into a hug. "I'm anxious to see where your dream goes."

She rested her hand on his chest. "Me too."

CHAPTER TWENTY-ONE

At the cabin window, Travis watched a sailboat cross the lake on the sparkling water until the potent scent of his brew drew him to the coffeemaker. He poured a cup straight black and took a sip. His tongue and throat burned, but he didn't care.

Sunday morning, all the goodie-goodies trotted to church. Hadn't he been a churchgoer at one time? He shoved the memory away and contemplated another chance to search the island.

The copy of the map from Blondie's office lay on the table. When he had ransacked her office in search of cash and found none, he'd stumbled across the paper. Not sure she had realized what she'd found, he had snagged it and dumped the book. With no luck finding the gold on the farm, in Blondie's yard, or on the beach, he planned to find a time to dig around in the cellar behind the General Store. His gut told him to search there next. Maybe the ladies left the small shovel he'd dropped in the cellar when he'd poked around. Good thing he'd hurried away before they came outside. How convenient for him to close them in, and then search Blondie's office.

He couldn't rely on his goons. They had ruined the chance of discovery at the farm, so he'd break into the cellar himself, but when?

Travis punched in one of the goon's numbers on his phone. "You guys are done. I don't need you anymore."

"Boss, we never found the box you wanted. We want to keep looking." The voice whined through the speaker.

"I said you're done. I'll meet you by the kayak hut in a half an hour and pay you." With a bad check from his fake account. "You get off the island today." He pushed the end button.

At the hut, he stood along the wall facing the beach and waited. The water glimmered like diamonds. His mom told him when the water shone, God smiled. Did He? Not on him. God deserted him long ago, when his dad left them poor and alone. He swatted and smacked the idea of a loving God away.

Twenty-minutes later, the two he had hired slunk around the corner.

"It's about time you got here." His eyes bored into them. He jammed an envelope into each of their hands. "Get off the island now, while all the good folks are in church. Don't draw attention to yourselves." He thrust his hands out as if to push them away.

Penny Frost McGinnis, Abbott Island Book 3

"We're out of here." The two ran off.

Travis hiked along the road to the middle of town and flipped his empty money clip in his hand. No one roamed the streets. The shops were closed on Sunday morning, and a quiet lull covered the town. The odor of dead fish hung in the air, a typical island smell.

He sneaked behind the General Store and strolled straight to the cellar doors. He'd picked the padlock the other day, when the ladies interrupted his search. Before the island flooded with tourists, he'd bring his lock pick kit back and sneak in and dig. He rubbed his hands together in anticipation.

Before he stepped away from the store, a memory of his mom seeped into his heart. "You be good and love Jesus. Then you'll have less worries." She'd whispered those words to him before she had passed away. Where was God when the only person who had loved him died?

He closed his eyes. "Mom, forgive me. This is our gold, and I think you'd want me to have the money. Wish I'd found it while you were still alive." He lifted his chin and sauntered along the street while he concocted a plan to dig in the cellar, certain the gold rested there.

~~~~~

The church doors opened, and Lucy and Owen stepped out. A soft breeze whispered through the trees and robins twittered.

Joel carried Gracie while Sadie, Marigold, and Johnny and his daughter, Alexa, followed. Johnny kissed Mari on her cheek. "I'm heading to the restaurant. We're open for lunch today. Anyone interested?"

Lucy turned to Owen. "Want to go? You can ask Aunt Marley and Uncle Jed. Maybe they'll join us."

Half an hour later, all of them gathered in the courtyard of Johnny's Place. With all the tables pushed together, they sat to eat.

Lucy pushed her hair behind her shoulders. "The day is amazing. Perfect temperature and breezy." She sighed.

Sadie elbowed Joel and Marigold. Aunt Marley grinned from ear-to-ear, while baby Gracie cooed. Every person at the table stared at Lucy and Owen.

Lucy glanced at her sister-in-law. "What?"

Sadie covered her mouth to stop the giggle. "Oh, nothing. Just sounds like someone is super happy today."

"Yeah, Sis. Anything you want to share?" Joel wiggled his eyebrows.

Owen leaned into her ear. "Want to tell them?"

Lucy stood and held her arms out. "I have a boyfriend." Her smile stretched from ear to ear.

Owen laughed and stood beside her. "And I'm him."

He side-hugged her, then the couple settled in their chairs.

Aunt Marley clapped her hands together. "I knew it."

Home At Last

Uncle Jed beamed. "I, for one, am happy for you. Let us know when the wedding will be."

Lucy and Owen shook their heads.

"Uncle Jed. Let's see where this goes first." He patted her hand.

A waiter delivered plates of hummus and pita bread and all the drink orders. Uncle Jed prayed for lunch, and they all dug in.

"I'd never heard of hummus until we ate at Johnny's. It's pretty tasty." Aunt Marley dipped pita into the smashed chickpeas flavored with garlic.

Lucy gazed from person to person. Joy filled her, and for today, peace flooded her soul. Good friends, a boyfriend, someone to buy her business, dreams of the future. What could go wrong? She hoped nothing.

Sadie held Gracie in the seat next to Lucy, and the little one patted Lucy's arm.

"Sweet girl, come to me." She took the baby from her mother's arms, then bounced her with a gentle hand and whispered love into her ear. "She's already grown so much. Four months old and she already knows her favorite person."

Joel cleared his throat. "Yep, she does." He pointed to himself. "By the way, the piece of rock we tested from the farm was fool's gold. Sorry, Marley and Jed, no gold in your barnyard. When Levi went over the area with a metal detector, I'm sure he told you he didn't find anything significant."

"He did. I went out with him and poked around, too. I didn't figure he'd find anything valuable. Just farm dregs." Jed leaned back in his chair.

The waiter served food to everyone. "Can I get you anything else?"

Lucy piped in. "We're good. Thanks."

The group enjoyed the rest of the meal in the quiet of the day.

After they left Johnny's Place, Lucy snagged Owen's hand. Warmth traveled from her hand to her heart. This man checked all the boxes. Kind, handsome, loved Jesus, worked hard, and so much more. She'd run her business for so many years, with no time to date, and now this sweet guy wanted to spend time with her. Plus, he held the possibility for her to follow her dream.

"Do you mind if we check on the store before we head to the farm?" They planned to survey the barn for what work needed to be done to make it into a celebration space.

"Sure. Any reason?" He wrapped an arm around her waist.

She snuggled against him as they walked across the street. "Just want to check in, make sure no one has bothered anything. I kind of made Andrew mad the other day. He was so pushy about buying the store. I told him to leave. I don't trust him anymore."

Inside the building, the two walked the aisles and checked the office.

Penny Frost McGinnis, Abbott Island Book 3

Lucy stepped out through the back door. "Owen, I'm out here." He joined her and they walked the perimeter of the small backyard. Something shiny lay on the ground. Lucy lifted the metal object and turned it in her hands. "I found a money clip over here." She held the piece of metal for him to see.

He took it and fingered the clip. "We messed up. We shouldn't have picked it up."

Lucy smacked her head with her hand. "I wasn't thinking."

"We should still take it to Levi." They locked the doors and walked to the police station. A few dark clouds hovered, and the morning breeze had turned into wind as cooler air covered the island. She shivered and rubbed her arms.

Inside, they found Levi hunched over his computer.

"Levi?" Lucy strode to his desk.

The officer raised his head and faced her. "Hey, what's up?"

"We were out by the cellar and found a money clip on the ground beside the cellar doors, but we both touched it. I didn't think to leave it lay and call."

Owen handed Levi the clip. "I doubt you can get anything off of it."

"Probably not." Levi examined it. "We haven't found any prints on anything we've tested. The ones I took in your office didn't produce anything. I'm not sure how we're going to solve this puzzle." He placed the money clip on his desk. "I'll bag it and see if anyone asks if one has been found. Thanks for bringing it in. Sorry I don't have more for you."

"We understand." Lucy crossed her arms. "How's Charlotte?"

A smile lit Levi's face. "She's great. We're making plans for our wedding in July. This may be my last case on the island, other than the smaller ones we experience during tourist season. Unfortunately, we still have a few shoplifters and fire bugs in the summer."

"I'm excited for you two, but we'll miss you." Lucy followed Owen to the door. "Thanks for all your help. We'll talk soon." He pushed the door open, and they stepped outside.

Lucy and Owen climbed into his truck and drove to the farm. No rain fell, but the clouds appeared to threaten the day. They matched the niggle of anxiety Lucy experienced from the found money clip. Instead of letting the day go south, she straightened her shoulders and prayed for joy to bubble in her. As soon as she laid eyes on the barn, her hope buoyed.

"You've seen the building when you came for dinner. I call it a barn, but it's a pole building. Uncle Jed had it built about fifteen years ago." Owen unlatched the door on the building and invited her to step inside. "We don't use it for much anymore. Uncle Jed used to keep a tractor and a small combine in here. He's moved them to the other barn since it's closer to the house and is about twice the size of this one. He doesn't grow

124

Home At Last

as much hay and produce as he used to, since he down-sized. The animals share the bigger barn, and everything I've purchased for landscaping and growing trees is in the big shed out back."

Lucy ambled around. "Is the barn insulated?"

"Sure is. Uncle Jed hung insulation when he added drywall for my cousin's wedding. Aunt Marley insisted Melody use the barn because she wanted to marry on the island. They had quite the celebration." He motioned to the floor. "This flooring is great, too. It's the kind you pour in a garage with the speckles. I helped apply it. I thought we'd never finish, but it was worth our time, because my cousin loved it."

"This is exactly what I need. Can we work out a price for rental? I'll clean it and refresh the paint. I want to find seating options and whatever else I'll need." She stopped and froze on the spot, then spun to face Owen. "I'm doing it again. Getting excited before I should. One thing at a time, right? Sell the store, then pursue a new business. Please, stop my babbling any time."

Owen's eyes twinkled, and he chuckled. "You're cute when you get excited, but you're right. One thing at a time." He opened the side door. "Let's tour the outside."

Green grass surrounded the building, and a flowerbed complimented the front. Peonies, foxglove, and lavender brightened the blue exterior.

"The light blue color is perfect, and we could plant more flowers. Are those Marley's?"

"Yes. She loves her flowers. I'm sure she'd help you." He wrapped his hand around hers and led her to the farmhouse. "Let's talk to my aunt and uncle and make sure they're good with all this. Did I tell you I'm swapping homes with them? They want me to take the farmhouse, and they'll live in the cabin. They said they don't have the energy to keep the house clean and repaired. I thought if you had a party of people who needed to rent a place to stay, I could sleep in the bunk in the barn and rent them the house. What do you think?"

"You'd let folks rent your home?"

"Sure. Why not?"

Lucy stopped Owen, took both her hands and placed one on each side of his face, then kissed his lips. "You're amazing. We'll talk about the possibilities once things start rolling. Thank you."

Inside, Owen and Lucy laid out their plans to Aunt Marley and Uncle Jed.

Jed nodded. "What a wonderful adventure for the two of you. Whatever it takes to keep this place going, I'm all for it."

Aunt Marley chimed in. "Me too. I hope I can help. You know I love to cook."

Lucy hugged each of them. "You two are wonderful. We'll see how this plays out. I know God is going to do something big with all of this."

After sharing cups of tea and cookies with Aunt Marly and Uncle Jed, Owen drove Lucy home. The clouds darkened and daylight dimmed. A few brave neighbors, on Lucy's road, grilled before the rain fell. The smell of burgers over a fire made Lucy's stomach grumble.

"Hungry?"

"I don't know how after our big lunch." She patted her stomach. "How is the softball planning coming?"

He pulled the truck into the parking spot by Lucy's home. "Great. Everyone is ready to practice this coming Wednesday evening. We can practice together, then let them choose teams afterwards. How have you split the teams in the past?"

"There's a good mix of ages who turn out, and we try to make the teams even by age, but however you all want to do it is fine by me." She looked forward to the first game every year. The teams played off and on all summer for fun and invited tourists to join them sometimes. She scooted over on the seat, and Owen placed an arm around her shoulder. "Thanks for all your help. You're an amazing man."

"Do you compliment all the guys?"

"Nope." *Only the one I'm falling for.* Was she letting herself hurtle toward love too fast? Unless she put on the brakes, she'd confess her love for him sooner than she wanted to. *Chill, Lucy. You have time.*

Home At Last

CHAPTER TWENTY-TWO

Rain spattered the windows and watered the May flowers. The blueberry muffin Travis warmed in the microwave fragranced the cabin. He poured coffee from the pot, black and rich. At the desk, he laid out Merrilee's letters and journal and perused them again.

Monday morning rain left him to sit in his room and stew. He opened a notebook he carried with him and jotted what he had learned. No bells rang clear, but the idea of the treasure being buried in the cellar made sense. The store had been a home at one time, most likely a summer home. The cellar provided additional protection. From the letters, his aunt seemed smart and sensible. When he studied the history of Abbott Island, the signs pointed to the General Store.

He closed his notebook. The rain had slowed, so he donned his raincoat and carried an umbrella. Without a car, he stayed on the pavement and hiked into town.

He passed Division Street and cut into the narrow, gravel alley behind the General Store. A shed sat in the corner of the yard across the alley. He stood beside the building and studied the back of the business. After a few minutes, he slipped around the building. An easy lock to pick and a window that faced the General Store. *Perfect.*

~~~~~

The infuser in the General Store scented the air with lavender. From the window, Lucy watched Andrew enter Johnny's Place.

Regina joined Lucy by the rain-spattered window. "What's he doing?"

"Eating, I assume. The more I'm around him the less I trust him." They turned and moved to the counter.

Regina straightened stickers on a spinning display. "I don't trust him at all. He makes me feel like gum on the bottom of his shoe."

"Yuck."

"Exactly." Regina picked up a duster and ran it over the top shelves. "Gio and I have an appointment at the bank in Sandusky tomorrow morning. I'll be back by noon."

Lucy swept the floor with a broom. "You do?" Her pulse sped. She prayed the banker saw potential in her dear friend and whatever collateral they had saved was enough for the loan. Of course, the building and business held value. The organizational skills and ingenuity Regina brought to the store proved her as a talented, dedicated worker with the gift of management. If she sold to Regina and Gio, the store would thrive, and she'd be free to pursue the event planning and venue.

Regina turned the *open* sign over on the door. "I hope I bring good news to you tomorrow. The store will keep me busy, but I can bring the kids with me in the summer and put them to work. They'll enjoy it. At least I hope so."

"I loved working here as a teen. Met some interesting people. Sadie and I worked together and have been friends ever since." Lucy carried sweatshirts to the back and stacked them on a shelf. "I'm going to work in the office for a while. Let me know if you need me."

"Will do."

At her desk, Lucy sorted papers. The hum of the shredder satisfied her need to discard old documents. The book on the history of the island lay at the bottom of the stack. She lifted it and thumbed through the pages. Dirt, from its venture outside, flaked off. She flipped to the index and searched for the word gold. Sure enough, a page number directed her to a section in the book about the woman who had traveled to search for nuggets during the Klondike Gold Rush. A photo of her dressed in furs and mukluks showed a glimpse of her face. Her eyes seemed familiar. Lucy never knew the woman or the family, but she recognized something about her. Determination glared at her from the photo. No doubt a trip to Alaska back then took a determined spirit.

Lucy browsed the story about her. *Merrilee Lester traveled with her brother and returned home alone. Some claim she buried a box of gold on Abbott Island near the summer home her family used for years. Where was the summer home? I wish I knew.* The author sounded convinced Merrilee had stashed a treasure on the island. Possible, of course, but wouldn't someone from her family have searched for it by now?

The General Store started as a house in the 1800s, but so did a lot of other buildings. She flipped to a map in the back of the book and studied the island. The author had included a modern map and one from the nineteenth century. *A map.* Lucy opened her phone and scrolled to the one she'd found and photographed. An X marked an area near where her store stood today. What if the treasure was buried on her property?

She hurried to Regina. "I'm going to talk to Joel. I'll be back soon." She darted out the door.

At the police station, Lucy shoved the door open and strode to Joel's desk. "Do you have a minute?"

He deposited his pencil on the desk and leaned on the back of his chair. "Have a seat."

She stood and paced.

"Or not. What's going on?"

Lucy settled her phone in front of him on his desk, along with the book. "Look at this."

"What are you showing me? I've already seen the map you found."

She pulled a chair beside him and sat. "I read through this new history written by one of our locals, and she mentions the Klondike Gold and how it might be buried on island property. The store used to be a summer home and one of the Xes on the map is beside my store. What if gold is buried on my property? Is it mine if I find it? Is that what the hole digger is searching for and why they broke into my office?"

"Slow down." Joel lifted her phone and studied the map, then took the book and read the passage. "The lady in this photo looks kind of familiar."

Lucy smacked his arm. "I thought so, too."

Joel woke the screen on his computer. "I'm going to bring up property laws in Ohio. Give me a minute." He typed and searched the page he called up. "The property owner holds the rights to something buried on the property, then sold with the property. If you find the gold, it would belong to you. You might want to hold off on selling until you investigate. I'm not saying the Klondike Gold rumor is true, or it's on your property, but if it is and you want to spend the time and money to tear up your yard, go for it."

"I'm not sure, and I don't want to destroy the backyard." She stood and paced across the room.

Joel joined her and stopped her with a hand on each shoulder. "Think it over and pray about it."

"Pray. Why can't I remember to talk to God before I jump?"

"We all forget sometimes. By the way, I ran into Andrew at the cabin this morning. I told him not to bother you or Regina anymore."

The man gave her the willies.

Joel touched his sister's arm. "He said he had no intention of bothering you."

"Good. Thanks for telling him to back off." She moved to the door. "I better get to the store. See you later."

Lucy walked into the store. Several people milled around the aisles. She sidled alongside Regina. "What's going on? We have a lot of customers this afternoon."

"Nate said they're shopping for shirts to wear for the softball tournament." She nodded toward the newest member of the police force. "I pointed them to the sale shirts. The ones you wanted to move before Memorial Day. I'm hoping there are enough and in the right sizes."

Lucy hugged her. "You're brilliant. Thank you. I wonder how they already know what teams they're on." She made her way to the customers. "Can I help you find anything?"

Penny Frost McGinnis, Abbott Island Book 3

The young officer's dimple showed when he smiled. "We all got calls from Owen, and he told us we're all on your team. I thought we'd get a head start and pick out shirts, if it's okay with you. We'll get them for the people who couldn't come. You have plenty of this one." He held up a shirt with a vintage vibe. "We thought we'd call ourselves the Souvenirs."

"Perfect. We sold a ton of those last year. I ordered more in August and had those left. Good choice. Are there enough in the right sizes? I'll give you an even better team discount." She carried an armful to the front of the store.

Regina scanned the tags. "What's my team going to wear?"

Lucy bagged the shirts. "I'm not sure. Owen will have to figure it out." Her laugh filled the store. At least Owen called all the players. Another plus for the man who had captured her heart. Except he forgot to fill her in. *Oh well, no one's perfect.*

Her teammates left the store, and Lucy sat on the chair behind the counter. "Regina, sit with me a minute."

"Sure." She lowered into the other seat. "You sound serious."

Lucy pointed to the book she'd tossed down after she returned to the store. "I was scanning the history book and found a chapter on the Klondike Goldrush. According to the author, Merrilee Lester buried gold in a box on a property here on the island, and the map I found has an X near this store."

"O-okay. What are you getting at?" She reached for the book and found the chapter. "What's that mean?"

Lucy ran a hand over her face. "It means if the gold is on this property, it rightfully belongs to me. If I sell the property to you, we need something in writing where we'd split it if we ever found it. I don't want to dig and destroy the store, but I'd like to check out a couple of places."

Regina's eyes rounded and her mouth fell open. "Wow. You'd split it with us?"

"Of course. Why wouldn't I?" Lucy took her friend's hand. "Let's not say anything to anyone until we figure out what to do. You can mention it to Gio, but please swear him to secrecy. I'm not much on keeping secrets, but for now, it seems best."

"I agree. We don't need a bunch of people snooping around." She squeezed Lucy's hand. "This could be quite the adventure."

"Sure could."

The bell on the door rang, and a new customer entered the store.

"How can we help you?" Regina called out.

Lucy hustled to the office and bowed her head. "God, I need Your wisdom."

CHAPTER TWENTY-THREE

On Thursday evening after work, the temperature lingered around seventy degrees. A white egret stood on the beach beside Lucy's tiny home. Her Adirondack chair welcomed her as she leafed through the scrapbook she'd created in high school. From old magazines, she'd cut and collaged ideas for weddings, birthday parties, and teen get-togethers. The styles had aged, but the ideas stood the test of time. She sucked in a breath when she turned to the collage she had made for her future wedding. She chuckled to herself about the style of dress she had glued on the paper.

Her ideas for a wedding had transitioned through the years. If she decided what to wear today, she'd choose less fluff and more simplicity. Her girlie self still loved the Cinderella style, but her adult self found the style too confining. She'd consider a knee-length dress with an A-line skirt covered in lace. Her mind wandered to herself walking down the aisle. She startled herself when the image of Owen, as the handsome groom, materialized. She slammed the book closed.

At the same time, a truck door closed and the sound of footsteps drew her attention to the man who walked into the yard—Owen.

Her cheeks warmed at the thought of her imagined wedding. She bit her lip to settle herself before she spilled about her vision of him at the altar. *Good grief. Get it together.*

"Hey, beautiful." He leaned over and kissed her on the cheek, then lowered himself into the other chair. "How was your day?"

Her heart tapped a fast beat. "Good. Nothing much happened. Regina and Gio went to the bank yesterday to see about getting a loan to buy the store. She seems confident, but wary. She doesn't want to get her hopes up."

"I don't blame her. It's best to wait." He stared at the water, then turned to Lucy. "By the way, thanks for telling me about your conversation with Joel. Have you decided to dig around the store to search for gold?"

She shook her head. "I'm not sure. What do you think?"

He drummed his fingers on top of the scrapbook she had placed on the table. "If you have one or two places you feel are worth your time and energy to dig, I'll help you, but I'd limit your efforts. You may be chasing a ghost."

She folded her hands and rested her chin on her fingers. "Sounds good. I'll think about where I want to dig. I guess I sound ridiculous, but I can't stop wondering about the possibility."

He reached for her hand and held it. "You have to satisfy your curiosity." Her book grabbed his attention. He lifted it from the table. "What's this?"

Lucy covered her face with her hand. "My dream scrapbook."

"Mind if I take a peek?" He waited for her to answer.

"Go ahead. It's a little embarrassing, but again, it's me." She leaned toward him.

Owen opened the book with reverence. He turned page after page and paused from time to time. "This is great. You spent a lot of hours putting this together, didn't you?"

"I did. While you were on a baseball field, I sat in my bedroom and cut out pictures." She took the book from him.

"Thanks for letting me into your world." His gaze held hers.

"You're welcome." She cleared her throat, unsure what to say next. So she blurted, "My team bought shirts for the game. What's your team doing?" Why was she so awkward? One minute her confidence rose, the next minute she nose-dived.

Owen let out the loudest laugh she had heard from him. "My team is wearing whatever they come up with. When I talked to Nathan, he decided to get matching shirts. He wants to look good for the ladies on the team. You have a couple of women his age who signed up. They live in Sandusky, and he recruited them."

"Seriously? He has been on the island for a few months. He must be lonely."

Owen stood and stepped in front of Lucy. He took her hands and lifted her from the chair. "So was I until you came along." He hugged her and in the next moment kissed her.

"You, sir, are smooth." She hugged his neck.

"Only because of you." He took her hand and led her to the beach where they watched the egret catch his dinner.

He wrapped an arm around her waist. "I'm glad I've gotten to know you, Lucy, and I hope you're happy too."

More than happy. Through Owen's encouragement, she'd not only drawn closer to him, she'd drawn closer to God. Prayers came easier and the joy Jesus promised flowed through her. Contentment like she'd not experienced before encouraged her. Her flightiness calmed—a little.

"I'm thankful we took a chance and got to know each other. You're kind and caring. I love the way you help your aunt and uncle and want to keep the farm viable." She hugged him. "I appreciate your willingness to help me if I decide to dig. What's one more hole on the island?"

Owen kissed the top of her head. "You make me laugh. Something I haven't done much of in quite a while."

The two of them sauntered along the water's edge. The fragrance of honeysuckle tickled Lucy's nose. She fingered a bloom. "This plant smells heavenly."

He turned her to him and wrapped his arms around her. "So do you."

Lucy prayed this wasn't a dream. She sought God's ear to guide her in her relationship with Owen. She didn't want to mess it up.

~~~~~

Darkness shrouded the woods, even as the moon shone. The shadows hid Travis among the trees. The two lovie-dovies had no idea he watched them from the woods behind Lucy's house. Their voices carried across the inky night. She mentioned digging around the store for the gold. The town's rumor mill flew with the story of his aunt's antics. Why couldn't the old-timers be quiet? The old man and woman on the farm must have told her. They'd be old enough to remember the stories their grandparents told. The gold belonged to him, because he was Merrilee's heir.

"Ugh." He stumbled over a dead log. His foot caught, and he hit the ground. The log rolled over his ankle. He twisted, but his foot wouldn't budge. Harsh words escaped his lips, then he fell back and lay on the damp, cool ground. Now what? He searched for something he might use to pry the log off, but no sturdy branches had fallen on the ground near him.

God, I'm not a praying man, but could You loosen my foot? A twinge of guilt shot through him. His momma taught him to pray as a child, and as an adult he had ignored her pleas to believe in Jesus. *What about now? You still could.* His momma's voice sounded in his ears.

~~~~~

Stars sprinkled across the sky as night enveloped the beach. Branches snapped, and a grunt echoed through the trees.

Owen stepped in front of Lucy and stared into the woods. "Did you hear a noise?"

Lucy peeked around him. "It sounded like something hit the ground."

"Stay behind me, please. I want to see if anyone is hurt or if it's an animal." He treaded through the yard to the edge of the woods. "I hear cursing and praying. Somebody's hurt." He shoved brush out of the way and searched the area. Then he stopped and listened for sounds of the person.

Lucy followed close behind. "Do you see anyone?"

Before Owen and Lucy discovered the person, a shadowy figure stumbled away from them and disappeared into the depths of the forest.

133

Penny Frost McGinnis, Abbott Island Book 3

"Whoever he was, he must be okay." Owen placed a hand on Lucy's back and led her to her house.

On the porch, Lucy collected her scrapbook from the table then opened her door. "Want to come in?" Owen followed her. "I'll make tea."

Her hands shook when she poured the heated water into mugs. "The thought of a person in the woods behind my house freaks me out. I've never felt afraid on the island, not even as a child. I hope we figure out why the holes and creepiness are happening." She rubbed her arms with her hands, then sat beside Owen on the couch.

He hugged her to him. "I'm sure Joel and Levi will find the person behind this. Don't give up."

"I won't." She sipped her tea. "You said 'he' when you referred to whoever ran from the woods."

"Yeah. The person was tall and moved like a guy. He limped too, but I couldn't see his features."

She stood and walked to Finn's aquarium, then sprinkled food in the water. "A man in the woods makes me wish I owned a dog instead of a fish. Finn's not a great defender, but I love him." The fish rose to the top to nibble his treat.

"He may not protect you, but I will. Do you want me to sleep on the couch tonight?" His eyes expressed a pure motive.

Lucy shook her head. "No. I'll lock the doors."

After Owen left, Lucy dressed for bed then watched out her bedroom window, which faced the woods. Nothing moved.

~~~~~

The cabin stood in front of him. A few more painful steps and he'd be inside. He pushed the door open and fell on his bed. His ankle throbbed worse than a toothache. Grateful he had maneuvered the log off his foot with his other leg, he whispered a prayer of thanks. In slow motion, he removed his tennis shoe and rolled the cotton sock off his foot. The ankle showed a bruise and swelling. He hobbled to the small refrigerator-freezer and gathered ice into a plastic bag. On his way back to the bed, he swallowed a pain reliever and downed a glass of water.

If Blondie and Hero-guy had found him in the woods, they would have discovered his secret. No way.

He fell onto the bed fully clothed, wrapped the ice bag around his ankle, and sank into his pillow. Aunt Merrilee had picked a great place to hide her loot, but the search might kill him.

~~~~~

The town buzzed on Friday morning. One more week until Memorial Day weekend when the tourists would flood the town. Several people gathered in front of Johnny's Place. Joel waved Lucy over.

She yawned on her way across the street. The smell of bacon drifted

Home At Last

to her.

"Johnny is serving breakfast today for all the locals. We're celebrating the last week before all the people who support the island show up." Joel grinned.

"Brother, you're silly, but it sounds good. Is everyone waiting to get in?" Lucy glanced at the crowd.

Joel fingered the rim of the police cap he held in his hands. "Yeah. I'm here for crowd control and pancakes."

"Before you eat, can I talk to you?" She wrapped her hand around his arm and pulled him away from the hungry crowd. "Last night, Owen and I heard someone in the woods behind my house. I realize the woods are public property, but it sounded like they fell, then took off. I may be overreacting, but it made me nervous."

"If you want me to, I can go over and look around, but I doubt I'll find anything." A frown crept onto his face. "I'll keep a watch for anyone who might be limping."

"Sounds good. Enjoy your pancakes. Love you, brother." Lucy dashed across the street. On the sidewalk, she crashed into Andrew. His hands reached for her arms, and he caught her before she fell.

"In a hurry?" He took a step back.

She smoothed her General Store t-shirt. "I guess I was. It's time to open the store. Are you going to Johnny's for breakfast? He's serving this morning to celebrate our last week before Memorial Day."

"Why's he doing that?"

"After Memorial Day, tourists swarm the island for the summer." She raised her hand in front of her. "Trust me, I'm not complaining. They keep the island afloat." She laughed at her pun. "We're thankful for the people who come and support our businesses."

"Makes sense. Too bad someone doesn't want me to buy their store." He sneered at her.

Lucy exhaled. "You have a great day."

He turned and walked away and favored his right leg. Lucy noticed a slight limp, or did she imagine it? Could Andrew have been the person in the woods?

CHAPTER TWENTY-FOUR

On the way to softball practice Saturday morning, Lucy's bike followed the curve of the road. Her backpack full of equipment swung to the left when she turned right. The bicycle tires wobbled. Lucy's legs peddled fast, and she righted herself before she toppled to the ground.

Out of breath and shaken, she rolled onto the ball field. Both feet on the ground and her bike's kickstand down, she pressed her palms on her knees and breathed. Footsteps caught her attention, and she stood.

Owen jogged to her. "You okay?"

She placed a hand on his shoulder. "Yes. I almost crashed my bike. This backpack is too full." She slung the pack off. "Guess I should have driven."

He lifted her pack from the ground and took her elbow. "I'll get you to the bench."

She twisted her lips. "So the competitor is my help."

Owen leaned away and donned a serious expression. "At least until the game starts." He let out a laugh. "This should be fun."

Once everyone settled in the dugouts, Lucy checked her list of players. She tapped her pencil on her clipboard. "I have everyone."

He ran his finger down the list. "Me too." Before he finished, Andrew walked on the field sans a limp and with a baseball glove.

"Hey, guys. Do you have room for one more?" He offered a weak smile. "Joel told me about the softball teams." He nodded to Joel and Sadie.

Lucy and Owen glanced at each other, then Lucy spoke. "I am one short. You can join us." Unsure about Andrew, she hoped his pushiness stayed off the field.

He bowed to Lucy. "Thank you."

Before the game started, Owen addressed both teams. "Today is our only practice before Wednesday, and we're not keeping score. The main objective is to have fun and get some exercise. My team take the field."

When all the players stood in place, Owen stepped on the pitcher's mound and faced Lucy at bat. "So you're the lead-off hitter?"

"Yes, sir. I am. Show me what you've got." She lifted the bat from her shoulder, took her stance and swung at the first pitch.

"Strike one." Lucy's parents visited the island today, and Dad called the pitches while Mom held Gracie.

She nipped the second pitch for a foul.

Owen tossed the ball for the third pitch and Lucy socked it over the shortstop's head. She bolted to first and jumped on the base, then wiggled her fingers over her head in a cheer.

In the third inning, Andrew slammed a grand slam. Not to be outdone, Owen returned with his own.

By noon, everyone needed a break.

"After sitting all winter, I'm out of shape." Lucy swiped her hair out of her face and readjusted her ponytail.

Owen patted her back. "Come work on the farm with me. You'll get plenty of exercise."

Lucy waved him off. "Yeah, yeah."

As the players packed their equipment, Andrew approached Lucy and Owen. "Thanks for letting me play. I haven't done this in a long time. Not knowing too many people on the island, it was nice to be a part of the game."

Lucy's conscience poked her. She'd thought bad things about Andrew. If she lived alone on an island full of year-rounders who depended on each other, she'd struggle too. Even though Andrew didn't live here, he'd been here long enough to get to know some folks. Had she misjudged him, or had he realized if he treated people with gratitude and kindness, he'd find more friends? Either way, she needed to check her attitude.

She stuffed her glove into her backpack, then faced him. "You did great out there. You must have played before."

"I played baseball in high school and some pick-up games wherever I could." A flush brushed his cheeks.

She loaded the pack on her back. "Be here Wednesday evening at 5:30, and we'll play an actual game. It'll be fun. We eat pizza and have chips and cookies. Bring what you want to drink, but no alcohol, please."

"Sounds good. I'll be here." He paused and stared at the ground. "Lucy, I'm sorry for pressuring you about the store. I don't blame you if you sell it to someone else."

"Thanks. I have a potential buyer, but maybe you'll find something else better suited for you."

Owen offered his hand to Andrew. "Great game. See you Wednesday."

Andrew shook it, then he turned and walked off the field.

Owen carried his equipment to the truck. "Want me to load your bike and backpack in the truck? We could grab pizza, then I'll take you wherever you want to go."

She unloaded her pack and climbed into the truck. "Sure. After we eat, I want to go by the store and check on Regina. She wanted to try a few

Home At Last

days without me before we get too busy, to see how it is to work full time. I missed her on the ball field, but understand what she's doing."

After lunch, Owen and Lucy entered the front door of the store and pretended to be customers. They browsed the shelves and studied the merchandise.

A look of amusement masked Regina's face as she moved from behind the counter. "How can I help you today?"

Lucy grabbed a stuffed bluebird from the shelf. "Tell me. Do you have any red bluebirds for sale?"

Regina pushed her lips together. "No Ma'am. Bluebirds come in blue." She burst with laughter. "Lucy, you're terrible."

Both of them bent at the waist and guffawed. When Regina caught her breath, she placed a hand on the counter. "Was this a test? To see how I might answer an interesting customer?" She used air quotes around interesting. "Or are you being funny at my expense?"

Lucy shook her head. "I was being funny, but not at your expense. Sorry." She shrugged. "We get some peculiar customers in here."

"I've experienced a few." She turned to Owen. "Anything I can help you with?"

Owen chuckled. "Not after that performance."

Lucy rested her hand on his shoulder. "He's nicer than I am, but seriously, how has the day gone?"

"We've had several customers this morning, which surprised me with the softball practice. A few softball players stopped in right after your game, and several of the older folks shopped this morning. Most of them bought cleaners, and a few picked out ornaments. They commented on the cute choices." She held out a list of items for Lucy.

"You have a knack for this. I sure hope your loan comes through." She sniffed the air. "You put vanilla in the diffuser. Smells good."

"I enjoy the clean scent it gives off."

"Me too. Are you okay for the rest of the day?" Lucy snatched a candy bar to share with Owen.

Regina smacked at her arm. "Shouldn't you pay for your purchase, young lady?" She grinned. "I'm fine. I'll close at four and lock the doors."

"Thanks." Lucy and Owen stepped onto the store's porch.

Owen placed his hand on Lucy's back and guided her to the truck. They each climbed in and he drove to her house. In the driveway, Owen leaned over the console. "Since you have the rest of the day off, do you want to help me? We can do some measurements on the event building and make a list of what needs fixing. You can help me set some trees and repot some flowers. A few of the businesses downtown hired me to spruce up the landscape in front of their buildings."

Lucy planned to spend the rest of her day cleaning and sorting

139

through a couple of boxes of papers, but spending time with Owen sounded better. "Let me take my pack in and change shoes, and I'll be right back."

At the farm, Lucy perched on a high stool at the work bench and transplanted seedlings into pots. The pungent odor of potting soil calmed her. The earthy scent grounded her and made her thankful for God's gift of nature. As a child on the island, she'd played on the beach and in the woods for hours each day. She and Joel had built forts and climbed rocks. They played pirate and pretended to search for gold.

"Has anyone found any more holes dug anywhere?"

Owen worked at the other end of the bench, drawing a landscape layout. "I haven't heard of any." He penciled in a window box on a building. "I was surprised Andrew came to the game today. He acted... nice."

"Yeah. He did. I'm glad he felt comfortable enough to ask to play. It's like he's had a change of heart." Lucy poked a seedling into a pot, then mounded the dirt around it.

Owen laid his pencil on the bench and walked over to Lucy. "I guess with time we'll find out if it sticks."

"I suppose." She brushed dirt from her hands. "When Joel and I used to play pirates and secret treasure, we overheard one of the older gentlemen in town talk about the Klondike gold. If I'm remembering correctly, he told his friends the gold had to be around the area of the General Store. I'm not sure why I'm remembering this now, except I was thinking about Joel and I playing..."

Owen patted her shoulder. "You're babbling."

"Sorry." She washed her hands at the wash tub in the large barn's corner. "Anyway, he believed it might be under or around the store because the house belonged to Merrilee Lester's family. You don't suppose it could be in the cellar, do you?"

~~~~~

Evening faded into night. Stars shone over the quiet island, and Travis relaxed in a chair beside the ancient cabin. The fragrance of honeysuckle drifted in the air and Travis, for the first time in a long time, valued the peace of a pleasant day.

He had watched the islanders interact at the softball game. They had simple, clean fun, which had eluded him for years. Instead of finding pleasure in simplicity, he had complicated his life with ambition and a constant longing for more. More adventures, more money, less personal interaction. The people on Abbott Island counted on each other. He might go as far as believing they loved one another. *Ugh.*

His mom had loved people and God. She had taught him, but he had ignored her beliefs. He thanked God or whoever listened for one good parent. Only the Lord knew where his father disappeared to, but his mom had stood by him, even when the police arrested him for theft at thirteen.

She had stood by his side, but at home she gave him a tongue-lashing and made him memorize Ephesians 4:28, "Anyone who has been stealing must steal no longer, but must work, doing something useful with their own hands, that they may have something to share with those in need." Then she'd made him mow and rake leaves for the neighbors on either side of them all summer and fall. By the time he graduated, he'd left the verse and his mom's wisdom behind and pursued whatever he wanted. Now his mom lay buried under six feet of dirt in northern Ohio. His heart ached for a hug from the precious woman.

Over the years, his soul had hardened, and he'd stolen from people who never saw him. He sneaked into their lives and removed items they had no idea existed or considered a myth. Him and his crew. He had dragged others into his deceitful life. Was it possible to start over?

Instead of the calm he experienced earlier, angst weighed him down like a sandbag. His head and neck ached. He rose from the chair, walked into the cabin, and slammed the door. Inside, he changed for bed, without turning on a light, and buried himself under the blankets. There in the still, dark night, he cried tears of sorrow for the disappointment he had inflicted on his dear, sweet momma.

CHAPTER TWENTY-FIVE

The church bells chimed on the cloudy Sunday morning, as Lucy met Owen on the steps. On their way inside, they waved to Miss Aggie, Miss Flossie, and Miss Hildy, who clucked and finger-waved back. They each wore a satisfied grin, as if their magic had caused Lucy and Owen to fall for one another.

Seated near the front, Lucy leaned toward Owen. "I've been thinking and praying about digging in the cellar. How about we wait until after the softball tournament in case we discover something?" She wiggled her eyebrows.

"If this will satisfy your curiosity, I'm in. Since the cellar is small, it shouldn't take long to find out the treasure isn't there." He wrapped an arm around her shoulders.

A pout formed on her lips. "Skeptic."

Piano music cued them to stand and sing. The congregation harmonized on *Power in the Blood* and *Whiter than Snow*. From the corner of her eye, Lucy saw Andrew as he scooted into the back pew.

The music quieted and the pastor shared about forgiveness and loving one another in a way to encourage hope.

Lucy's heart ached for the way she had thought about Andrew and the time she yelled at him. *God, forgive me.* When the service ended, she turned to catch his eye and wave, but he was gone.

Owen rested his hand on her back. "You okay?"

She lifted her face to meet his. "Yep. I saw Andrew come in, but he's already gone. I wanted to apologize to him for my reaction at the store the day I raised my voice."

"I'm sure you'll catch him another time. He'll be at the game on Wednesday." He guided her out of the church.

She stopped beside Sadie and lifted baby Gracie from her sister-in-law's arms. "How's my girl?" she cooed to the little one. "You're wearing the outfit I got you."

Dressed in a lavender flowered dress with a cotton lavender coat to match and a bonnet with ribbons, Gracie wore a toothless grin as Lucy kissed her cheek. She cuddled the baby and bent her head sideways to motion Sadie to her.

"What's up?" Sadie frowned.

Lucy patted Gracie's back. "Nothing to be worried about." She leaned close to her sister-in-law. "How long is Andrew staying on the island?"

She shrugged. "I'm not sure. He's paid through the end of May. Why?"

"Just wondered."

Sadie squinted and looked at Owen, then Lucy. "I thought you and Owen were dating."

Lucy swayed with Gracie. "It's nothing like that. I am dating Owen and enjoying his company. I thought I'd talk to Andrew about us getting off on the wrong foot and me being rude."

"Oh." Sadie raised her eyebrows and made an O with her mouth.

"Yeah. I can be a bit over the top at times." She hugged her niece. "Don't be like your Aunt Lucy, little one."

Sadie laughed. "You... over the top?"

She handed Gracie to her mom. "I'll find him and talk to him. He was here at church this morning." She had not seen him at the church before. Was he a believer? Whatever his status, she determined to pray for him and talk to him.

~~~~~

Settled at a picnic table on a quiet part of the island, Travis watched the water ebb and flow. The roast beef and cheese sandwich he picked up from the local store had lost its flavor, or his appetite waned. He tossed the half-eaten meal in the trash and carried his Pepsi with him to the shore.

He trundled across the beach as a warm breeze ruffled his dark hair. Eyes on the sand, he meandered around a dead fish, then spied sunshine reflecting on an item in the sand. He leaned to pick up the shiny object. Lake glass littered the area. He gathered several pieces and held them in the water to wash the sand away. Shards of blue, green, white, and brown clung to his hand. Some people considered the glass a treasure. Though most pieces held little monetary value, the thrill of discovery made the finder happy. He shoved them in his pocket.

Similar to his search for treasure over the years, he loved the hunt. The actual finds left him disappointed when his hunt revealed an empty vessel or little plunder. What about the gold said to be buried on this island? Did the nuggets exist or did his family trump up the story? His mom told him not to waste his time and to seek the treasure of Jesus' love. How could he not search? He had his minions dig where he thought the map pointed. They either blew the searches or found nothing. One other place tempted him to break the law. One last holdout coaxed him to step foot on another person's property and trespass.

If anyone else found the treasure, he'd have heard. What if the mistakes he and his dimwitted minions had made had caught the interest of the islanders, and started rumors about the treasure circulating again?

Home At Last

He crumpled the pop can and tossed it in the trash, then trudged onto the road. Sunday afternoon, most island folks stayed home. In a short time, tourists would swarm the island. Determined to check out the one last place he planned to search before a host of people invaded, he set his plan into motion. Before Friday, he'd break into the place and dig. A thrill ran through his veins as he heard his mother's voice in his head. "Be a good boy and do the right thing."

He ran his hand over his face. "Not now, Mom."

~~~~~

On Monday morning, the General Store hummed with activity. The early birds had arrived before the crowds showed, to enjoy the first full week of pleasant weather. Lucy greeted several return guests. A lady in a bright green Abbott Island t-shirt approached Lucy.

"Do you have any hot pink shirts, dear?"

"Sure do." Lucy led her to the neon colors.

Another customer fingered every Christmas ornament, then left without a purchase.

The store quieted after lunch. Regina and Lucy sat at the counter and rested their feet on a shelf.

"Wow. What a morning." Regina wiggled her toes. "It's exciting to see folks who haven't been here since last year. The Dodson's kids have grown."

Lucy rubbed lotion into her hands. "I noticed, and Mrs. Livingston still wears her bright colors. I'm glad I ordered some shirts in the hues she wears. The one she bought matched her lipstick."

The bell on the door chimed. "Hello, ladies." Owen wore a t-shirt with a tractor and the slogan, *Farming isn't for everyone, but hay it's in my jeans.*

Lucy hopped from her stool and greeted him with a kiss on the cheek. "Hello, handsome." A blush reached her cheeks. Never a flirt, she tried, but felt silly.

Owen gave a toothy grin. "Hi, beautiful."

Regina stood and placed her hands on the smooth wooden counter. "Okay, you two, go to the office. I'll handle the customers." She pointed to the back of the store.

He grabbed Lucy's hand and led her. In the office, he sank into the comfy, flowered chair, and she rested her bottom against the desk.

Lucy leaned her hands against the desk. "What have you been up to today?"

"I've been working on our event center. I cleaned out all the debris and junk we had stored and swept the floor. I used Aunt Marley's dust mop to knock down cobwebs." He leaned his head on the back of the chair.

Lucy clasped her hands over her mouth, then dropped them to her sides. "Wow! You're amazing." She sat on his lap, then hugged his neck. She didn't deserve a man who cared so much, but she thanked God he came into her life.

Owen wrapped his arms around her waist. "I like this." He smiled, then kissed her. "I should have cleaned the building days ago."

Lucy rested her head on his shoulder. "I don't know what to say. You're helping me make my dream a reality. I'm anxious to find out what Regina can do. She said her husband was talking to the bank this morning, so I should hear soon. I pray they buy me out." She pushed her lips together and raised one finger to her mouth.

Owen took hold of her hand and pulled it away from her face. "It's okay to babble, as you call it, especially when you're excited. I love your enthusiasm. As a matter of fact, I love you."

Lucy stilled and stared at the man. "You do?"

He put a finger under her chin and drew her face closer to his. "I sure do." He met his lips with hers.

After the kiss, Lucy looked into his eyes. "I love you, too. I never thought I'd say those words to a man, especially one who said them first." She hugged his neck.

Regina hurried into the room. "Lucy, you need to come out here."

A chill ran down Lucy's spine. She and Owen rushed to the front of the store. The romantic moment dissipated like a wisp of smoke.

Regina's husband stood beside a display rack. His face wore a grim look. "I hate to bring bad news, but the bank is asking us for more money for the down payment. I'm not sure what we can do." He rubbed his hands together. "I haven't given up, but we need more time."

Lucy's heart ached for Regina and Gio. When she had purchased the store, she ran into the same issue. Her parents had helped her figure out the financing using the inheritance from her nana. Without another serious buyer, she had time, but then she'd have to put her dream on hold. The Holy Spirit nudged her. *God's timing is perfect.* Of course. Trust God. Have faith.

"No worries. I'm not in a hurry, and I'll be happy to help in any way I can." She reached for Owen's hand and he squeezed it. "We'll figure this out."

~~~~~

Afternoon sun shimmered through the front window of the store and shined a beam on Regina and Gio. Owen stepped to the man and shook his hand. "I want to help. Let's grab a coffee and talk?"

Gio's face relaxed. "Sure."

Owen turned to Lucy. "Can you come to the farm after work? Aunt Marley is making her fried chicken. Best on the island."

"I'd love to. See you tonight."

146

Owen and Gio stepped out to the street and headed to Catie's Cafe. Inside, they ordered coffee and found a table. Seated in a corner, Owen sipped from the paper cup.

"Good stuff. Catie makes the best Americano."

"The lattes are good too." Gio rested a hand on the table.

Owen leaned toward his friend. "I don't want to overstep or get involved where you don't want me, but I am in a position to loan you money, no interest."

Gio dropped his head and stared at the table. After a moment, he raised his head. "I can't ask you to loan me money."

"You didn't ask. I offered." Owen longed to make Lucy's dream of event planning a reality. He loved her and wanted what she wanted. If it meant loaning Gio and Regina money, he'd do it. His sign-on bonus had languished in the bank long enough. Sure, he earned interest on it, but he'd love to use part of it to help. Plus, when Lucy opened the event space, she'd spend more time on the farm.

The man let out a breath. "We're talking thousands of dollars. At least six thousand."

"Do you have the paperwork from the bank?"

Gio reached for papers in his back pocket. "This is what they gave me. If you're serious about it, take a look." He handed the thick packet of papers to Owen.

After several minutes, Owen handed them back. "We can make this work."

"Why do you want to do this?"

A slow smile crossed Owen's face. "Because I love Lucy."

Gio's mouth fell open. "Okay, then. Sounds like you're smitten. Is that the word?"

"Sure is." Owen tapped the table with his hand. "Lucy wants to open an event planning space and invite people to use it for weddings and parties. I want to help make it happen. If I can loan you the money for the store, then she can get her new business going."

Gio reached across the table and shook Owen's hand. "Let's do this. Regina is going to be thrilled."

"Other than Regina, let's keep it between us until we get the final approval. I don't want Lucy to be disappointed if the bank balks for some reason. I don't think they will, but you can't be sure." He gulped the rest of his coffee. "Call the bank and set up an appointment. Let me know when to meet you. This is gonna be great."

CHAPTER TWENTY-SIX

A nod to spring escorted Lucy along the driveway to the farm, as late daffodils bloomed in clumps of yellow and white. She parked in front of the event barn where Owen pushed a wheelbarrow of crushed stone.

Outside the car, she hustled to meet him. "What are you doing with the rocks?"

He set the legs of the wheelbarrow in the dirt. "A few spots in the driveway, close to the house, have thinned out. I'm adding some gravel until we can get someone here to add a substantial amount." He pulled off his work gloves, then flexed his arms. "Keeps me buff." He let out a laugh.

Lucy chuckled. The man had no idea how handsome he was.

He slipped his gloves on, lifted the handles, then carted the stones to the driveway. Lucy trailed behind him.

"I want to finish. Should take a few minutes, if that's okay. Aunt Marley is in the kitchen, if you want to head on in." He rested the wheelbarrow on the ground.

"Okay." Lucy planted a kiss on his cheek, then went to the door and peeked her head inside. "Hello."

"Do I hear the sweet Grayson girl?" Aunt Marley wiped her hands on a dishcloth, then greeted Lucy with a hug. "Come on in here. I'm glad you could join us. Our boy has been working his buns off in the barn. He says you have ideas to use it. I can't wait to hear them over dinner."

Lucy returned the hug. "I'm happy to be here and to share my plans. I hope you and Jed approve." The fragrance of fried chicken made Lucy's stomach grumble. "Do I smell cherry pie?"

"You have a good sense of smell. I had some cherries frozen from last year. Jed and I go to an orchard on the mainland a couple times a year and gather fruit. I love to have it in the freezer for days when I want to bake." She stirred a pot on the stove. "I hope you like mashed taters and gravy."

Lucy's mouth watered. "I do. I'm a potato girl. Is there anything I can do to help?"

The woman eyed the table. "If you don't mind, you can set out the plates and silverware in the dining room. You know where it all is."

Lucy found four plates in the cabinet. She set them across from each other, two to a side, for better conversation. If she and Owen married, she'd spend a lot of time at this table. *Wait, slow the thought train. No one mentioned marriage. Calm yourself.*

Uncle Jed and Owen tromped into the house and wiped their feet on the rug. Lucy had not noticed how much the two men favored one another. If Owen aged like Jed, he'd keep his handsome features. She'd love to see a photo of Jed and Marley when they married. Both of them looked much younger than their age.

At supper, the fried chicken rounded the table.

"Aunt Marley, you've outdone yourself." Owen stabbed a chicken breast and placed it on his plate.

Lucy took two legs. "The leg has been my favorite since I was a little girl." She piled potatoes, gravy, and green beans on her plate. "I agree with Owen. You've fixed us an amazing dinner."

Aunt Marley clapped. "If I had a nickel for every piece of chicken I've fried, I'd be a rich lady."

Uncle Jed patted her arm. "I've sure been blessed by this young lady." He pecked her cheek.

"We better get to eating." She straightened her napkin. "Lucy, tell us your ideas for the barn."

For the next half an hour, Lucy discussed her business plans. "I'm praying it all works out. I need Regina and Gio or someone to buy the business, so I can move forward with this one. I hope you all are okay with me renting your building."

Aunt Marley finished her last bite. "No, we aren't all right."

Lucy's face dropped. Tears stung her eyes. Owen had told her he had worked and prepared the space for her to execute her ideas. If they didn't approve, what would she do?

The woman touched Lucy's hand. "We want you to use the space rent free. We don't use it for anything else and we'd love for you to have full access. Plus, when Jed and I trade houses with Owen, we'll be far enough away the noise and traffic won't bother us." She eyed Owen. "By the way, when are we switching? I've been sorting and packing."

"Soon, I promise. I have more work on the barn and landscaping jobs, but I'll pack as I go along. You'll be out of here before you know it."

A dreamy look crossed Aunt Marley's face. "Jed and I set up housekeeping here. It would be wonderful if another young couple did the same." She winked at Lucy.

Owen rose from the table and gathered dirty plates. "Thanks for the delicious meal."

Lucy stood to help him. Her cheeks burned. "Yes, delicious." She grabbed the silverware and followed Owen from the dining room to the kitchen.

"Excuse my aunt, please. She's never been subtle." He ran water and poured in detergent.

Home At Last

Lucy pulled a dish cloth from a rack. "No worries. I love how she's herself, and what a generous gift. I can't believe they want me to use the building for free."

Owen pulled her into a hug. "They are the most generous people I know. I'm thankful they love you as much as I do."

"Me too." She reached into the sink and scored a handful of bubbles. Before he could stop her, she covered his nose in them.

He leaned in for a soapy kiss.

Clapping drew the two apart. Aunt Marley stood and applauded the young love. "You do my heart good. Now let's have pie."

After they finished the dishes, Owen held Lucy's hand as they meandered to the event barn. "Building or barn? Which sounds better?"

Lucy tapped a finger on her mouth. "Event barn sounds more inviting. I'm thinking about calling the business Island Charm. I could offer western, lakeside, or a farm theme. Whatever the couple would want." She paused her steps. "I'm going to have to scour thrift shops to find props. Want to shop with me?" She batted her eyelashes.

"We'll figure it out as we go. You aren't in this alone. I'm here for you." He tugged her hand, and they stepped to the barn. "Come see how it looks."

Lucy stepped in and Owen flipped on the lights.

She spun in a slow circle. "This is amazing. It's so clean." Above her, fairy lights twinkled. "Oh my, you hung lights. They're perfect." Tears stung her eyes and spilled across her cheeks. She sniffed, then sobbed.

"What's wrong? I thought you'd like the lights."

"I...love...the lights. I'm overwhelmed to have someone care about me so much. I mean, I know my family loves me, but I never expected to have a man care so much. This is amazing." She flung herself into his arms.

Owen held her. "You are worth whatever I do to show I love you. No one has seen me for me, except you. You don't have agendas."

She leaned away and kept her arms around his neck. "You are the kindest man I know, and you have a heart for God."

They held hands and wandered under the twinkling lights. "I wonder if Sadie would paint a backdrop for me. Something neutral I could deck out with whatever the couple wanted. We could have a trellis or a canopy. This is gonna be fun." Lucy let go of him and twirled with her arms out.

Owen took her hand and pulled her into a hug. "It sure is."

~~~~~

White billowy clouds floated across the azure sky. A great blue heron sailed above the lake. Wednesday morning, Travis had hiked along the boardwalk through the woods and found his way to the small hidden beach on the north edge of the island.

He planted himself on the sand and filtered bits of broken shell through his fingers. What was wrong with him? For the first time in a long time, he found himself more centered and calmer than he had in years. On his walks on the trails and through the woods, even when he spied on people, or sneaked through town the music of the birds and sight of deer reminded him of time with his mother. What if he stopped stealing, settled down and... what?

He stood and paced along the edge of the water. A stick floated in, and he picked it up and tossed it back in the water. Would the people here want him to stay? If they knew him and his evil ways, they wouldn't.

He trudged to the boardwalk and tromped back to the cabin. Dismay rumbled through him and anger welled up in his heart. He was meant for a life of crime, yet he longed to be free.

~~~~

A few weeds sprouted in Lucy's flower beds around her tiny home. She sat on the ground with a spade and dug the green monsters out. Beside the foxglove, she pulled tufts of grass from the bed, then checked around the lavender, and the pink and yellow tulips. In the corner, the lily of the valley thrived.

Because of the softball game this evening, she had closed the store. She took her time in the yard and admired the work of Owen's hands. The promise of summer excited her for the garden surprises she'd find. After she finished the weeding, she washed her hands and sat at her tiny kitchen table. She checked her to-do list. All done. Time for a quick run.

She rounded the corner near Sadie and Joel's home. Her heart pounded and her blood flowed. Lucy found a short run invigorating. Not one for long marathons, she had participated in the island's 5K last November. She slowed her pace and walked past her brother's home.

Someone walked toward her. She squinted at the person who approached. Andrew strode as if he was on a mission. Should she dart off the road out of sight or talk to him?

Before she decided, he stood in front of her.

"Afternoon. It's a beautiful day." Lucy lifted on her toes.

Andrew held her gaze. "Yep, beautiful." He glanced at the sky. "Do you have a minute?"

"Sure." *As long as we stay in public.* Even though she wanted to forgive him, he still gave her pause.

"There's a picnic table across the road, under the trees."

Lucy followed Andrew through the grass to the table and settled on the opposite side. She folded her hands in her lap and waited.

He rested his elbows on the table and focused on her. "I... um... want to say I'm sorry. I pressured you to sell the store to me, and I didn't mean to upset you."

152

Lucy let her shoulders relax. This man sought her forgiveness. His aggressive approach had given her anxiety, and his insistence had annoyed her. *Lord, I want to forgive. I even planned to, but I can't get my mouth to speak the words.*

He sat across the table, his head bowed and his hands clasped. Was he praying?

She cleared her throat. "Thank you. I forgive you and wish you well. I hope you find what you're looking for." She rose from her seat and stepped away from the table. "I'll see you at the softball game this evening." With a wave of her hand, she darted off in a run.

As she headed home, anxiety niggled at her. An uncomfortable tug at her gut told her even though she'd forgiven Andrew, she had best stay away from him. The sincerity of his confession hadn't reached his eyes. They grew almost black when he said he hadn't intended to scare her, like he enjoyed inflicting fear.

She neared her house and tried to shake off the creepy vibe, but it clung tight.

Home At Last

CHAPTER TWENTY-SEVEN

Two dozen people hustled around the baseball diamond and prepared for the game. Dust flew when Joel and Levi set the bases, and Lucy arranged the bats on the fence for her team. Owen sorted equipment and Lucy's dad donned his umpire gear. Sadie's golden retriever, Rosie, chased a loose ball across the field. Excitement stirred as the teams came together.

Lucy called her team roster to set the line-up. Andrew stood at the back of the group, with his eyes focused on her. She shook off any negativity and plowed ahead with plans to beat Owen's team.

"Okay, guys, is everybody ready to play? Who's here to win?" She raised her clipboard over her head.

The team shook their fists in the air. "We are!" Laughter broke out among the players.

Lucy adjusted her ball cap then trotted to the batter's box. She set her feet at home plate, lifted her bat from her shoulder, and gave Owen the stink eye. He tossed the first pitch.

"Strike."

"Dad?" Lucy glared at her umpire father.

"I call them as I see them."

The second pitch sailed in. Lucy swung and knocked the ball into right field. She hustled to first base.

"Safe."

After five innings, Owen's team led by two. The players batted and fielded as if they'd played all winter.

Owen took the plate and faced Levi on the mound. On the third pitch, he swung and knocked the ball out of the field. With players on first, second, and third, he celebrated a grand slam.

Lucy shook her head. As much as she loved the man, her competitive spirit screamed. After the third out for Owen's team, Lucy's bottom three were up to bat. Before they did, she stood in front of her team in the dugout.

"Looks like they have a new pitcher. My brother. We need to hit the ball out of the park." She rubbed her forehead. "Guys, I don't want to be beaten by my boyfriend and my brother." The team chuckled, then sobered and agreed.

Andrew took his place at the plate. On his first swing, he slugged the ball into the left corner and rounded the bases to second.

Lucy jumped and cheered. Maybe she could forgive him after all.

Marigold hit a single and Sadie singled by error. Bases loaded. Lucy stood and faced her brother. She lifted her bat to swing, then stopped.

"Ball one."

Lucy sauntered to first base after Joel threw three more bombs. She waved at her brother as she passed.

Joel rolled his eyes. "Yeah, yeah."

In the end, Owen's team won twelve to ten.

Abbott Island Restaurant delivered several large pizzas to the picnic tables beside the field.

Lucy touched her dad's arm. "You want to bless the pizza?"

"Sure. Lord, thank You for fun and fellowship. Bless this food and all the folks here. Amen."

Owen pulled Lucy's ponytail. "Good game."

She turned and touched his arm. "It was. Everyone had fun. Congratulations on your win."

"Why, thank you, ma'am." He bowed.

"Oh, brother. Speaking of brother, where's mine? I thought he'd harass me by now." She looked around the tables.

Owen pointed across the field. "He's preoccupied with important business."

Lucy's gaze followed his. Joel stood at the back of their SUV changing Gracie's diaper. "Good for him."

Amy, Lucy's mom, rolled up in her chair. "Sweetie, you played a great game. I was rooting for you." She held her daughter's hand. "What's this I hear about you starting a new business and selling the store? Your dad told me."

Lucy sat on a bench to face her mom. "I'm sorry, Mom. When I called to talk to you and Dad, you weren't home."

Her mom patted Lucy's knee. "No worries. I'm excited for you, and I want to help if you need me."

"I'm sure I will." She leaned in and hugged her. "I'll call you soon."

The team members tossed their garbage and cleared their gear.

Lucy gathered stray plates and napkins from the tables. "Owen, are you coming over tonight?"

Owen folded pizza boxes and deposited them into a large trash can. "If you want me to."

"Of course I do. Even if you did beat me."

~~~~~

Purple and pink streaks crossed the darkened sky. The north star shone near the full moon. An owl hooted and leaves rustled in the woods. On the porch, Lucy handed Owen a sweet tea, then settled in the chair

Home At Last

beside him.

"Thanks, Lucy." He reached for her hand. "I had fun at the game. When you asked me to play, I wasn't sure I would. My mind still plays tricks on me."

Lucy's thumb stroked his. "In what way?"

"When I think about taking the mound, my heart races and my chest tightens. Doubts fill my head, even though the game was for fun. The whole not-good-enough scenario plays like a movie in my mind." He turned to her. "You are what got me through. Knowing you love me anyway."

Her heart hurt for him. "You're an amazing man. Never doubt the gifts and opportunities God has given you."

"Thank you."

Lucy stood and paced across the porch. She stopped in front of Owen. "Is everything okay?"

She nodded. "Yeah. I want to dig in the cellar before the weekend gets busy. Want to help me tomorrow evening? I have a shovel."

Owen stood and took her hand. He guided her to the beach. Waves churned as if a storm brewed. The odor of electricity in the air hinted at rain.

"I thought we should talk about the cellar away from the road where someone might hear us." He wrapped an arm around her shoulders. "Of course I'll help you. I'll bring the flashlight we use when we work on equipment. It shines bright as the sun." He pinched his lips together.

Lucy wiggled out of his hold and faced him. "What's wrong?"

He stepped to the water's edge, picked up a rock, and tossed it in the water. A splash and ripple crashed the waves. She joined him and held his arm.

"I don't want you to be disappointed. If by some ridiculous chance we find gold, you could use it for the event planning business, but it's probably not there."

She scooted away. "You think I'm foolish."

"No. I'm simply stating the facts. Sorry if I'm too practical." He folded his arms over his chest.

"You could have told me you thought I was wasting my time." She propped her hands on her hips.

He reached for her and she backed away. "I didn't want to discourage you, but I can't imagine a buried treasure on the island."

"Never mind." Lucy took another step away from Owen. "I'll do it by myself. I have my own flashlight. Don't worry about me. I might tell you what I find." She stomped to her house, went inside, and slammed the door.

At the window, she watched Owen's taillights sail away.

157

Before tears formed, she grabbed Finn's food and sprinkled the flakes over the water. "I wish you could talk, Finnegan. You'd tell me if I was foolish or not. On second thought, it's best you don't speak."

She slumped on the couch and punched a pillow. "Why do I overreact? I realize I might not find anything. I'm prepared if I don't." She flopped her head on the pillow she had assaulted. "Now Owen is upset because I mouthed off. What am I going to do, Finn?"

~~~~~

The dark woods shadowed Travis from Owen and Lucy. As still as a tree, he listened to them. Blondie planned to dig in the cellar tomorrow. Her hero boyfriend backed out. Perfect.

After Owen drove away, Travis crept out of the woods. One more try, and if nothing surfaced, he'd give up and live a life without crime. What if she found the treasure, the gold his aunt buried so many years ago? His mind whirled at the idea of what kind of life he'd live as a rich man. Problem was, if she found the gold on her property, the treasure belonged to her. Stupid laws.

He trudged along the road, uncertain what time she planned to dig. He'd stake out the back of her building tomorrow. The neighbors behind her had a shed he'd hide in and when she started her endeavor, he'd give her time to dig, then he'd surprise her. If she found the box, he'd knock her out of the way, then grab it and go.

In his cabin, he packed his belongings in his backpack. He'd carry the pack with him and be ready to escape the island. Over his days of watching, he had pegged two boaters who hid their keys under their seats. Either one would work, and he'd leave the boat where the coast guard could find it. No harm in preparation.

He laid the map out one more time and studied the Xes. One marked the spot behind the General Store. Tomorrow, he hoped to be a rich man.

~~~~~

Rain poured outside Lucy's window, Thursday morning. She lay in bed and watched drops drizzle down the glass. Her mood matched the rain. Sad and dreary. Why had she raised her voice to Owen? He deserved better. The man wanted to protect her, even from herself.

She raised herself up in bed, then let her feet hit the floor. Downstairs, she dressed for work and ate one of Sadie's cranberry muffins with her coffee. She'd warmed the baked item, and the house smelled of cranberries and spice. She breathed in the scent, and the tenseness in her shoulders eased.

Dressed in her purple Abbott Island raincoat, she trotted to her Jeep, then drove to work.

Lucy parked in back and ran through the pelting rain to the office door. Inside, she shook her coat and hung it on the peg.

Home At Last

"Morning." Regina stood in the doorway. "Yucky day, isn't it?"

"Sure is. I doubt we'll get many people today." Lucy's computer hummed after she pressed the power button. "I'll work in here for a while."

Regina clasped her hands in front of her and bounced on her toes. "Before you start, I have news."

Lucy walked around her desk and leaned against the edge. "Are you going to share?"

Her coworker's voice rose an octave. "Yes. We're buying the store."

Lucy hugged her, and they both bounced on their toes. "I don't know what to say, except I'm super excited." Regina fell into the comfy chair and took a breath. Lucy held her hand on her chest. "My heart's beating out of my chest. When did you find out?"

"Last night. Gio and I talked, and we decided to take Owen's loan to help us with the down payment." She beamed.

Lucy's brow furrowed. "Wait, what? Owen loaned you money to buy the store?"

Regina covered her mouth with her hand. "He didn't tell you?"

Lucy shook her head. "No. He didn't."

"It's a few thousand dollars so we could make the down payment. No interest." She stood and placed a hand on Lucy's shoulder. "Don't be mad at him."

She eased into a slight smile. "I'm surprised, not mad. He wanted me to chase my dream."

The man she had accused of thinking she was a fool had provided the means for her to sell and then pursue the desire God placed on her heart. More than words, he was a man of action who loved her more than she imagined. He'd admitted he was practical, in the heat of their argument. She understood that even better, now, to mean financing rather than gold nuggets.

"Lucy, you okay?"

"I'm fine. Humbled, but fine."

Regina left her to her office work. Lucy punched in Owen's number. No answer. No point leaving a voice mail. She'd catch him later.

By noon, the rain had stopped and dark clouds floated north. Lucy stood outside by the cellar doors and debated. To dig or not to dig. Owen knew she'd go in after work. Uncertain if he'd help her, she was determined to plunge a shovel into the dirt after Regina went home. No one would question her working in her own cellar.

Her online search, yesterday before the game, had instructed her to soften hardened dirt by soaking it with a mixture of baby shampoo and water. She had filled a large spray bottle with the two and hidden it behind the store with her shovel on the way to the game.

159

Penny Frost McGinnis, Abbott Island Book 3

She snatched the spray bottle, then closed her eyes for a second. "God, give me guidance. Please." Lucy unlocked the padlock and climbed into the cellar. She sprayed a large area with the baby shampoo, then retreated and locked the doors.

A little after five, she'd learn the truth. A treasure or a waste of time.

CHAPTER TWENTY-EIGHT

The gray day offered more cover for Travis. In a yard behind the General Store, he concealed himself in a shed where the smell of gasoline and oil emitted from an old lawn mower. Earlier, he had watched the owners of the shed drive their car onto the ferry and skim across the lake to Marblehead. His observation skills paid off every time.

Around noon, his stomach growled. He plucked a protein bar out of his pack and chewed his lunch. Through the peephole in the shed, he watched Blondie lean on the doors to the cellar. She bowed her head. Was she praying? What was with her? Mom had prayed over everything, even him. His lip quivered at the memory of his kind, loving momma. He smacked himself in the face to stop the pathetic emotions. A real man didn't weep over losing his mother, yet a tear hit his cheek.

He glared out the hole and watched Blondie raise her head, unlock the doors, then descend into the cellar. His gut told him to stay put as he considered a confrontation. Before his patience wore thin, she emerged, pushed the door closed and clicked the lock, then scurried into the back door of the store. More waiting.

The clock ticked off another hour. At 3:30, Travis's head jerked. He had fallen asleep against a smelly tarp. Pain shot along his neck as he stretched to remove a kink. He tore a water bottle from his pack and chugged a long drink.

The store closed at five. She'd search then. From the argument he had eavesdropped on, she'd dig alone. He'd let her wield the shovel for a while, then emerge from his hiding hole and confront her. He rubbed his palms together and anticipated the weight of gold in his hands.

~~~~~

Even with all the foot traffic in the store, the day dragged. After lunch, Lucy restocked household goods and rearranged Christmas ornaments. She spent an hour reorganizing t-shirts and jackets, then dusted clean shelves. Regina waited on the last customers of the day.

Lucy turned the sign to *closed* after their feet crossed the threshold. "We've had a busy day. Thanks for all your hard work. Just think, you'll be on my side of things soon."

Regina tidied the counter. "I'm excited and nervous. You make it look easy." She dug her purse from a box under the counter. "The summer staff starts tomorrow."

Lucy tapped her foot. "When we interviewed them, they were a great crew." A few of them lived on the island, but most ferried from the mainland. One, like Sadie, lived on the island in the summer with her grandparents. "An FYI, I provide passes to the students who live on the mainland so they can afford the ferry. Otherwise, they couldn't swing the travel back and forth."

Regina looped her quilted purse straps over her shoulder. "They've all been in for at least one training and caught on without issue. As long as they can run the cash register, they'll be fine. I may get some part-time help for fall from this group." She moved to the door. "I'll see you in the morning." She waved and walked out.

Lucy bolted the door and hustled to her office. *Take a breath. You're simply digging a hole or two in your own cellar.* What if the ground was too hard? She'd figure out what to do.

At her desk, she bowed her head and shored up her strength. If only Owen had joined her.

She stepped outside to the back of the store and locked the back door. From her key ring, she secured the key to the cellar. She scanned the neighbor's yards, on her way to retrieve the shovel she'd hidden behind the oil tank. No activity. Good. She dragged the shovel to the doors, unlocked the padlock, then climbed in. Her flashlight lit the cave-like opening. The dirt in the area she sprayed appeared wet. After arranging the light to shine on the spot, she plunged the shovel into the dirt. Nothing clanged, no hard surface met the tip. She scooped a shovel full and dipped the spade to drop the dirt in a corner.

After several tries, she discovered nothing but bugs and worms. She wiped her face with a handkerchief her mom had given her. Mom and Dad had shared their opinion of a treasure on the island. Dad had laughed and said, "If there's gold buried behind the store, I'll mow your yard all summer."

As her dad's words wounded her ego, she plunged the shovel deeper. This time the tip hit something hard. The vibration she felt in her arms from the connection energized her. She poked the tip in and hit another spot. With a burst of energy, she disposed of the dirt on top and stared at a burlap covered object. On her hands and knees, she brushed dirt away, then untied the bag. She sat back on her heels at the sight of the primitive carving similar to totem poles she'd seen in art books. On her feet, she grabbed the flashlight and shined the beam on the wood. The carved eyes of a fox stared back.

Footsteps sounded behind her. *Owen must have come.* She swung around and froze. "Andrew. What are you doing here?"

A loud, harsh laugh echoed through the cellar. "You can call me Andrew or Travis. Andrew Travis Jones, as a matter of fact."

Home At Last

She clutched the shovel like a ball bat. Lucy's hands shook and perspiration covered her face. "Whoever you are, get out of my cellar and off my property. Now."

"Not when you have something that belongs to me. My great-whatever aunt Merrilee buried gold here, and I'm taking it with me." He peered past her and shined his cell phone's flashlight on the box. "It's like she described. Keep digging."

Lucy lifted the shovel and swung. Travis raised his hand and stopped the swing in midair. Lucy jerked the shovel away.

He pulled a revolver from his pocket and aimed it at her. "I said dig."

She bit her lip and shoveled. After a half an hour of loosening the soil, the box broke free. Travis shoved Lucy to the corner behind the hole, then extracted the box. He pulled a knife from his boot and pried open the lid, while he kept the gun trained on Lucy. Gold nuggets shimmered under the beam of the flashlight.

Lucy gaped. "It's real."

"Yeah, it's real, and it's mine."

"No. Technically, it belongs to me. I own the property." Lucy's ire rose, and she planted her hands on her hips, even as she clutched the shovel.

"Lucy." Owen's voice carried into the cellar, and his footsteps followed.

"I'm down here and so is—"

"Shut up." Travis shined his light in Owen's face.

"What's going on?" Anger pierced Owen's voice.

"Your little girlfriend found my gold, and I'm taking it with me and locking you two in here."

Travis lowered the light.

Owen stepped to the dirt floor. "Andrew?"

Lucy shook her head. "Andrew Travis Jones. He's the great-something nephew of the woman who brought the gold back from the Klondike, or so he says." Her grip on the shovel caused her hand to ache. She had one more chance while he addressed Owen. Lucy lifted the spade in the air and swung. She lost her grip, and the shovel sailed through the air.

"Aw, too bad," Travis sneered. "You shouldn't have tried to hit me." He kicked the shovel away and faced Owen.

"Call me Travis, I go by Andrew when I'm playing nice." A raucous laugh escaped him as his beady eyes stared at Owen, then he shoved him to Lucy and planted himself between them and the door, his gun on Lucy.

Travis squatted in front of the box and ran his fingers through the nuggets. Lucy kept the gun in her sights and inched her way out of the corner to face the man who claimed the gold. *Try a different tact, maybe play*

163

Penny Frost McGinnis, Abbott Island Book 3

to his softer side, if he has one.

Owen followed and touched Lucy's arm, but she shook him off. "Andrew, did I see you at church on Sunday?"

His shoulders stiffened, and he glared at Lucy. "Why do you care?"

She fixed her eyes on his face. "Did you go to church as a boy? I bet your mom took you."

The corners of his mouth dropped into a frown and a far-away look filled his eyes. "Yeah. She taught me verses, too. I got saved when I was twelve years old and vowed to take care of her, but I turned bad, and she died and left me with a mountain of bills."

Owen slipped past Lucy and stood between her and Travis.

Travis's hand hung at his side, and his grip on the gun loosened.

Owen bent to make a move, but Lucy shook her head.

Her voice softened. "What would your mom tell you if she saw you today?"

His eyes hardened. "All I wanted was for you to sell me the store, once I figured out the gold had to be buried here, but no. You had to sell to the woman and her husband." He grunted. "There you are, digging the treasure before it left your hands. You're no better than me." He gripped the gun.

Owen placed his hand on Lucy's back and pleaded with Travis. "Let's talk about this. We can come to an agreement."

"Not happening. The gold is mine. Get out of my way, so I can carry it out of here."

Lucy's voice quivered. "What verses did your momma teach you?"

"Stop asking about my mom. I broke her heart." He sniffed and wiped at his face.

"How long has she been gone?"

The man's shoulders shook. "Too long, and now it's too late."

Lucy inched closer to him. "It's not too late to seek forgiveness." She knelt beside him. "God, we know You forgive, and Andrew here has a burden he's carrying. Please show him Your mercy and grace and open his heart to You."

He sank to his knees with a wail of agony. "I'm sorry, momma. I've stolen and cheated and broken your heart. Forgive me." A sob poured from him and his shoulders shook. "All I see is her disappointment in me and how I failed her. I promised myself this would be my last crime." Another sob escaped him. "I don't deserve forgiveness."

His gun dropped to the floor. Owen ducked down and recovered it.

Lucy knelt beside Travis. She kept her eyes open as she continued to pray for the broken man.

She rested her hand on his shoulder. "We can help you get your life back on track. Seeking Jesus' forgiveness is the best place to start."

Home At Last

The man's face turned to her, then to Owen. "Why would you help me?"

Lucy rose and took Owen's hand. "Because Jesus forgave us and God wants us to love people. I'm not worried about the gold. The hunt was fun, but I want to use it for good. We have homeless folks and low income on the island, and the money could assist them. If you have bills to pay of your mom's, we want to help you, too."

Andrew hung his head and wept.

Owen closed the box and peered at Andrew. "Let's get out of the cellar." He nodded to the steps.

All three climbed out. Owen locked the doors, then called Joel and Levi.

Lucy sat beside Andrew on the back step of the store. He held his head in his hands. "I've made a mess of my life. I tried to get you to trust me, but you didn't."

Lucy brushed dirt from her hair. "You're right. Too many strange things have happened since you came to the island."

Joel and Levi trooped into the yard. "What's going on?"

After Lucy told the story, Andrew held his hands out and Levi cuffed him and told him his rights.

Joel looked at Lucy. "It's Andrew's eyes we saw in Merrilee's photos. No wonder she seemed familiar."

"You're right." Lucy rubbed her temples. "We need to figure out what to do with the gold. I want to divide it between Andrew, Regina, and myself."

Joel drew Lucy aside. "I'll bring the car back in a bit to pick up the gold. We'll lock it up and find out where to go from there. I'm glad you didn't get hurt." He hugged her. "I gotta say, you're a mess. Your face looks like you slid through a pig sty."

She slugged him on the shoulder. "Funny, brother."

The three men left, and Owen and Lucy sat on the cellar doors. "I'm not leaving here until my brother comes back for this crazy treasure."

"Neither am I." Owen crossed his arms.

"I'm sorry I got so mad."

He scooted closer to her. "I shouldn't have reacted the way I did."

Lucy bumped his shoulder with hers. "I thought you weren't coming today."

"I wasn't, but something nudged me off the tractor and into town." He wrapped his arm around her shoulders. "I believe God gave me a shove in the right direction. I'm not sure you needed me. The way you talked to Andrew broke something in him."

Lucy rested her head on his shoulder. "When he visited church, he appeared so forlorn. Something clicked for me and the words flowed."

Penny Frost McGinnis, Abbott Island Book 3

He picked a piece of dirt from her hair. "You know you're a mess, right? A beautiful mess." He planted a kiss on her cheek.

"I dug for an hour before he came in. He had to have watched me." She shivered. "I guess he wanted me to do all the work." A giggle crawled from her belly to her mouth. "I must look a sight and I'm so tired. How did I get myself into this?"

Owen wrapped her in a hug. "You're Lucy. Wild, crazy, gorgeous Lucy. I wouldn't want you any other way. By the way, how did you get the ground soft enough to dig?"

"Baby shampoo."

"O…kay. You never cease to surprise me."

She wrapped her hands around his neck. "I hope I haven't scared you off."

He rested his forehead on hers. "No, Lucy. I'm looking forward to what comes next." He pulled her close and stole a kiss.

Home At Last

CHAPTER TWENTY-NINE

Birds chirped a song of joy to awaken Memorial Day weekend. Poppies and irises swayed in the warm breeze. Lucy sipped from her coffee mug and watched the waves splash the shore at seven o'clock in the morning. Every muscle in her body cried with pain from wielding a shovel yesterday.

After Owen followed her home last night and hugged her goodnight, she'd tossed her filthy clothes in the washer and stood under the shower. Dirt had sailed down the drain, along with the stress of the day.

Tires crunched in her driveway. She watched Joel exit the cruiser and trek to her deck.

Joel lowered himself into the chair beside her. "Morning, sis."

She angled her chair toward him. "Good morning. It's a beautiful day, isn't it? Can I get you coffee?"

He smiled at his sister. "Thanks, but I'm good." He pulled out his smart phone. "We need to discuss a couple things. I figured you'd be up and ready to face the first day of tourist season."

The last first day she'd open the store for Memorial Day weekend. Excitement and sorrow twisted through her. She'd miss the store, but not the chaos. Happy to turn the reins over to Regina and Gio, she planned to celebrate with them and Owen soon.

"I'm more than ready." A huge smile feathered her lips. "With the mystery of the gold solved, and Andrew or Travis or whatever he goes by in your custody, I can breathe. If I hadn't seen the map I found in the woods, I never would have gotten involved. I'm thankful it's over."

Joel grasped Lucy's arm. "Now, if I can talk for a minute." He let go. "Andrew will be extradited to Colorado, where he stole jewels from a rancher's property, plus he has other warrants, along with trespassing and destruction of property. He'll be behind bars for a while. I'm hoping he'll get some psychological help, as well as spiritual."

"Good to know. When you find out where he ends up, can I get an address? I want to write to him and encourage him."

Joel nodded. "Will Owen be okay with you staying in touch?"

"It was his idea. We hope to help him move forward with life and not get stuck in the past and his mistakes."

Owen understood Lucy's soft heart for hurting people. After Joel and Levi had walked Andrew off the property yesterday, Owen had held her hands and they prayed for Andrew, then he suggested they write to him when he landed in jail. Her love for the former baseball player had overflowed from her heart even more.

Joel tapped on the back of his phone. "The other thing we need to discuss is the gold. I'll call one of my buddies who has information about selling minerals and gems and ask him the best way to proceed."

"Thanks for checking. My mind is still reeling from finding the nuggets."

"Levi and I counted more than one hundred small, raw pieces and a few larger ones. Hard to believe they've been buried there all these years. With so many, you should be offered a healthy return." He squeezed his sister's shoulder. "I'm proud of you, sis. Your portion will help a lot of people, plus paying off Travis's mom's bills. You amaze me sometimes."

Lucy's eyelashes were wet with unshed tears. She and Joel stood, and she wrapped her brother in a hug, then stepped back. "That means so much to me. You're the best."

Joel's phone pinged. He glanced at the screen. "Gotta go. Tourist season has begun." He jogged through the yard and jumped in the cruiser.

Lucy watched him leave, then went inside to prepare to face the day.

~~~~~

The ferry docked as Lucy peddled her bike along Main Street. Cars and trucks drove onto the dock and bicyclists and walkers descended on the island.

Fifteen minutes later, Lucy watched Regina flip the *open* sign over on the door and prep the summer staff. "I'll be your supervisor for the season. We see a lot of foot traffic, so keep your eyes open, be prepared to help the customers, keep a positive attitude, and have fun."

Lucy stepped beside her and addressed the new employees. "I'm glad you've chosen to work here. Some of you worked for me last year and for others, this is all new. This will be my last month to own the store. I'll be in and out."

Several of the teenagers moaned.

"The good news is Regina and her husband, Gio, will be the new owners. I'll be around as I start a new venture. Now, let's make this the best summer ever." She raised her hand and shook it like a tambourine.

The employees scattered to their positions, and Lucy heard them welcoming customers. She leaned toward Regina. "It's going to be a great season."

By six o'clock, Lucy's feet hurt worse than her shoulders. She locked the store's door and sighed. Before she and Regina retreated to the office, someone knocked on the door. When she peered out, an enormous bouquet of wildflowers hid the person behind them, but Lucy recognized the man's blond hair. She swung the door open and Owen stepped into

Home At Last

the store.

"I'm making a delivery for the most kind-hearted, thoughtful, and beautiful woman on Abbott Island." He held the flowers out for her.

"These are gorgeous. What sweet man sent them to me?" She buried her face in and breathed in their fragrance.

Owen peeked around the flowers, and his brown eyes glimmered. "Someone who loves you, Lucy." He took the flowers and placed them on the counter, then held her hands. "I figured you'd had a long day. I hope you'll let me take you to dinner."

"I'd love to go to dinner with you. I want to freshen up and change clothes." She picked up the flowers.

"You look amazing, but I understand." He followed her to the office. "I saw your bike around back. It's in the truck."

Regina cleared her throat. "Someone's an amazing boyfriend."

Owen's cheeks pinked. "Hi, Regina. I do what I can." A grin split his face.

"You two have fun. I'm heading home to my kiddos and Gio." She hugged Lucy. "We had a fantastic first day. Can't wait to see what tomorrow brings."

Lucy gathered her purse and jacket and they walked into the backyard. She eyed the cellar. "I can't believe we found gold yesterday. Feels like it was months ago, except for my back and shoulders. They've hurt all day." She rolled her shoulders.

He opened the door for her, and she hoisted herself into the truck. "I'm glad it's behind us."

In the driver's seat, he shifted into gear and drove to Lucy's.

When they arrived at her place, he walked her to the door. "I'm going to visit your beach while you get ready."

"Sounds good. I'll be quick."

True to her word, Lucy hurried to change clothes, then wandered to the beach and found Owen scouring the sand for lake glass. "Find anything interesting?"

He turned and watched her walk to him. "A few pieces. Pretty small, but beautiful." He opened his hand and revealed a pale blue piece the size of a pencil eraser and a bigger brown one. "You can add them to your collection." He dropped them into her palm.

She admired them, then tucked them in her pocket. "The gold pieces weren't much bigger than the brown piece of glass." She stared at the lake, then turned to Owen. "We've had our hands on genuine gold."

In all her years, she never imagined she'd be involved in a treasure hunt. When she had met Andrew, she sensed something was off, but couldn't pinpoint why. Something about him had given her warning signs. He had avoided eye contact and evaded personal questions. At least

Penny Frost McGinnis, Abbott Island Book 3

he understood he had done wrong.

Owen twined his fingers with hers. "You okay?"

She leaned into him. "I'm good. A little sore, and I can't stop thinking about Andrew and how he tricked us. I thought I was a better judge of character. Now I pray he finds his way back to God and to an honest life."

Owen dropped her hand and placed an arm around her shoulders. "You had no idea, and neither did I. I'm thankful you weren't hurt." He pulled her into a hug.

She rested her head on his chest. "Thanks for coming when you did. I didn't think he'd hurt me, but I wasn't sure. The whole situation seems surreal."

He kissed her forehead. "Sure does. I'm glad it's over and we can enjoy the summer. Let's go get some food."

A short time later, they placed their names on the waiting list at the restaurant.

Lucy glanced at the diners, then waved. "Charlotte's here with Levi." She pulled Owen to the couple's table.

Charlotte stood and wrapped Lucy in a hug. "It's so good to see you."

"You too. When did you get in?"

Owen shook Levi's hand.

"I came over on the ferry this morning. I saw you on your bike." Charlotte motioned to their table. "Want to join us? We haven't ordered yet."

"No. We don't want to bother you."

Levi stood. "It's no bother. We want to ask you something."

Lucy glanced at Owen. "Sure. If you want us to. Let me take our name off the list." Owen hurried to the front counter, and Lucy sat.

Once they had all settled into their seats, the waiter took their orders. After he walked away, Charlotte spoke in a low tone.

"I heard you've had an eventful week. Levi was telling me about the treasure."

Lucy touched her fingers to her cheek. "Yes, we were saying how surreal it all seemed." She moved her hand to the table. "I'm thankful we are all okay and the gold is in a safe place. Once Joel figures out our best move for cashing it in, it will help a lot of people."

An old fifties song played in the background while they talked about Charlotte's school year. The waiter placed their hoagies on the table and the fragrance of the red sauce enticed them to eat.

After a few bites, Charlotte patted her mouth with her napkin. "Levi told me you're opening an event venue on the island."

Lucy chewed a tasty bite. "I am. Owen has a newer barn for me to use. I want to host weddings, anniversaries, birthdays, whatever anyone would like." She paused and sipped her Pepsi. "I'm going to work on it this summer while Regina gets used to running the store."

Charlotte's eyes sparkled with excitement. "I'm listening and hoping you'll be ready soon."

Lucy blurted, "Do you want your wedding on the island?"

"As a matter of fact, I do." Charlotte wadded her napkin. "Can you get the barn ready by the end of July? It's less than two months, but I love the island and my family does too." She grabbed Lucy's hand. "I'll be working for Marigold this summer until the big day." She glanced at Levi and let go of Lucy. "We could plan it together."

Lucy covered her mouth to keep from whooping, then fist bumped the air. "Charlotte, I'd love to help you with your wedding. You and Levi can be the first couple married in the barn." She took a breath. "Have you chosen the date?"

Charlotte reached for Levi's hand. "We want to get married the last weekend in July. I'm hoping it won't be too hot."

Owen said, "The barn has an overhang with vent ridges and a commercial dehumidifier to help lessen the humidity and fans for air flow. If you plan it for the evening, it'll be cooler."

Lucy patted his knee. "What he said." She shrugged. "This is going to be so much fun." Her first wedding in the barn. Lucy's mind reeled with ideas. Twinkle lights on the ceiling and tulle, lots of tulle. She'd find chairs to rent or buy and tables. Johnny could cater.

Charlotte interrupted her thoughts. "Lucy, when can we meet?"

"Oh. Um. How about Wednesday evening?"

"Sounds good. Let me put the time in my phone right now." Charlotte tapped on her smart phone and added the information. She tucked the phone in her pocket and leaned into Lucy. "You've had quite a busy, crazy spring."

Lucy shook her head. "I've never experienced anything like it. Did Levi tell you much?"

"No. He couldn't share details, just that the treasure was found." Charlotte bit into her sandwich.

Lucy shared what happened in the cellar and explained how Andrew had tried to finagle his way into buying the store.

"Thankfully, Regina and her husband purchased the General Store so I can open the event venue." Lucy rubbed her hands together. "I'm so excited you two will be the first ones to get married there."

For the rest of the meal, the couples discussed possibilities for the wedding and the probability of the Guardians getting into the playoffs.

After some insightful conversation, they paid their bills and said goodnight.

Owen drove Lucy home, and they sat on her porch steps and listened to the waves wash the sand. "Sounds like you lined up your first event."

Penny Frost McGinnis, Abbott Island Book 3

She nestled into his shoulder. "I'm not going to sleep tonight."

He kissed her temple. "Whatever you need me to do, I will."

"Thank you for offering me the chance to make this work. Without your barn, I couldn't pull this off."

He hugged her to him. "I'm blessed to spend time with you. You are one amazing woman."

CHAPTER THIRTY

The last weekend of July

Eighty-three degrees and no rain in the forecast fashioned a huge smile on Lucy's face. She and Owen had worked all week on the final touches to the Island Charm Event Venue.

Tulle crisscrossed the fairy lights strung from the top of the walls to the rafters. On one of her scavenger hunts for decorative items, Lucy had found an old crystal chandelier at an estate sale for a reasonable price. Owen and Uncle Jed rewired it and hung the dazzling light display from the center of the ceiling.

In June, Sadie, Charlotte, Joel, Levi, Owen, and Lucy had painted the drywall pastel blue-green and trimmed the baseboard in warm-white. Lucy had purchased twenty-eight folding chairs from a local church when they replaced theirs. The Nifty Thrift Shop in Sandusky tracked down two rustic eight-foot maple dining tables. Several islanders and relatives donated mismatched wooden chairs. Aunt Marley gifted her with tablecloths she had hand crocheted over the years.

On a Saturday at the beginning of July, Miss Aggie, Miss Flossie, and Miss Lottie had carried in three sets of vintage dishes they no longer used. Enough to serve over fifty people.

"I can't take your family dishes." Lucy had shaken her head.

Miss Aggie edged close to her. "Of course you can. None of us have children to leave them to. We want you to have them, so they'll bring joy to your patrons. You're doing a good thing here. The island needs more people like you."

"I don't know what to say." Lucy hugged the neck of each woman, then she lifted a plate from each of the three boxes. "These are beautiful. I love that they're all different."

"They are quite lovely, much like you." Miss Flossie tittered.

~~~~~

On the last Saturday of July, Lucy stood in the center of the barn. Tears filled her eyes as she took in the incredible reality of the moment. Soon, her first event would take place.

Charlotte and Levi had discussed their needs for their small wedding and given her the freedom to design their special day. They expected thirty guests, so Lucy had arranged chairs to face a large trellis, draped in tulle and flowers, where the bride and groom would stand.

Charlotte's family stayed at the rental cottage she had for the summer, and a few guests rented Sadie's cabins.

Lucy and Owen had set up the tables and chairs outside under the oak trees, where Johnny and Henry would serve their Greek and American specialties. One of Marigold's friends had delivered the wedding cake. Three layers of chocolate cake iced with almond butter cream. The baker had created lavender hydrangea sugar flowers and added them to each layer.

Lucy left the back of the barn's floor open for dancing. A group of local musicians had volunteered to play instrumental bluegrass for the reception.

Two hours remained until Charlotte and Levi would tie the knot.

Lucy's heart soared at the thought of hosting her friend's wedding.

In June, Regina and Gio had officially purchased the store and given her more of a financial cushion. Once Joel had found how to cash out the gold, he and Lucy paid off Andrew's mother's debts and given a chunk of the money to the island library, a local homeless shelter, and to a program at the church which helped veterans and widows. Plus, Regina and Gio paid Owen back with their share.

Thank goodness Andrew had come to the island, so the gold was unearthed. Otherwise, it would have lain in the ground for who knew how long.

In June, Lucy and Owen had written to Andrew. In a few weeks, he had replied. He apologized again for the difficulties he had caused and thanked them, several times, for their kindness. A man and woman came to the prison once a week and read to the prisoners from the Bible, answered questions, and prayed for him. His life had gone haywire, but he thanked God someone cared about him.

Before she went to Owen's farmhouse to change, Lucy sat in a chair at the front of the barn and breathed in the aroma of gardenias and lavender, then she bowed her head and sought God's ear.

"I'm not sure I can ever thank You enough, Lord. You heard my cries of discontent, and You answered. You've blessed me more than I ever imagined. I ask Your blessing on the couple getting married today. They are two of the sweetest people I know. Thanks for letting me be a part of their special day. And, God, thank You for Owen. I never thought I'd meet someone so right for me. Help me not to be a bonehead in our relationship. I love You. Amen."

Footsteps sounded behind her. "Don't call the love of my life a bonehead." Owen placed his hands on the back of the chair.

She stood and faced him. "You heard me, huh?"

"Sure did." He turned and looked at the lights and decorations. "You

Home At Last

created an incredible venue." He took her by the hand and led her to the trellis. There, he knelt before her on one knee.

She widened her eyes. "What are you doing? We have to get ready for the wedding."

His eyes met and held hers. "We have time." He reached into his pocket and pulled out a small blue velvet box. "Would you open this?"

Her fingers fumbled as she lifted the top of the box. "Oh, my." A diamond solitaire, with a bezel-cut of white gold surrounding the diamond, glimmered at her.

He grasped her hand. "Lucy, will you marry me?"

Her hand shook and tears trickled down her cheeks. "Yes, yes. Of course I'll marry you." She bounced on her toes.

He rose from the floor and took the ring from the box. Then he held her hand and placed the diamond on her finger. He pulled her to him for a kiss.

Owen leaned into her ear. "I wanted the first event in the Island Charm Event Venue to be ours. I love you."

"I love you, too." She embraced him and grinned to herself. Last winter, in all her loneliness, she didn't have an inkling the summer promised hope and love. She'd found both in Owen.

~~~~~

At six o'clock in the evening, Charlotte's dad escorted her down the aisle. Her niece, Lottie, danced to the front of the barn and scattered flower petals on the floor. Lottie's dad, Peter, stood in as Charlotte's man of honor, since she had no sisters. Levi asked Joel to be his best man.

The pastor from the local church guided the couple through traditional vows.

Levi held his bride's wedding band and placed it on her finger as he repeated after the pastor. "I give you this ring as a symbol of my love. I cherish and honor you in the name of the Father, Son, and Holy Spirit." Charlotte repeated the words and put a ring on Levi's left hand.

"You may kiss your bride."

Levi dipped Charlotte and kissed her.

After the bridal party posed for photos, the guests gathered at the tables to eat an abundant meal and delicious cake.

Lucy scurried from one table to the other, checking on guests and making sure Charlotte and Levi had everything they needed.

After the evening ended and they wished the newlyweds well, Owen and Lucy cleared the barn of all the trash, then locked the door.

Owen tugged Lucy to him. "You did it."

"We did it. I couldn't have pulled the wedding off without the help of you and our friends." Her eyes burned from weariness. "I had so much fun. I'm going to love this."

Penny Frost McGinnis, Abbott Island Book 3

They held hands and meandered to the porch at the farmhouse. The baas of sheep called from the field. Crickets chirped in the yard. They settled on the porch swing.

"I enjoy the sounds out here. When I hear the animals or the rustling leaves, I feel closer to our Creator."

Owen rested his arm on the back of the swing. "I'm hoping you'll be living here soon. I'd like to set a date for our wedding."

She leaned her head on his shoulder. "When are you thinking?"

"Is October too soon?"

She sat straight and turned to face him. "The farm in fall would be gorgeous. I don't want a much bigger wedding than Charlotte and Levi's. We could do this."

She placed a hand on each side of his face and kissed him. "I can't wait to tell Sadie, Marigold, and Regina. They'll be so excited."

"I noticed you didn't show your ring off tonight." He reached for her left hand.

"I didn't want to take away from the bride."

"Understood." He kissed the knuckles on her hand.

"Let's invite our friends over tomorrow evening and share the news." She clasped her hands together.

~~~~~

On Sunday evening, Lucy and Owen's friends gathered at the barn. Except Levi and Charlotte, who flew to Charleston, South Carolina, for their honeymoon.

Marigold sliced the left-over wedding cake Charlotte's family had left behind and poured coffee. "Thanks for inviting us for cake, but I have a feeling something else is brewing."

Owen and Lucy stood under the trellis with Cheshire Cat grins. Lucy wove her arm through Owen's. "We have an announcement." She held her left hand out, and the ring sparkled.

Sadie handed Gracie to Joel and ran to hug Lucy. "Congratulations." All their friends embraced them, patted their backs, or shook hands.

"How soon is the wedding?" Marigold hugged Lucy.

"Have you told Mom and Dad?" Joel piped in.

"Yes. We called them last night." Lucy patted her brother on the arm.

Owen squeezed out of the circle surrounding Lucy. He called over their voices. "Could you all sit?"

Everyone claimed a chair. "We have decided to get married in October. Not a big wedding. My parents and sister will be home then on furlough and my only other relatives are my aunt and uncle. Who are thrilled, by the way. Aunt Marley claims she brought us together."

Laughter rolled through the barn.

Lucy wrapped an arm around Owen and he hugged her back. "We

176

Home At Last

may need your help. Even with a small wedding, there's a lot of work. And since I'm the bride this time, I'm not sure I can get it all done. What do you say?"

They all chimed, "We do."

Lucy pumped her fist in the air. "Yes!"

October

Scarlet, gold, and orange leaves painted brilliance across a cerulean blue sky and gave way to a perfect day for a wedding. A sixty-degree breeze drifted across Abbott Island and the sun shone.

Lucy stood in front of a full-length mirror in her future bedroom. "Mom, I can't believe I'm getting married."

Her mom rolled her wheelchair to Lucy's side. "You are so beautiful. Your grandmother's dress fits you perfectly. With the updated neckline and sleeves, it suits you. I know you talked about shortening the A-line skirt, but I'm glad you didn't. You've had an old soul since you were a little girl, and I'm thankful you found someone who loves and understands you. We couldn't be happier for you."

Lucy bent and kissed her mom on the cheek. "Thank you, Mom." She fingered her necklace. "I was so surprised by this. Joel told me it was your idea to have the smallest gold nugget made into a necklace for me. I love it, and I love you and Dad."

"Speaking of your dad, he's waiting to walk you down the aisle."

Lucy followed her mom to the living room.

Her dad, dressed in his Sunday suit, helped both ladies outside. Joel walked beside his mom's wheelchair into the barn.

At the back of the barn, Lucy stood out of sight until she heard the wedding march. At the first note, she and her dad stepped into the aisle.

Owen's eyes brightened, and a smile stretched across his face.

Lucy's dad held her arm and walked her to the front, where he gave his girl to her groom.

Levi officiated. When he had learned the couple would be getting married, he'd asked if he could be the one to pronounce them husband and wife. After all Lucy had done for him and Charlotte, he wanted to give back. Along with plans to finish his teaching degree, he had asked his church to ordain him, then he applied for his Ohio license to perform weddings.

Under the trellis Owen had built, he and Lucy held hands and exchanged vows they'd written. Their words promised a life of faith, hope, and love. Before he kissed his bride, Owen turned to the folks in attendance. "We want to thank you all for making this day possible." Then

Penny Frost McGinnis, Abbott Island Book 3

he wrapped his arms around Lucy and kissed his bride.

Lucy's heart thumped. She couldn't wait to move into the farmhouse with the man of her dreams and be home at last.

THE END

ABOUT THE AUTHOR

Penny Frost McGinnis, author of *Home Where She Belongs* and *Home Away from Home*, books 1 and 2 of the Abbott Island series and picture book, *Betsy and Bailey: No One Will be Just Like You*, has lived in the world of books most of her life. She retired from the library life, then launched her writing journey. She and her husband live in southwest Ohio with their golden retriever, Rosie. She embraces and enjoys her family, fiber arts, and baseball. Her life's goal is to encourage and uplift through her writing.

THANK YOU!

Thank you for reading this book from Mt. Zion Ridge Press.

If you enjoyed the experience, learned something, gained a new perspective, or made new friends through story, could you do us a favor and write a review on Goodreads or wherever you bought the book?

Thanks! We and our authors appreciate it.

We invite you to visit our website, MtZionRidgePress.com, and explore other titles in fiction and non-fiction. We always have something coming up that's new and off the beaten path.

And please check out our podcast, **Books on the Ridge,** where we chat with our authors and give them a chance to share what was in their hearts while they wrote their book, as well as fun anecdotes and glimpses into their lives and experiences and the writing process. And we always discuss a very important topic: *Tea!*

You can listen to the podcast on our website or find it at most of the usual places where podcasts are available online. Please subscribe so you don't miss a single episode!

Thanks for reading. We hope you come back soon!

Printed in the USA
CPSIA information can be obtained
at www.ICGtesting.com
CBHW011947250724
12177CB00026B/780